Colony

a story by

Colin Hodgson

Published by C E Hodgson
Colchester,
United Kingdom
www.private-people.co.uk

First edition November 2011

ISBN: 978-0-9569498-3-7

ACKNOWLEDGMENTS

Again, many thanks to the people of Wikipedia. A true fountain of knowledge and resource.

And heart felt thanks to my friends and family who continue to encourage and support my writings, especially my Dad.

Cover designed by Colin Hodgson

FROM THE AUTHOR

"Hi, I'm Colin Hodgson. This, Colony, is my second book, and I have again truly enjoyed the writing of it. It is one of my surreal fairytale-type stories which looks closely at the beginnings of life, love, and emotion, as well as at the cruel reality of mankind. Colony covertly peers in on mankind's cruelty and dogged determination to better themselves, which make the human race the most powerful life-form which has ever been know to any God.

My first book, Saint Ninah, is another story which sits outside of the main stream, eddying along in the shadows and appealing to a growing number of readers who do not want to read the run of the mill 'trade' books which are written to a formula.

The two titles are not part of a series, but both enhance the enjoyment of the other, enjoying common characters and beliefs. Read them both."

Contents

1 -- COLONY

March 1972, Essex, England.

As Uncle Steven and Katie entered the graveyard the rooks called. They circled overhead looking down on the two visitors with intrepid interest but when Katie twisted her deformed neck up to look at them, and waved, they quietened and returned to tending their young. It was a cold spring morning, and the little blond-haired girl shivered as her distorted body giggled with excitement.

The tiny eight-year-old held on to her uncle's hand to steady her walk, one leg slightly dragging, and she swayed with every step, but her face gleamed as she slowly headed towards the grave. And on the other side of the graveyard, snuggled below a stately **old** conker tree, was her khaki army tent.

"I need to sit down, Kate," whispered Uncle.

The frail old man lowered himself onto a bench, and Katie, grinning, struggled on by herself. The journey across the grass was gruelling.

"I'm nearly with you," she uttered.

As the grave became within reach, Katie stopped and looked over to the little tent and observed, "A new dawn approaches." She took the final painful steps and dropped down onto the grave, laying face down on the un-tended mound. She whispered, "I hope you are behaving yourselves." The chit-chat went on for several minutes. "I'm going home

7

soon, just to change, but I'll be straight back. I'll think of you both wherever I am." She held her ear to the earth. "Don't be silly. Now I've got your emotions, I'm never gonna let them go. Love you, my impetuous pinky-tickler." She started to giggle, but was distracted.

"What are you doing? Get off the grave!" shouted the vicar. "Come on, off with you."

She strained to turn her head enough to see the vicar's legs towering up over her. "I'm talking to my friends." She pushed herself over and rolled off the mound. "I'll miss my friends, and their love." The little blond girl lay on her back and grinned up at the vicar.

"Well you can't treat a grave like a playground."

"I can, it's *God's* playground, and I'm talking to my friends." Her speech was slurred and the cold ground was sending her into shivers, so the vicar held his hand down, and she took it.

"Come on, child, I'll take you to your father."

"He ain't my father. He's Uncle Steven."

The vicar could not understand her deformed speech, and so just smiled. As he looked towards the bench he exclaimed, "Oh, he's gone."

"No, he'e still there. He would never leave me."

2 -- THE CAVEMEN'S PAINTINGS

February 1971, an Essex Approved School.

The boy's eyes were reaching straight into the clear blue sky, then came the blow. A fist shot from the heavens and his vision blurred, then again, and the skies turned dark. Peter jumped up from the beaten boy amidst cheers and screams. The other children shouted for more, but Peter left the boy for dead, suddenly realising what he had done.

"Don't *dare* move from that seat," growled the headmaster. "Your uncle is coming."

"Uncle who?" asked Peter. "I haven't got any uncles."

"Be quiet."

The knock came on the door, and the head walked over to it. There was a middle-aged man, quite tall but wiry, and he introduced himself as Steven.

"Come in, sir. We have a rather bad boy to contend with, here. This is Peter, in case you don't recognise him."

Steven stood and stared at the fourteen-year-old boy, then smiled. "You were not much more than a baby last time I saw you. I don't know if you remember me."

"No." Peter was in a huff. "Never seen you before. What do you want?"

The headmaster gently reminded Peter, "You are in trouble, and your uncle is the only person in your life. So give him a chance."

"I've got a sister!"

"But your sister can't help you, can she." The head raised his eyebrows.

Peter looked down at his lap. "Don't remind me."

Uncle Steven broke the ice. "I remember your mum. She was beautiful. You must have missed her these past seven years and I want to help to make up for it."

"So what were you to my mum, then?"

"I'm her older brother. Remember?"

Peter's face lit up. "Mum mentioned you. You're a murderer! That's brilliant."

Things suddenly went quiet. The head left the room to get some coffees, so Steven was able to talk to Peter in confidence, and Steven's mood instantly changed. "Please help me, Peter. I need your forgiveness." Steven was close to begging. "I killed your father. I *beg* your forgiveness."

Peter's face faded and frowned. Steven had killed the boy's father. Forgive? "Forgive? You prat."

"Please listen. He beat your mum up so badly she died, and hurt Katie. I've seen Katie today, and I cried. Please forgive me, I had to do it. He killed my sister and now look at Katie. She's as good as dead."

The headmaster walked in with the coffees. The atmosphere froze.

"Are you two getting on?" he asked. The two lads just looked hard at each other. "Does Peter know the circumstances of your conviction? I think he needs to know. It might just help him to understand his own anger."

Steven took a deep breath. "If I explain, will you listen?" Peter nodded, so Uncle continued. "You were about five, and your father was a drug dealer. He was also a user. His moods swung full circle every day and he was hitting both your mum and Katie, so she made the big decision to leave, with you and Katie. As you all got ready to leave for that new life, he turned up and beat her up, and Katie was dropped down the stairs. They were both very badly hurt. But you got out of the back and ran round my house." He studied Peter's body language.

"You don't remember do you. Anyway he came after you, but my Mary let you in and locked the doors. She phoned me at work and I got straight home. When I went round to yours he was gone, but Trish and Katie had just been left, unconscious, so I ran to the phone box and called the ambulance. Trish recovered partly, but as you know, died when you were about seven. Katie never fully recovered. You know what she's like now." Steven sighed. "So I killed him. Please forgive me."

Poor Peter had been through the coals since his mum died. The school to which he had been sent, by the courts, was an approved school, a place for bad boys, an institution. He had constantly been in trouble, always because of his protective nature, fighting the bullies. On that day he had again witnessed his best, and only, mate get a beating, and so returned the favour by breaking the bully's jaw, nose and cheekbone, then ending up in the head's office. And there he was, sitting with his long-lost uncle, the murderer.

Peter avoided the request for forgiveness. "I beat Jonesy up. I don't want his forgiveness, he deserved it. And I'm already locked up in this hole, so they can't do any more to me."

Steven reached out and put his hand on the boy's shoulder. Peter winced.

"Peter, I'm a convicted murderer, but I've done my time. I'm now out after seven years. I don't know if that's justice, but I'm out. Now I've been open with you, about my reasons for doing such a terrible thing in the eyes of God. Why do you keep fighting? I need to know, for my own peace of mind." He waited for a response, but none came. "I'm family. We all have only the three of us. I'm on your side."

Peter looked up, frowning. "If I tell you the truth, will you believe? Nobody else does." He looked at the head. "Sometimes the head does, but not often. You know, I was going to kill Jonesy. That's what I wanted to do, but something stopped me. Wish I'd killed him."

"But why?"

Peter huffed, "They're killing Stuart. Jonesy and his two wankers. They're killing poor Stuart. Bullying him to death." He stopped.

After a while of silence, the headmaster stressed, "We have that under control."

"Shit you have."

Uncle snapped, "Peter! Mind your tongue."

Peter stretched a wry smile. "They're bullying him so bad. Jonesy's face might stop them for while. But not for long, so I'll have to do it again."

"You can't keep taking the law into your own hands," whispered the head.

Peter fidgeted, and replied very deliberately, "So what would happen to him if he ran away from the bullies? You know, away."

The head leaned forward, "You know he would be returned and punished."

"So, what would happen to him if he stayed here, and not run away?" No answer came. "So he's locked up in a personal hell; can't fight it, can't run away from it. What has he done to deserve all this abuse?"

The head sat up straight and replied, "We are considering a different approach to your mental state. Your uncle has an offer of a new job."

Uncle Steven smiled. "It's a new life. We could all go, the three of us. I've spoken to the clinic about Katie."

"She's crippled, a spastic. How the hell can you take her anywhere?" Peter leaned back and crossed his arms. "Unless there's a clinic there."

"There is. The company has a clinic of its own. It's a mining community, and they mine izaline. It's good money as well."

"I've heard of that stuff. It's from away."

Uncle jiggered a bit. "It's definitely away. There's a new colony, all it does is mine the precious metal. It's a job for life, and they discovered another deposit, apparently. What do you think?"

Peter thought about his little sister, slumbering around on her rug, lonely and desperate. "I suppose if Katie's gonna die, it could be somewhere else. She might even be able to stop crying."

The seeds were sown. Peter began to think about spending time with his little sister, who was robbed of normal life by her father, and who never stopped crying. After considering the vague proposition for all of thirty seconds, Peter made his decision. "We'll go."

The headmaster smiled, but secretly mourned the going of Peter; he was the little boys' protector. He prayed for another like him, to deter the bullies, to punish them, to teach them. Maybe his prayers asked for a little too much. But he would carry on praying, anyway.

"You'll look after Stuart? Promise?"

The head made his solemn oath to protect Peter's pal the best he could.

The next day the children at the school saw Peter off. They quietly watched him walk away with his small briefcase bearing his life's belongings, but with his heart bearing the real jewel, his sister. He had escaped, and maybe so had she!

Uncle Steven had been right up front about the job, and the offer was genuine, so they registered with the company in readiness for the trip to the colony. It was so exciting, a far away world full of mystery and promise, in a community of adventurers, like one big happy family. They would fight the world together, tend each others wounds, laugh and play amongst the strange plants and fauna, and be happy. And perhaps the different climate would suite Katie's nervous problems.

"She is responding to these new drugs," said the nurse, smiling. "Katie, say hello to your brother."

Katie managed to lift her blond head in response. Her eyes were large and grey-green, and they looked deep into Peter's heart. He could hear her saying *'help me Peter',* but he could not hear the rest.

He whispered in her ear, "Tell me later, sis. We're going to a new colony."

She grinned and looked into him. *'I want to go there. But never leave me.'* Peter gave her a hug.

"You will need to take a supply of her pills; she's got so much better since we have had these ones. And when you get there, make sure she is properly registered with the clinic, and also that there is a forward order for further supply. Other children with similar disorders have made outstanding progress with these." The nurse was sad to see the unfortunate little eight-year-old move away as she had tended her for over three years. "Please, Steven, make sure she has the correct drugs."

They spoke to Katie's consultant.

"The girl's problem with her nervous system is so rare. We have been in contact with the other two known cases, and they have all benefited from changes in their environment." The doctor sighed. "Normally I would be fighting to prevent you from taking her. But she may respond to a total change. She has made slight improvements on the new medicines, but not enough."

Peter smiled, "I'll look after her. All she's done for years is lay around here; it must be hell for her, like being in a spider's web, waiting for the inevitable. If she doesn't go she might as well die."

Doctor Franklin wished them the best.

The trip was long and arduous. During the many days in the cabin they slept as a result of the additives in the drinks, and that made the journey easy, well, for some of them. Katie never slept. She had to sit in what looked like a child-seat, strapped upright with her head supported by a collar, and so watched the stars as the ship silently sped towards their new life. As the Earth was lost from sight, she wept.

At last, touchdown. As they stood up from their seats the stewardess offered to take Steven's hand luggage while he carried Katie out and, when they emerged into the steamy atmosphere of their new colony, the captain was waiting.

"Sir, welcome to New Bury. Did the children have a settled trip?"

He looked at Peter as if to say 'Well?'. Peter just shrugged his shoulders. He had slept the whole time.

"Anyway, the reason I have met you off the ship is to ask if you have sufficient equipment for your daughter. There is very little here, particularly for children."

Oh dear. Uncle Steven looked at Peter, and Peter at Uncle Steven.

"I take that as a no. Well, I think you'll find that you are the only family here with children, so I can safely offer you our wheelchair. It is the seat on which your daughter sat, which attaches to a wheeled base. It is very adaptable. It's yours if you would like it."

Peter asked with a shake in his voice, "No other children?"

"I'm sorry, but I think that is the case. Have you been led to believe otherwise?"

Peter stroked Katie's long blond hair. "The brochures showed a school and playing grounds."

The captain was sympathetic. "There used to be. The colony is almost depleted. Very little left here, and our shuttle is not scheduled to come back for another six months." He could see the concern on Uncle Steven's face. "The ship is not full for our return. You *could* go straight back home."

The adult and the teenager were left in a bit of a quandary. "What can we do, Uncle?"

"The captain has been really kind to warn us. I think the company has conned us over here." They had to think of Katie. "Do we have six months supply of pills for Katie?"

"Yes. And the clinic should be able to get us more if need be."

The captain reminded them, "We will not be back for about six months, and we are the only transport. They won't be able to get anything in sooner than that so I would suggest great caution here. You're not the first people who have been disappointed with this colony. The way things are going, you could be the last, but it is only for six months. But you do have a disabled child, and that will make it harder for you."

Peter put his head close to Katie's and asked her, "What should we do, sis?" She looked hard at him, and smiled. She seemed to say, *'stay and search'*. But Peter wasn't too sure. He suggested to his uncle, "We could stay for the six months. You do the work and I can look after Katie. I've never spent much time with her so it'll be good for us both." Katie grinned her approval. "I know what'll happen if we go home, same as has happened last few years. I would rather take our chances here."

Against Uncle Steven's better judgement he agreed to stay. "Thanks for your concern, Captain, but we'll stay for the duration."

The captain showed them how the wheelchair went together, bid them well and promised to be back in six months. The adventure had begun.

The site manager showed them to their accommodation. It was a large tent!

"Brilliant!" shouted Peter. "It'll be like a camping holiday. We've never done that." Little Sis' grinned, and with a bit of help, they did a high five. "We're gonna have a whammy of one!"

It was warm, but humid, with lush vegetation and the horizon showed some low mountainous areas. Not far into the distance was the sea.

The other workers were rough, hard men. They were loners, staying there on their own, for whatever reason, and none seemed very happy. They were mystified as to why Steven had taken two children to such a colony and they just thought he must be mad. Steven was beginning to ask himself why. But the shuttle had gone, not to return for about six months.

"Don't worry, uncle, we'll be ok. Me and Sis can have an adventure, especially since she seems to be getting a little better each day with her drugs. She's sitting up and sort of talking, and I'm beginning to understand a lot of it."

Uncle Steven sat down on the floor with the children. "I start work tomorrow. No rest for the wicked. Hope I'm ok." He hadn't worked for seven years, since going into prison. "It's nerve-racking."

Peter was holding Katie on his lap. "I think Katie wants to say something to you."

Peter leaned over to offer her mouth up to Uncle's ear and she struggled with, "I love you, Uncle."

He hugged her, and then said, "I love you, too. I can actually understand you." She had never spoken to Steven, and he was a little emotional.

"Do you know what your job is yet?" asked Peter.

"I've been told that I'm with the 'extermination' crew. There's a load of dangerous creatures here and we go in ahead to clear them. Apparently this's the only area where they still exist." He looked sadly at Katie. "I think they're almost extinct. And he also told me that this is the last known deposit of izaline. Some job for life, hey?" The company had duped them, probably because nobody else would take the job. "Whatever happens, we'll be going home on the next shuttle. They're probably shutting up shop here."

With work starting the next day, Steven thought it 'family-like' to spend the rest of the time together so they assembled the wheelchair and went for a stroll around the camp. There were only eight tents, but there was a brick and wooden school large enough for several children, and it was sadly derelict, just like the playground. A large shed comprised the bar. Everywhere needs a bar, it is where they meet and socialise, and get pissed up. Steven took a look through the door.

"Good morning, sir. Saw you coming down the street." There was an old, grey-haired gent behind the tiny bar. "I suppose you can call it a street."

"Hiya. I'm Steven."

"Heard you'd arrived. I'm Old Dick." He held his hand out and shook Steven's hand. "This my little patient?" He leaned down towards Katie.

"How d'you mean?" Steven frowned. "It's Katie."

"I know. And this is the clinic. And the bar. And the courthouse. Not just a shed, you know."

The adventure was getting more disappointing by the hour. Peter looked down at Katie and wondered if she knew what was going on. She looked up at him and grinned. "Yes," she uttered.

Steven was becoming increasingly concerned. "This is *the* clinic? Where?"

Old Dick pointed to a grey cabinet. "That's the medicine cabinet." He raised his eyebrows. "It only has the basics. The old clinic fell down, and we rescued some bits."

"Didn't the company send more supplies? The shuttle has just been; we were on it." He looked around the shed and realised that the cabinet was the only piece of furniture besides the four-foot wide bar and the shelves of beers and spirits. Those shelves were full.

"No, we haven't used anything from it for ages, nothing to replace. These blokes only use the odd bandage. But don't worry, I used to be a doctor. You're in good hands with Old Dick. Drink?"

Steven felt in his pocket. "Got no money with me."

"Don't need it. All the food and drinks are free, well, sort of. We get stopped money out of our wages for it. Just ask me though, don't help yourself. I've got to keep some sort of job." The old man poured a whisky for Steven and himself, and orange juices for the two children. "Cheers, hope we see more of you at Old Dick's."

"Sir," Peter asked, "is it safe for us to walk about? Uncle was told of the dangerous animals."

Old Dick leaned on his bar and scratched his chin. "I think so. I think the creatures are all gone, you know, killed. They were supposed to be ferocious fighters, cut you to bits, so they had a massive cull. They only found a handful, but we haven't seen any since."

Steven asked, "Then, why do you think they've given me the job of exterminating?"

"It's a job, isn't it? You've got to have a job out here else you'll go mad. The company don't know that they're all gone, so you got the job. We're all doing the same, really. Nothing. All the deposits seem to have gone, and if no more are found, we're going home. Shame, but all good things come to an end. This place has been good for me. I love socialising, but only for a little. And that's what I get here, a little."

"Sir, how many people are here?"

"Including you three, eleven. That's enough. When there were over a hundred, there was loads of trouble. This's a nice bunch."

"And who lives in that tent?" Peter pointed across the 'street' at a tiny khaki army tent, sheltered below a conker tree.

"Hmm, well, I don't really know. It's been there for some time, never seen anybody at it."

Katie managed to raise her hand and point at the tiny tent. She twisted her head towards Peter, and he put his ear to her mouth. "Mummy," she whispered. Her eyes were excited, but damp from a recent bout of crying. "Mummy, you know," she whispered.

"Don't be silly, Sis. We'll talk later, when we're on our own."

Old Dick was a good introduction. He knew everything, apart from the little tent, and so he told the newcomers about the caves where the precious metal was prospected, and about those tankers across the street which were full of ionacin, a seriously corrosive compound.

"Those tankers over there are excess to requirements, and unstable, but I don't think they know what to do with them. The chemicals inside are so bloody poisonous I think we will all just move out and leave them here to the elements, and to God. Peter, you mustn't take your sister near them, I mean it. They are beginning to leak, so stay away. One miner got some on his foot a couple of years back, and it just ate the foot away. I had to cut his foot off, without getting any on me, but it had got into his blood and went all over his body. I've never heard a man scream like it before, as he spent several hours just rotting from inside. We all had to go away and leave him, couldn't stand it."

Steven asked, "Why didn't you kill him? That would've been kinder."

"We thought the insurance wouldn't pay out if his death was not from the gunk. That's what we call it, gunk. It's fluorescent green."

Peter whispered to Katie, "Stay away." She turned her head and grinned.

"That little tent turned up a little while ago, and no-one knows where from or who from. Some strange things happen here, but we just ignore them all."

"Sir, where is it safe for us to walk? Katie's getting so much better every day, I want to let her see around. I think she has a sound mind behind this poor old shell."

"I'm Dick, not sir." He stepped outside the shed door and pointed towards some hills. "They're not far away, about half or so hour walk, bit more with a pushchair, and there are loads of old caves, apparently some with wall paintings from millions of years ago."

"Wowee. Cave men? We'll have some of that, Sis."

"But be careful, you could get lost in the caves. The team will be prospecting there soon, and if nothing's found, that will be our lot here. That's the last section left, so when they turn up, if you are there, come home and leave them to it. Your uncle is going to have to go in and clear any of the local creatures."

Steven raised his eyebrows and, "Hang on, you're telling the kids to go there exploring. What about the creatures?"

The old man grinned, "I've already told you there are none left. All you have to do is go in ahead, to show the company that we are working to the H & S rules. Just don't tell anybody, especially in any letters. They'll be covertly scrutinised, and you'll probably be sacked, excess to requirements. Use your noddle."

They all stood and drank their tipples, and then Katie, with a smile on her face, gave Peter's arm a gentle tug. She whispered to Peter, who asked on her behalf. "Err, Dick, Katie wants to know if she can talk to the creature if we meet one?"

"Now, lad, that would be daft and dangerous. But they've all been killed, so don't worry about it."

Katie's smile turned to sadness. Peter picked her out of the wheelchair and cuddled her as she cried, and whispered into her ear to calm her down, "We can at least look out for one. Don't cry." She clung to his neck and sobbed.

"That's why I never had bloody children," huffed the old man. "Where's your wife Steven?"

"Oh, she left me many years ago, when I did something terrible. But these are my nephew and niece, not my children. I owe them a life." He realised what he had said. "I know, and I brought them here. I think I'll regret that move."

The two men left the children standing outside, looking at the distant adventure playgrounds, while they discussed Steven's new role. Old Dick had been on the colony for over twenty years, and in that final site for two years. He knew the routines. He explained that the gunk was a chemical which had been manufactured to dissolve everything, except lead and izaline. It was used to dissolve all the rocks and minerals, particularly granite, from around the izaline, leaving the precious metal intact and ready to be harvested. The metal was so precious that the investment had been enormous, manufacturing tons of the gunk, only to find that the presence of izaline was so sparse on the colony that most of the gunk remained sitting in degrading tankers at the various spent mining sites. One day they would do something, like explode, or vaporise, or something, but by then the colony would (hopefully) have been deserted by the miners. Only the natives of the colony would remain to suffer it.

"But the gunk has been used for other things. Your gun is like a flame thrower, but throws gunk instead of flames. It does those creatures so effectively, there's nothing left of them after. But you won't have to use it."

He kept reminding Steven, or was he reminding himself?

Steven and the kids completed their walk around the site, keeping clear of the tankers. Katie, however, was fascinated by the little tent. They looked inside, and it was empty, but little Katie was so thrilled that she was unable to stop giggling. Peter didn't worry about what she was giggling about, she was laughing instead of crying. Her improvement since the new drugs seemed to have accelerated since their arrival.

Night fell almost instantly, and up sprung two moons, turning the landscape a yellowish blue. Then they both fell over the edge of the world, leaving total darkness. They snuggled into their camp beds for comfort.

"Night, night, sleep tight," whispered Steven.

"Nigh, nigh." Katie was uttering discernible words and sentences.

"Don't let the bedbugs bite," Peter replied, and smiled, believing that maybe the colony *was* the right move for Katie, and for them all.

The morning switched on as quickly as the evening had turned off. And there was noisy activity outside so Peter pulled himself up and looked out of the flap. There were six scruffy-looking workers outside, loading up a motorised cart. It was Uncle Steven's work crew.

Katie looked up at Peter through her lovely grey-green eyes and she smiled. "'eter," she said and held her hand towards him. He held it and grinned.

"Once I've washed you, we're off creature hunting." The teenager was just as excited as his little sister at the thought of searching for a creature, however dangerous. But he still remembered Old Dick's words *'But they've all been killed'* so he wasn't going to worry about it.

"Get up Uncle!" He clapped his hands. "Time for work."

God, poor Steven, who had not worked for years, was about to meet the miners. He jumped up and washed, then went outside to introduce himself. Peter heard a load of laughs as he washed Katie, and they could be heard cheering about something, so he looked out of the flap to see Steven with a pack on his back which had a flexible pipe going to a chunky fat shotgun with a bulbous pump in front of the trigger. He was waving it around like a kid, laughing with the others and he seemed to have struck up an instant friendship with those burley looking miners. I'm sure they were a lot nicer than they looked. Old Dick came out from his shed and handed them all a package, probably their lunch.

"I think, Sis, that Uncle Peter is gonna have a whale in this place. I hope so."

The men hitched up a small bowser to the motorised truck, and they embarked on their trip from the camp, towards the hills. All they needed was some miner's marching music.

"They're going our way. Wonder if they will be at the caves."

Old Dick called them over, and the children ate a full English breakfast between them. "Dick, my sister is getting so much better. This is a brilliant environment for her. She's even eating better."

"It's not so bad here. I think you'll have a great time. Do as much as you can, we've only got six months, less if they don't find any izaline very soon." The old man wasn't looking forward to going home. He had become 'institutionalised' on the colony, with little or no worries. "I don't want to ever go home, really."

Katie leaned forward from her wheelchair, and stroked his hand. Her distorted smile said *you'll be ok'*. The old man smiled down at her and ruffled her blond hair.

"If you go to the caves, be careful not to go too far in. You could get lost. They're not massive, so you'll find your way out eventually, but it could be scary for your sister."

The two adventurers set off from the shed, and Katie waved her hand at the tiny khaki tent as they passed. She muttered something, but Peter could not understand.

The place was just like home, but warm and fairly humid. The plants were green, but in many places they were entangled by spiny brambles which caught Peter's clothing if he moved anywhere from the centre of the path. The woodlands had a sinister air, foreboding, private.

"We'll stay out of there, Sis." But Katie giggled as they passed a particularly dark part of the woodland. "Ok, you're braver than me. But tell me if you see anything."

They left the wooded part and the land opened out to heath land, dotted with yellow-flowered gorse. It stretched down to the small mountains ahead, and to the sea to the right. It was much less intimidating. The path ended abruptly, so they had to travel over the short grass and heather. Katie grunted and pointed towards the mountain to a dip in the rocks.

"You wanna go there?" Peter pushed hard, and they set out towards the dip, as Katie became increasingly excited. "Well, Sis, you're having a great time." He was so pleased that they had gone to the colony. Katie had spent years on a mattress, and it must have been like a living hell for her, like living in a cocoon, with just two eyeholes through which to connect to the outside world. But the new drugs were kicking in, and she was becoming alive.

"Mummy."

Peter frowned as he looked at his sister in disbelief. "I'll ignore that for now."

They reached the dip. It was just a dip in the rocks, running down to a small pool which collected the water from the towering cliff. But Katie began jigging in her chair, and giggled constantly. So Peter pushed her down to the pool, and as they stared into the dark hole a reflection showed some hot air ripples wafting out from the cliff above. They both looked up, and there it was, warm air blowing out from a hole and refracting the light to display a distorted face. Was it a miracle or a mirage? They both just stared, but the wind blew and the warm air dispersed, and the face was gone.

"Come on, it's the cave." Peter lifted his sister from the wheelchair, and he scrambled up the gentle slope to the entrance, which was hidden behind a rocky upturn. "Wow. It's so warm." The air puffed from the cave, brushing their faces with dry, warm gases which smelled like toffee. "Perhaps we can get a toffee apple," joked Peter.

He dipped his head under the low entrance, and stepped into a large cavern, and they waited for their eyes to adjust. As they did, the cave paintings appeared.

"We've found them, Sis." They stared at the ancient murals which could have been millions of years old. "We are some of the only humans who have ever seen these. We'll need to come back with a camera. They're fantastic." They were dimly lit from two holes further up the cliff, and the light shone directly onto the paintings. They must have been painted with a view to being highlighted by those roof lights, to heighten the onlookers' experience. "I wonder if they tell a story." Katie pulled his arm and pointed to the left, where maybe the sequence began. Peter walked, with Katie in his arms, to the first picture to the left.

It was a simple picture, depicting a large, bulbous being, surrounded by many smaller beings. The sun was high in the sky. The second showed the large being looking out to a wavy sea, where a vessel bobbled. The third was very red and the large being stood with a large hole through his torso, and all the smaller beings cowering away from him, covering their faces. The fourth and final one was of the large being lying down, with the smaller ones bowing their heads, as if in mourning, and standing over the head of the large being was a figure with a bright ginger head and a brilliant green face. Large tear drops hung from the cheeks of the ginger-headed person. The series of four pictures was of simple depiction, but the story behind it clear. The people had welcomed somebody, but had then lost their leader or God, maybe after he had fallen for somebody of a very different structure. It was one of those stories which could be expanded in a thousand different directions, with a thousand different endings, all of which would probably be wrong. It was far too simple to be simple.

"Wonder what it means, Sis." He cuddled the little girl.

She grinned and pointed to the first picture. "God," she whispered, pointing to the large person and then to the smaller beings, "Children." Then she scowled and pointed to the vessel in the second picture. "Us." She pointed into Peter's face, then into her own. "Us." They nervously moved to the third picture and there she pointed to the large being with the hole. "God." Her face was sad, and she had begun to weep. Then the smaller beings, hiding their faces, "Us. You, me." Her whispering was becoming a little stronger as her earlier excitement changed to anger. "Uncle 'teven," as she pointed at one of the smaller beings. The tiny, stricken girl was becoming stressed. They stood in front of the final picture and she held her hand out towards the ginger-headed being. Peter moved forward so that she could touch the feet of the being in the picture. She said nothing, so after a while they moved back to have a better overall look. She pointed to one of the mourners and sadly said, "'eter. You." Her hand then moved slowly across the painting and pointed at the ginger-headed being, and almost with a sigh of relief, she whispered into Peter's ear, "Mummy."

Peter never said a word. He just gazed at the ancient cave painting, at the fallen God, and at his mother. Ridiculous! He began to smile, and playfully waved his sister from side-to-side, rubbing his nose on hers as she passed and she grinned, biting her bottom lip.

"You prat! You really had me going then." The two of them chuckled and cuddled. "You're coming back to life, aren't you." They looked at the four paintings for a little while. "Come on, we'd better get back to the camp. I think you've wet yourself."

They climbed down from the cave entrance, and Katie was sat back into her wheelchair. They laughed and joked all the way home.

Colin Hodgson

3 -- THE NEW BURY MONSTERS

"Uncle. It's great here. We found the cave paintings!" Peter held Katie tight as he ran to meet the returning miners. "What about you?"

Uncle Steven grinned, "I got through the first day. We'll take it from there."

The other miners all smiled at the children and said 'Hiya' before piling into the shed for their after-work pint.

"You should see the paintings. They're *millions* of years old." Peter sighed as Katie laughed and put her thumb up to her uncle.

Uncle Steven was totally knackered. He had just completed his first proper day's work for many years and was very proud of it, but *oh* so tired. "We'll get some grub, then I've got to sleep. Come on." He took the children to the shed where he ordered their food from Old Dick.

The sun suddenly disappeared and the two moons rose, but they quickly disappeared below the horizon leaving total darkness. It was a little scary for the two adventurers. On the first night they were so tired that they just instantly went, or one of them did, but that night they were awake, excited and fidgety. Peter crept over to his sister and lay beside her.

"Shush, mustn't wake Uncle. He's gotta be up again in the morning." He lay with Katie, looking towards the window. He could see some stars, but nothing else. "It's so quiet here. At the borstal I always heard owls, and even some nightingales. But nothing here."

Katie put her mouth to his ear and he heard, "They've nearly all gone."

"Really? How do you know?"

"The 'ictures said, silly." Her nose was tight against his head and ear. "That's why they 'ainted them. To tell us." She chuckled. "We can go 'ome now."

Peter frowned, and bit his bottom lip.

"'eter, you were in the last one, so was Mummy. She not here any more." She held Peter tight. "We'll go home."

The poor boy was becoming confused, but put it down to his sister's illnesses. He ignored her.

"Peter." She actually managed to get the 'P' out, she was improving rapidly. "Sorry. I love you, and uncle." She was close to crying.

"Hey, don't cry. We're like on holiday. We'll go home in six months, and enjoy the place 'til then. You mustn't keep crying."

She sobbed, "Sorry. Brought you here cos I'm selfish. Thought you were someone."

"I am. I'm your brother. You're all I've got and I've got to get through this shit life somehow. Help me?" He had a tinse of begging in his voice. "Please help me."

The roles seem to have reversed, maybe just temporarily, but Katie replied, "I will. Always."

Morning broke, and Peter looked at his sister who lay smiling, wide awake. She whispered, "Looked after my brother all night." She grinned up at him.

The routine was much the same as the previous morning, except that Steven already knew his mates, so they didn't cheer. They went off to work, and Peter washed himself and Katie, then wandered over to Old Dick's shed. He made them breakfast, this time a full English breakfast for Peter, and scrambled egg on toast for Katie. They ate heartily.

"We found the cave paintings, Dick," said Peter, proudly. "They were massive."

"Really? I've never seen them. Some people say they don't even exist, just myth."

"I'm taking my camera today. I'll show you them." He looked at his sister, "And you know what, Dick, Sis can read them. Like a book." He glanced a sideways look at Old Dick, "Know what I mean?"

The old man retorted, "Perhaps she can. Give her a chance. Tell me what you saw, Katie."

She sat in her wheelchair and bit her bottom lip as she grinned. "Mummy. And you." She pointed at Dick. The two 'older' ones patronised her with some smiles. "We can go now." Her voice was weak, but clear. "Go home."

Peter held his sister's hand and asked, "Do you want to go back to the cave, for some photos?"

She just shook her head.

"Oh. I wanted some photos." Peter was disappointed. "I wanted to show Dick."

Old Dick interrupted, "Don't worry about me if she doesn't want to go. It must be tiring for her."

Peter insisted, "No, we'll go." He looked at Katie. "It's not too tiring, is it?" She glumly shook her head.

She held her hand out to Peter, "Look after you." He nodded in appreciation.

The old man sighed and said, "You must look after each other. And I bet when I see you next, Katie, you'll almost be walking. Your change is amazing, and just three days." He bid them farewell.

The warm air still wafted out from the cave, but the toffee smell was stronger. Peter carried Katie through the entrance and they waited for their eyes to adjust. Horror! No cave paintings!

"It's the wrong cave!" shouted Peter. "It *must* be!" They stared at the bare cave walls and Peter was huffing with anger. "Where are they?"

Katie pulled round to his ear and whispered, "They told us."

Peter frowned, "Who told us? Don't understand."

"They told us the story. Mummy has gone. Gone. Lost again." She pointed to the way out. "We must go. Now!"

"But she just stood there, in the picture. Why has she gone?" He wasn't believing his sister. "Tell me!"

The tiny blond bit her bottom lip, and whispered, "Her tent had gone. Let's go home. Quickly."

As they held each other in that smelly cave, the warm air movement increased. And they heard voices, angry ones, and then screams. They seemed to be coming from behind the wall where the pictures were. Katie pointed to the exit, so Peter began to move towards it, towards their escape. But the shouting and screaming turned to crashes and rumbles and then a muted explosion rocked the cave, sending hot dust to cloud their vision, and then darkness. Peter froze, clenching Katie to his chest, and the noise tuned down to only a scratching sound. It came from behind them.

Peter stood motionless and whispered, "Not a sound."

Suddenly they were hit. Something knocked them from behind, then grabbed them tight and swung the two children round. They landed behind a rock, against the wall. In a blind fear, they lay there in the dark as movement swirled around the cave like a demon of the night until, amongst a volley of screams, the thing vaguely lit up and melted into the ground. The toffee smell was overpowering. Peter shielded his sister's head beneath his upper body while the shouting slowly depleted back into the darkness behind the painted wall. It was quiet again.

Peter began to cry. "Katie." He shuddered as he spoke. "Sorry." He slowly released her from his desperate hold. "You ok?"

The dust began to clear, and they both coughed up some of the dust. Katie had hit her head, and was bleeding, but smiled at Peter, and then kissed his lips. "I look after you, my brother. Go home now." She pulled her hand up to his face and wiped his tears from his cheek, then, "But we mustn't leave the children. Poor children."

Peter frowned. He stretched up to look over the rock, and in the middle of the cave floor lay a creature, bubbling and steaming. It was large, much bigger than a human, but was slowly disappearing as it was eaten away by a green 'gunk', and the ground around was becoming pitted as the rock melted. The creature had been shot by the miner's gunk thrower. Uncle Steven!

Katie began to cry. They had found their creature, just like the God in the painting, and it was dead, killed by their own family. She whimpered, "Mustn't leave the children," and Peter just stared in horror, witnessing the last few moments of the being's existence, and then it seemed to run down into the holes which the gunk had created. The green stuff dissolved everything, almost. He wondered if the gunk would eat six feet into the ground, to lay the creature properly to rest. Katie just stroked his cheek.

"What are we going to do, Sis? There might be more." He looked over to the wall, where a ragged hole had been blasted. "We'd better go and find the men." But there was no sound. "Or we'll have to take our chances going out the front."

Katie whispered, "She saved our lives. We can save her children. Look." She pulled at his neck and he looked round into the dusty hole in which they sat. He caught his breath and held Katie tightly. She said with a smile, "Our friends." She stressed, "Friends. Children."

The dust slowly settled and there in the corner of the cave were two creatures. They were sitting upright, one hugging the smaller one and both looking sadly at the two humans. They were a bit smaller than Peter, had dark green skin, a bit wrinkled, but smooth, and their necks were thick, almost straight down from their heads, and their arms and legs long. So similar to a human, but very different. They looked at Katie with a longing despair, and Katie's twisted smile invited them over to her. As the bigger one leaned forward Peter panicked. He pulled Katie away and moved sideways, and the sudden movement frightened the little being. He opened his mouth and whimpered, clutching his little mate. Peter moved back and relaxed.

"Hello," chuckled Katie. She grinned at the frightened beings. "I'm Katie. This 'eter. No, *Peter*." They all stared at each other for ages. She pointed at herself, "Katie." The bigger one slowly moved his hand and pointed at his little partner, but said nothing. She looked up at Peter and suggested, "We call him Mo?" She giggled, and the bigger one smiled, then she pointed at the little one and said, "Mo."

Peter held her head and pulled her ear to his mouth. "We need to go home."

"No!" She bit her bottom lip, "We *must* look after babies. Mummy is dead."

"Sis, these are alien creatures. The mum was massive. They'll grow up and eat us both." He looked to the middle of the cave, and all he could see was a steaming hole in the floor. But then he suddenly realised what had happened: two little children had just lost their mother, as he had done seven years earlier. He looked at the little things and wondered. "Do you think they grieve?"

"Course. They're people." She looked at the little one and carefully said, "Mo. You are Mo." She waited for a response, but none came. "They're babies. They'll learn."

"What are we gonna do, Sis? Can we take them to the camp, do you think?" They both shrugged their shoulders. "I've got an idea. We can go back to the camp and test the ground a bit. See what they would do if we took them back."

The two children left the other two children in the cave, and set off back to the camp. They had decided to take things very sensibly, after all. The adults had just killed their friends' mother, and would probably kill their friends if they ever found them. They had to be sure.

"Dick, if you met a creature what would you have to do?"

"Kill it. Before it kills me." He smiled, "Why ask?"

"But if it wasn't going to kill you, what would you do?"

"How do I know? How do I know if it's gonna kill me?"

"But do the creatures kill people?" Peter looked at the old man in expectation.

"Well, they have, once. We found a deposit and the creatures just wouldn't let us anywhere near to it, so we went to battle with them, and we killed several of them, but they killed two of our comrades. They swiped them once and they were in shreds." He shook his head.

"How many did you kill of them?" asked the little adventurer.

"Must have been about twenty, maybe more."

Peter raised his eyebrows then snarled, "They had to defend themselves. Didn't you talk to them? They were probably just scared of you."

"Don't be silly. The company ordered the extermination of the species. They were getting right in the way. We had deadlines to meet, and they were a bloody nuisance. We killed them all."

"You bloody didn't!" Peter got a poke in the ribs from Katie. "I mean, there was still one left, cos they killed it today. Wait till they get back and you'll hear." He had almost given away the little babies. "So now the last one is dead, you can leave them alone."

"They won't do that. If they've found one alive, there'll be others, and the company want the vermin removed. They've still got places to prospect."

Katie pulled Peter to her and whispered, "They are in danger. We need to look after them, and keep quiet." She looked at Old Dick and said, "You scared?"

He shook his head and grinned. "I don't think they're as dangerous as humans." But he would still have killed them if he had the chance. He was institutionalised, brainwashed, and to him they were lower orders, to be used, abused and killed. That was his outer shell, anyway.

Katie pulled Peter to her mouth and asked him to speak to Old Dick for her. He stood up and said, "Katie says, 'You won the war, leave them alone now. Your people went to war with loads of countries, but you don't carry on killing them now.' That's what she thinks."

That shocked both Peter and Old Dick. The brain was finally escaping from the confines of a useless body. Wow!

Old Dick moved over and shook the girl's hand, "You have a point. But you won't convince this lot. They just brainlessly toe the company line, unlike some of us." He scratched his chin. "If you've found some, don't tell the others." They'd got him wrong. "Be very careful, but keep quiet."

Katie smiled at Old Dick. She could see something in him which he probably didn't allow many people to discover. "Thanks, Dick."

The mining team returned home with big stories to tell. They had made a kill, and the enemy was depleted, on the run, and their advanced forces were hot on the trail of the rest of the reprobates. The battle would soon be won. That was the gist of things in the shed that evening.

Meanwhile, back in the tent, "The truth, Uncle." Peter pushed Steven to tell the real story.

"We were at the end of a long, deep cave, and there was a feint signal on the detector. We thought it was probably a falsey, cos it was so feint, but the others say they haven't found anything for months and the company is getting impatient. Anyway we had a glimmer of hope. We went along this really narrow bit and it opened out to a cavern, where we had the signal from. We set some explosives to break through the end of the cavern as the probe showed a hollow behind the wall. And the izaline detector still showed a feint signal. So we were ready for the hole to blow, and whoosh, something rushed past the front men. It stood in front of me, with my thrower in my hand ready. It was half dark, but I could see a large thing, must have been ten foot tall, and it was staring at me." He stopped for a while. "I've only ever killed one thing before, your dad. I didn't know what to do, nor why. So I just stood there. The others were shouting at me, but I couldn't shoot it. It was like it was talking to me, silently, just saying nothing. But the detector was still bleeping weakly, so I stood aside to let it past, and I could then go to the front with the others and use the detector. Anyway, I went to the front and it moved down the cave. The others were mad and were shouting and screaming at me. But they blowed the hole through, and the detector showed something in the other side. Suddenly the creature pushed past me and the others, and went through the hole. In the screaming I pointed the gun through the hole and let fly with that gunk. A horrible, husky scream came out, then loads of hot air, and a stink of toffee apples. They say that it's the smell of one of their nests." He looked at the floor. "I must have killed it. We're going back first thing to check out the nest. See if there are any more creatures, and check that detector signal."

Oh dear. Peter looked at Katie who was curled up on her bed and sighed. They had to get back very early to move the babies, or they would be lost.

Katie asked, "Uncle, were you scared?"

He had a proud smile on his face. "Not me. I don't think it would ever have hurt me. It could have done, but it just looked. I couldn't see very well, but I think it was smiling at me. I wish I hadn't killed it. I wish I had said hello to it." He was showing some regret. "I wonder why it had to rush back and go through the hole. Must have had something in there."

Katie, as so often, had a tear in her eye. "What if we were in the cavern when you throwed it?"

Steven looked at both the children and whimpered, "I would've killed myself. But you weren't."

Morning arrived and as the sun shot up from its hiding place Katie crawled over to Peter and poked him. "The men are getting ready. Quick."

Too late, one of the miners was outside the tent calling for Steven. He shot up and sped out without even a wash. Old Dick gave them their pack-ups and they were off.

"Oh no! They've gone already!" Peter panicked. He threw some clothes on, and changed Katie's nappy. "We're gonna lose them, Sis."

He almost threw her into the wheelchair, and they sped off down the lane, with Old Dick waving from his shed, and praying for them. But they suddenly found themselves close to the gang, as they were taking the same route, and heading for the same cave. They slowed. There was no way of getting past them with the woods so full of brambles. As they all entered the heath land Peter called out.

"Uncle!"

The group stopped and turned around. Surprisingly, the burley miners all smiled and said 'Hiya kids', and then looked at Steven.

"What're you doing? We're going to be working down here today."

One of the other miners, probably the boss-man, suggested, "They can come along if they stay out of the way while we work." He grinned, "If they can *catch* us working, that is." They all had a bit of a laugh, and then moved on. The kids strung along.

"What're we gonna do, Sis? They're gonna kill them when they find them. Do you think that if we explained about yesterday they would let us look after them?" She shook her head. "Then we'll have to be a shield, in front of them."

Katie held her hand up for him to move down to her face, and she gave him a loving kiss. "You always stick up for little ones. I love being your sister." She bit her bottom lip. "I'll look after *you* when you need me." Peter was confused, but he felt a warm shudder run through his heart.

The miners arrived at the pool, where the detector was pointing. The signal suggested that the izaline, if any really existed, was deposited in the deep, black hole, which collected the water from the cliff. The men never knew of the cave entrance, hidden from view by the small rocky outcrop, so Peter picked Katie from her wheelchair and covertly carried her up the slope. The smell was still there but the air was cooler, as the wind blew through the newly blasted hole in the wall. They stood still, just inside the entrance, while their eyes adjusted and as the cavern revealed itself to them, they gasped. There were two new paintings!

"Go over there," Katie urged.

"Wow! Hell!" Peter stopped dead as he saw what was ahead of him; a hole in the floor where the poor being had been killed. It went down into the darkness, and they could see some glistening which looked like water. The gunk had corroded the ground right down to the underground water-way, the one in which the miners were about to enter in search of izaline, and they could hear them talking through the water.

Peter thought quickly, "The gunk. The water might be poisonous." He hurried out of the cave and down the slope to the men.

"Stop!" He approached his uncle. "The water. Stay out."

The men were very responsive, and they stopped lowering the chain ladder.

"What's up, lad?" asked the boss-man. "You seen something?"

Peter smiled as he panted. "I don't know. But the poor thing that you killed yesterday. It might have gone into the water. I'll show you."

Oh dear. He suddenly remembered the little babies, in the cave. He looked into Katie's face, but she just smiled and whispered, "Show them the hole." Peter relaxed a bit and walked round the rocks and up the slope to the entrance. The men raised their eyebrows, but waited for Peter to enter before they were prepared to; the cowards. And as Peter's eyes adjusted, the pictures became very distinct, by their absence. They had gone. He stood with Katie and waited for the first brave miner to enter.

"Look. That's where you killed it yesterday. It's gone right down to the water."

The miners walked around the hole, sniffing the air. They all had their turn, and then the boss-man said to Peter, "Well done. I bet that water is lethal. You know, you might have saved our lives." He walked to Peter and held his hand out, then they shook firmly. "Thank you, lad." I think Peter had, at that very point in time, become one of the boys, maybe one of the men. He was very proud of himself. "I don't think the small amount of metal is worth our risking ourselves. We'll leave it there for posterity." He grinned and looked around at the others. "I have this strange feeling that this was the last detection of izaline we are ever likely to get from this colony. I think we'll be going home soon." He winked at the little girl.

The men looked around the cavern, but there was nothing there, except for the smell of toffee, the smell of the creature's offspring.

"I'd like to know how you knew about the creature, and the hole." The boss-man raised his eyebrows, expecting an answer. He urged Peter to reply. "Come on lad. Whatever it is we won't hold it against you. We're all in this together."

Katie whispered into her brothers ear. He then spoke to the boss. "We were in here when you killed her." Katie whispered, and he spoke. "We saw her get torched. It was horrible. We stood right where the hole is when she came through the wall."

Uncle Steven butted in. "Please don't say that." He remembered Katie's question the night before about them being there, and being killed. "I could have killed you." Nobody knows what could have been going through his head.

"Stop!" ordered the boss-man. "It's a good job you killed it, Steven. You saved their lives." He turned to Peter. "You're very lucky to be alive. Perhaps we are all gonna see some luck from now on."

"But you already have. I saved you from the water." Peter shouldn't get too smug, these were rough, fighting miners. Katie whispered, and Peter told the boss-man, "My sister would like to save your lives again, if you don't mind. Can she?"

The miner frowned a little and then replied, "S'pose so."

"If you're thinking of going back into the cave behind that wall, you know, through the hole, don't. It is too dangerous. That's all." Katie whispered again. "And if you don't want to take any notice, then we won't stop you. But we *will* stop our uncle. We love him."

Everybody was quiet, looking around at each other, until one of them suggested, "Let's call it a day. Have a day in the shed, on the beer."

The boss nodded. "But we'll be back tomorrow to route out these creatures, the smell is still fresh."

They all left the cave, and as Peter put Katie back into her wheelchair, Uncle asked, "Are you coming back with us?"

"No, Uncle, we'd like to take a look around for more paintings. I've got my Polaroid today."

4 -- THE WILD COLONIAL BOY

As the gang disappeared into the wooded area the two newly formed heroes relaxed.

"Sis, that was brilliant. It kept them out of the other cave. Let's go and get the babies."

"No." Katie grinned and whispered. "It's not safe. We'd be hurt."

Peter snapped quite frighteningly, "It's me! I don't need that shit."

She dropped her grin as he snapped, and then held her hand to his face. "No. I didn't make it up. The painting said."

They looked up the slope towards the cave. "So, tell me what the pictures said. Please." He rubbed his nose on hers; he was sorry for frightening her.

"The first one had some people laying down, with a big rock on top of them and some smaller people standing by, with tears dropping from their faces. It was Uncle laying under the rock. He has warned us." Her speech was almost normal. "The other picture showed a tree like an elephant head, with big ears and a trunk, and a bright light at the base. It was a sign of love." She had a glow in her cheeks. "They are our babies."

Peter hugged the little one as he picked her out of the wheelchair. "Let's just check the cave." He had every faith in his sister, but…

They carefully walked around the hole in the ground, to the other hole in the wall. Very gingerly he stepped near to the opening and leaned forward to see inside. It was pitch black. He could not see a thing. Katie squeezed his arm to stop him going any further, so they moved away. "I'll take your word for it, Sis." They then walked over to the hidden part where they were thrown. As they slowly peered around the rock, they expected, but there was nothing. They had really gone. "Oh God, they've gone into the other cave," exclaimed Peter.

"No. Under the tree! The *picture* said." So they went out of the cave entrance and stood looking out across the horizon for a tree which looked like an elephant. Loads of trees, but no elephants. A little despondent, they returned to the cave to look for some clues. And there it was; a painting showed the tree, and the yellow spot of light at the base, but Katie had a longer look and could see some wavy lines behind the tree. "It's the sea," she said, and so they left the cave and moved down the slope and out towards the open heath to where the sea was in sight.

"There it is, Sis." Not very far away there was an African elephant, with enormous ears and a trunk hanging low down. That was their tree, and in their hearts they both knew that the babies would be sitting below it, waiting for them, and hoping.

Peter had to push hard to move the wheelchair through the long grass and heather, and he began to sweat and puff. It was not a long distance, but torturous. He was only a child so they decided, at about halfway, to sit down and rest.

"Peter, what if we don't get back tonight?" Katie was a little concerned about their uncle, and about worrying him unnecessarily. "When we get to the boys, you can go home and explain to uncle that you left me sleeping."

"What? Leave you out here alone? Never. We'll both go home, or both stay out." He abruptly stood up and huffed, "Let's get going."

He pushed for a while, and then picked Katie out of the wheelchair and carried her, pulling the empty chair behind. That was a lot easier.

They arrived at the tree. Everything seemed deserted, not a creature in sight. The little bit of shrub around the base was not enough to hide the two of them.

Katie leaned back and waved her head about to look. "Mo! Little Mo!"

Then they heard a wheezy noise, a bit like a baby crying with a very sore throat. It was them. They had nested away from the tree, in amongst some dense gorse, and were calling the kids over to them, so Peter took Katie and they carefully pushed through a break in the spiny barrier. There they were, at the back of a grassy kindergarten, secured by the spikes of the thick gorse scrub. They were all elated.

The little green people cuddled each other, and seemed to be inseparable, clutching onto everything they had left after the tragic loss of their mother. The orphans looked to their new adopted parents with hope. Their small eyes were dark and their necks thick, but apart from that their overall appearance was of thick-set, dark green children, but with no genitals, at least not in the same place as us. Katie wanted to be put down with them. She leaned over into them and they all held each other tightly. Peter just sat back and admired the instant affection which they all shared, and perhaps felt a little jealous. But he let them have their moment, like a grown-up might have done.

Peter had taken his Polaroid camera out of the bag and was playing with. He took some pictures of the three children, and then sat down close to them while they developed. He showed them the photos and the babies were quite amazed, and could recognise that it was them, pointing at Katie and chuckling.

"Mo," she said, looking at the little one. He smiled back. Then she said to the larger one, "Stumpy. You are stumpy."

She pointed to him. "Stumpy." He seemed to be trying to repeat it, but gave up. "My little children. I'll look after you."

Peter was a little concerned at their new family members, wondering what their uncle would think to his new nephews. He would probably think of them as pets, or even pests. And the other miners, well, they would just kill them. It seemed that they were in the middle of a real thicket in more ways than one. It was going to be a hairy time for the little ones, but Peter was aware that they, at least, were at home, unlike him and his sister.

Katie had managed to open up the camera bag and had pulled some pictures of Uncle Steven. "Uncle Steven." She pointed at his face. Then another one of him. Katie told them, "Our Uncle Steven. He looks after us." The two babies were quite fascinated by the camera and the photographs, but were not freaked in any way. And when a picture displayed with Peter in it, they both pointed to Peter. Katie said "Peter," and pointed to him. Little Mo attempted to say Peter, but it came out quite different as his tongue was trying to talk in quite a different manner. But they continually tried, each time getting a little closer to the English version, and giggling in between along with their new 'Mummy'.

"Katie, we need to get going soon, or do something. It'll nearly be dark by the time we get back. And you know how dark it gets when the moons go." Their first major problem. But the two babies slowly got up and walked hand-in-hand to a scrape in the ground, and lay down, pulling some dry grass over. You would never have known they were there.

They decided that the safest place for them, for now, was where they were in the scrape, protected by the gorse thicket. After all, the only dangerous creatures remaining on the colony were those two little babies. Or was it the humans?

The journey back was hard, and they were getting tired, but they just made it before the sun-down, just as Steven was beginning to worry.

"Now, kids, I'm not gonna have this. It's about half hour from dark. You could have been stranded out there. The others were gonna come after you some time back, but I didn't want any fuss. I said I knew where you were."

"But, Uncle," snapped Peter, "There's nothing out there to hurt us, is there."

"That's not what the others are saying. We're out in the morning to search out the young of that creature. They're dangerous!"

Peter jumped, "What is it with you lot? You said the creature didn't harm you, but you killed it. That's typical fucking human."

"Now listen! We are here with the mining company. We'll *stick* with the mining company, or we're in the bloody shit up to our necks. The izaline is believed to be spent here, no more big enough deposits to be economical and they're saying about a ship picking us all up on the way back from another drop. We're going home very soon." He looked into Peter's eyes, "That's good, isn't it?" He could see Peter's eyes wetting. "Isn't it good?"

Peter blinked to clear his eyes. "Don't know. Will we be going back to what we had?"

Steven dropped his head.

Peter asked, "How will it be different? You've got out of your prison, which allowed you to walk, talk, have friends, and laugh and I've got out of mine, which allowed me to walk, talk, have friends and even play and laugh. We could even wank. Sis will go back to hers, where she was trapped in a chrysalis, seeing and hearing, but not talking, not walking, not laughing, not playing, not loving, just nothing. She was like a caterpillar waiting, but waiting forever, waiting to die."

"But she's getting better with the new drugs."

"It's *not* the drugs!" He put his head into his hands. "It might be part the drugs, ok. But it's more than that. She was making slow progress at home, hardly any. She could move her head, great! And that was after months on the drugs. Look! Look at our Katie."

Katie was sitting upright, and she grinned, biting her bottom lip. "I feel good." She was slowly transforming, and although her limbs were twisted and deformed, they were beginning to work.

"It must be the atmosphere, or water, or something. Old Dick, he said that the medicine cupboard wasn't used, the odd bandage. Why? They're all so healthy. There's something in this colony helping Katie and all of us."

Katie leaned over and pulled Peter's arm, for a cuddle. She put her mouth to his ear and whispered, and Peter seemed to drop down a few degrees.

"She says that we ought to go home. Me and you, not her." That was too big for a fourteen year old boy. He looked into her grey-green eyes and asked, "Why? We've found each other. Why?"

Steven suggested, "*We'll* make the decisions, Katie's too young."

"But you know then, it'll be *our* fault if she turns back into a spirited, vigorous brain living in a lump of lard." Peter looked at Katie and tried to smile.

She put her mouth to his ear and whispered. "I can get home alone, but I'm not going without you."

He frowned and asked, "What are you talking about?"

"I can get home, but I'll never leave you here." She kissed his cheek. "Tell you later. No more talk about it."

Uncle Steven needed to sleep, so they finished the food and waited for the lights to go out, and then, by the time the two moons had dropped, he was soundo. The hard work and a couple of beers sent him off to another world, just for a while.

Peter lay with Katie. "Sis, I'm a bit scared."

She laid her head on his neck and whispered, "I know. I'm sorry." She changed the subject. "They're going out for our babies in the morning. We might lose them."

The two 'parents' could only wait, and hope for the safety of their adopted children, and eventually Peter went to sleep, while Katie watched over him. She never slept.

The light returned. Steven, for once, was awake before Peter.

"Morning Katie. Sleep well?"

She nodded, and squeaked, "Like an avian explorer, been all around the galaxy." She giggled. "Where you been?"

Uncle Steven frowned as he replied, "Had a nightmare. Don't know where I was."

"Make sure you don't go back there, then."

Steven went out to meet the gang, and Peter awoke to the morning chores. He cleaned himself up, gave Katie her drugs and then cleaned her up. They went to see Old Dick in the shed. He was morose.

"What's up, Dick?" asked Katie, her head swaying from side to side.

"Hmm, don't ask."

She giggled, "But I *am* asking."

"Bloody going home, ain't we. Home. That fucking shithole." He suddenly awoke. "Oh sorry, the language. I'd better watch me tongue" He at last smiled. "Yeah, going home. Be good for you two. Nothing here for you." He looked out of the door, at the khaki tent. "I'd like you to have something. They're no use to me." He went to the medicine cabinet, and took out a paper bag. "Once we found some izaline which wasn't buried in a cave. The izaline was shaped like a small bone. And all around it was this white stuff, powdery stuff, so I took it and made it into these tablets. Wasn't sure why at the time. But as the years went by I found out why. The earth's core is mostly iron, and it features heavily in the make-up of our planet. But here, the core is believed to be nearly all caskin. And it's in the air, only in minute amounts. But the powder we found is crystallised caskin, and we've found it at every izaline deposit. Well, those which haven't been gunked. Not sure what it means, but I'd like you to have the tablets. Take them home with you when you go, and I think, Katie, you'll find a use for them."

Peter asked, "Can we eat them?"

Dick shook his finger. "No, no. One of the miners tried it and he said it was lovely, like strong peppermints. But he went mad and dropped dead after a few days. His liver had almost exploded." He sighed. "I think it's the caskin which causes all the miners to get cancer as soon as they go home. That's why I don't want to go home."

Katie put her arms up for Peter to lift her out of her seat, and he did. "We don't want to go home either. Well, I don't but I want Peter and Uncle to." She bit her bottom lip. "Do you know why?" Her weak, deformed arms held Peter tightly.

The old man, even with the whisky in him, still had a sharp mind. "Why what? Why you want Peter and Steven to go home, or why you want to *stay* yourself?"

"Both."

The old man gave a wry smile, "Of course I know why." He thought carefully, through the alcoholic haze. "First, the cancer. The caskin cancer. I know, we all die when we go home. They don't tell anybody that when they come, nor when they go home, but I've kept in touch with some old mates. You know, I've never told anybody here, no point; it's too late once they've been here for more than a few months. Now Peter and Steven could go home now and be ok, but if they stay much longer….. Second, you've found some friends. And I don't just mean me."

"What do you mean, Dick?" she quizzed.

"You know what I mean. You're an intelligent girl, more than anybody realises, and more than anybody else here. And you've found some babies. D'you wanna tell me about it? Won't tell the others. On my heart."

She stared hard into his eyes. "I know you won't. We have some babies."

"Sis, what the hell're you doing?"

"He's like us, he likes them. Why do you like them, Dick?"

He shuffled his feet and leaned hard on the tiny bar. "One saved my life, some years ago. I was with the gang in a cave and there were big gaping cracks in the floor. Anyway I fell down one, and lodged on a bit sticking out. I hurt my leg and arm and couldn't move, but I didn't hit my head, so I survived the fall. But the others must've thought I was dead, so they left me for dead." He looked out towards the little tent. "I laid there for ages. Felt like a lifetime, then something touched me on the face. Don't know how it reached me but it was one of the creatures. They're big, and very strong. It spat in my face and I thought I was going to get torn to bits." He cocked his head to one side. "I don't think they've ever torn *anybody* to bits."

Katie grinned.

"Anyway, it didn't tear me to bits, cos I went right out when he spat me, and woke up being carried by someone. I must have been delirious cos the person was strong enough just to carry me on his own and was bright ginger and the face was a green light. I don't think it was one of the creatures, and I looked around and there was nothing, just space. Endless space. So weird. I think I was carried back to camp and put inside the little tent, where they found me next day." He chuckled. "They saw my feet sticking out of the tent, under the flap. They thought someone was having a joke, so they just left me nearly all day." He poured himself a drink of whisky. "Haven't drunk properly for two years now." He smiled at Katie. "*You* know they don't hurt anybody." The old man knew more about the little girl than he realised. "You have a kinship with them, I can smell it." He looked at his feet in shame. "But we've got to kill them. Don't know why."

Katie waved her head about. "As a human, you should know that it's because."

Old Dick looked at Peter as if to say, 'What?' but Peter just smiled. He knew what Katie had meant; you do as you've been conditioned to do. And that's what the miners were off to do that morning.

"I think," Peter remarked, "they are going to find the children, and kill them."

Old Dick nodded. "I think you will lose them. I'm sorry Katie."

Katie whispered into Peter's ear. He conveyed, "Katie thinks they will look after themselves, and survive. She's hoping. We should all hope. Do you pray, Dick?"

"No, but if it helps, I can begin. Who do we pray to?"

Katie chuckled, "God, your God."

And Old Dick raised his glass of scotch nectar, "To God, our God."

Meanwhile the mining group had neared the rocky area and then were stopped by the boss-man.

"Right. I think this is a good time to tell you lot. I got a message today from the company. We're being pulled out. We've hardly found any izaline for months. Just *three ounces* and they think it's depleted. A ship passes tomorrow, and it will pick us up."

One of the miners shouted, "Tomorrow? That's a bit short notice."

The boss-man grinned, "Why? What've you got to do before you leave?"

Nothing at all. They lived in tents, as bachelors, had a handful of luggage, and only memories to take home. That is, apart from the illnesses which would take them to their graves!

"So make sure you are *ready* for the morning. We'll have a leaving party tonight, clear Old Dick's shelves for him, and it's 'goodbye New Bury'."

They all faltered for a few moments, and then cheered.

"But we've been instructed to cleanse the area of the enemy. The future plans for the colony are unsure, so they don't want to come back here in a few years time and the new residents be faced with ten foot tall monsters. The babies we are looking for today are the future enemy, and they must be eradicated. *Today!* Got that?" He looked around at the 'enthusiastic' band on hunters. "Well? Are we up for some cleansing? These are lower beings, and are excess to God's paradise. They must go." He again looked around at the 'enthusiastic' band of hunters, at their faces which promoted their barren emotions. They were not convinced. "And to help you to do God's work, the company has pledged a bonus of six month's wages for all of us, if we can today eradicate these evil low-lifes." Their dire facial emotions changed to smiles. When faith fails, money triumphs.

The two babies were still in their kindergarten in the safety of the gorse. They had collected some rocks and had built a small mound which stood about two and a half feet high, on which they had placed several very large dark brown mushrooms. They sat down by the mound, clutching each other, and waited for the return of their adopted parents.

The eradication team entered the cavern where they suspected the babies may have returned to. Gunner Steven, the man with the gunk thrower, went in first, followed by two comrades. As he stood for a few seconds, while his eyes adjusted, he saw a wall painting. It was a ring of gorse bushes with two little men in the middle. But as his eyes adjusted to the light, the painting faded, and disappeared, leaving Steven blinking and rubbing his eyes in disbelief.

"Careful Steve." His comrade pointed to the hole in the floor, the grave. They searched the cavern, but found nothing. "Let's get out of here. It stinks."

"Right," said the boss-man. They stood away from the rocks surveying the heath land which ran down to the sea. "We'll do a pincer-type beat. You three spread to the left, and we'll do the right. Steven, you stay dead centre, with the gun, and any body sees anything, shout, and Steve'll be right there. All understand? We must find these today."

The group spread out, and Steven looked ahead at his route. It was going to take him towards a tree which resembled an elephant and as he looked down the gentle slope towards the sea and the tree, he noticed that there was a clump of gorse bushes to the left. The wall painting showed a ring of gorse, and he remembered that there was something inside the ring, two things. He could not take his eyes off the gorse clump. Not knowing why, he just *had* to get to it before anybody else did.

As they moved forward, they all poked around in the shrubs and kicked the clumps of dead grass. They were on a shoot, the beaters intent of flushing out the prey to expose to the gunner, and they went 'heyup' and 'weyhey' as they pushed the line along. Steven kept a bee-line for the gorse thicket, hoping to be the hero of the day as he was when he shot their mother, and as the beaters to the left moved too close to his line he waved them to spread to the left. He wanted the gorse thicket, and something was guiding him there. The boss-man shouted for them to slow on the left, and allow the right flank to catch up with the line. Suddenly the right flank shouted and jumped up and down as a creature shot from a clump of grass. It sped back towards them and they yelled and jeered to frighten it around towards the gunner and it passed like lightning across Steven's path. He raised the gun, but it was only a hare. Panic over.

One of the beaters yelled, "You could've got some shooting practice, Steve." They all laughed.

The line moved on with no other excitement, until it reached close to the elephant tree. They slowed, but for some reason Steven had to get to the gorse thicket before the others. He raised his hand for the line to halt and then walked to the thicket, and they all stopped their beaters' chants. Silence. He looked over the five foot shrubs and could see that there was an area in the middle. *'It's the painting. The ring,'* he thought. He found a weak part between two plants and pushed through. He stopped dead. The others could see his head and shoulders, and kept quiet in anticipation. He stared in awe, and in fear, at two little green creatures who sat by a pile of stones and mushrooms, and they stared with their tiny eyes into his. He was mesmerised. His hands began to shake as he turned the gunk thrower towards the babies and he gripped the trigger. And then…..

"Uncle Steven." The little one, Mo, spoke very quietly, but he heard him.

Steven caught his breath, began to shake and his finger lost the trigger.

"Uncle Steven," Little Mo repeated, quietly.

This time Steven *clearly* heard him. He began to sweat, his forrid furrowed deeply as his brain became confused. He began to panic, and found the trigger.

"Uncle Steven."

The trigger finger would not work. Steven tried to speak, but could not get anything out. The boss-man called to him, which awoke him, and he put his hand in the air to acknowledge. Suddenly he managed to speak. He just said, "Peter?"

Little Mo smiled and turned his thick head towards his big brother, who also smiled and slowly stood up. Stumpy waddled over to Steven, who was at a point of collapse, and held his hand out. Shaking violently Steven responded and Stumpy placed something in Steven's hand, then waddled back to Little Mo and helped him up. They quietly moved into the thick shrubs and disappeared into hiding.

"Steven!" shouted the boss-man and as he did Steven pulled the trigger. He blasted his target with the gunk, and they began to melt, bubbling and hissing.

"Got them?" shouted the boss-man, and Steven just about managed to nod, and the men all followed Steven's route into the thicket. They stared at the target which spat and bubbled, and at the mushrooms which had liquefied, running down the disintegrating body of rocks like melting flesh. The flesh covered rocks could have been *anything* in that state, even two little dark green babies.

One of the men raised his camera. "We need this for our bonus."

All the men cheered, and pulled at Steven's hand for a shake, from the one who had killed the last of the New Bury creatures. "He'll be a colonial hero. The wild colonial boy!" They shouted and danced around the smouldering gunge as it began to eat down into the soil. They were the ultimate victors and the fox was quite literally going to ground.

But poor Steven had broken. His brain had shut down, and all he could see were his two children, in alien bodies, smiling at him, and escaping.

As the men danced, they began to realise that Steven didn't. The joy eddied and began to flow back to concern; their new friend and hero had gone over the top. They carefully took the pack off his back and relieved him of the gun, and then walked him out from the thicket. The boss-man gathered them all together.

"I've seen this before, after killing the creatures. He's in shock." For a bunch of rough, tough, burley, God-fearing miners, they were very gentle with Steven. He had had a nervous breakdown. He could only see his Nephew and Niece, sitting in front of him with dark green skin, and he constantly whispered 'Run, run fast.' That was all he said as his mates walked him slowly back towards the camp.

When they arrived, Old Dick left his shed to greet them. He looked at Steven and frowned. "You got them, then." There was no air of celebration amongst the group, the initial fervour of the 'kill' had died and they now concerned themselves with the health of their gunner. "Bring him in for a stiff un," suggested Old Dick.

"Come home," whispered Steven, and Old Dick instinctively took his hand.

As Dick clutched the broken man's hand he slowly pointed out, "The kids have gone out hunting cave paintings." He looked down in shame. "I tried to talk them out of it, but they went anyway. I'm sorry Steven."

Poor Steven may have understood, but maybe not, anyway he smiled at Old Dick, carefully removed his hand from

Dick's and accepted the glass of scotch. It went down the hatch, and the others gave a cheer.

"Let's party! Home tomorrow." They all squeezed into the shed, began their farewell drink, and the children soon melted from their thoughts as they pickled their brains with the alcohol.

While the miners were heading back to base, the two adventurers had hidden themselves in the woods at the top of the heath land. They waited their chance to make the trek across the open land to the elephant tree.

When they got there Peter was panting and sweating.

"Let's sit under the tree for a few minutes, Sis." He picked her out and they sat looking at the thicket. They watched, wondering if the babies were still there, or if Uncle had made a kill.

"I think they are," said Katie. "I don't think Uncle would kill them." But as she spoke, Peter was asleep. "My poor baby, just sleep. I'll look after you." Katie sat rigid as his head fell onto her shoulder. "You're safe with me."

But the day was coming to a close, and the sun suddenly disappeared below the horizon. Peter continued to sleep as the two moons raced across the skies, and then it was totally black. The night was so dense. Katie held Peter tightly, and kept watch.

Back at the camp the men turned out of the shed, for bed. They were totally smashed, and not one of them could put two words together. Old Dick was back on the bottle, but was just about able to help Steven to find his tent. None of them even missed the two children. Typical bunch of piss-heads.

Colin Hodgson

5 -- THE PASSING OF DICK

Peter slept for several hours, almost until sun-up. As he awoke, he shuffled around but felt so snug and warm, he drifted off again. Katie grinned as she stroked his forrid. Then a few moments later, the sun shot up above the horizon, and the colony came back to life. Peter fidgeted. Then he scratched his nose, and put his hand down beside him.

"Ahh, what's that?" He screeched and shot up, knocking poor Katie to the floor, along with Stumpy and Mo. "What?" His face lit up. He had been snuggled up, all night, to his sister and two baby creatures. He gasped with his mouth wide open, and then he almost cried. "You're here. Come here."

All four of them cuddled, and rolled onto the grass like little pups, but then suddenly stopped. They all sat looking at each other, and even Katie sat upright without support. Her face was a joy to witness, with her open grey-green eyes shining through her blond hair, and a smile which could have spanned the universe. She was in heaven.

The men in the camp were waking up, their heads banging and throbbing from their hangovers. None of them were fit to travel, but they had no choice.

"The ship will be here in just forty minutes," shouted the boss-man. "Grab your bits, we're going."

But Peter and Katie were in a world of their own, playing with their children, giggling and fighting, and teaching them new words.

Then Stumpy looked out to sea. He could hear something. "What is it?" Katie asked.

He pointed, and a long way off there was something in the air. Within seconds it was above them, and slowing down to land. It was their transport home.

"Go, Peter. Go. Now!" Urged Katie. "Go home!"

"What about you? Come on, we've got about two hour walk from here."

"You can get there in an hour without me."

They looked at each other.

He grabbed Katie by the waste and picked her up.

"I'll run with you. It'll be quicker." He held her to his chest and they set off, followed by the two babies. "Stay here, they'll kill you both!" He stopped. "They *can't* come, Sis!"

"I know. I'll stay with them. I can get home later. Please." She kissed him full on the lips. "Please go home, or you'll never get there."

The poor boy was confused by what she was saying. "I can't leave you here on your own. You're my sister." He would not move an inch. The two babies put their arms around his waist and wheezed. I think they were crying. And then Katie began to cry. "I'm staying with you!" stressed Peter.

But as they stood clutching each other, the ship roared, lifted above the distant woodlands, and it was gone. *None* of them were going home!

"I'm staying with you," whispered Peter, and suddenly burst out laughing. They just fell about in stitches, and rolled onto the grass in fits. They were all staying on that distant colony, New Bury, maybe until death. That was *so* funny, apparently.

But the giggles slowed and Peter stood up. "We're all staying." Suddenly they were not laughing. The realisation of what had just happened sunk in, and Katie began to cry. Peter picked her up. They looked over towards the camp. "What're we gonna do?"

She carried on sobbing. "Sorry, Peter."

They said nothing as he put her into the wheelchair. The two babies stood one each side of Peter as he set off towards the camp, and then they both put a hand onto Peter's hands as he pushed the little girl through the grass. Their spindly little fingers were rough, and thicker at the ends, but they were gentle, and Peter felt a comforting warmth as they held him. There was a lot of love ready to bloom from inside those leathery carcases.

Tired, and a little apprehensive, they approached the camp. From that distance everything looked quite normal, the miners were never there during the day, anyway, but Peter was concerned.

"The babies must hide here while we check out the camp." They crept into the woodland. "I'm scared, Sis." He reached down and held her hand as he pushed her into the camp. Everything was as it was the day before. Maybe they hadn't gone, after all.

"Peter!"

"They're still here!" Peter almost screamed with delight.

But Old Dick shuffled out of the shed, distraught. "Peter, oh dear, Peter."

Peter could tell from Old Dick's reaction that they had all gone and the brief moment of hope was dashed. They stood and looked at each other.

Old Dick hobbled into the shed and beckoned them inside. "I couldn't stop them. I tried." The old man had begged the miners to go looking for them, but the boss-man gave them an ultimatum; home now, or stay forever. And old Dick stayed, alone. "I can't go home, and I'm glad I'm not alone, but you should have gone." He made some food for them as they had a drink. "Please be my friend. There's nobody else." He was still drunk from the night before. "Please be my friend."

Katie hadn't said a word until then, but she pulled herself up from her wheelchair and almost stood. "Look, Dick. I can nearly stand." She grinned at the old man. "Your friend can nearly stand." That broke the ice, and Dick cheered up. She turned her nose up and said, "We can have a good time, here together. All five of us."

Dick chuckled, "You can stand, but you can't count."

She just giggled as she pointed out of the door. There stood Stumpy and Mo and the old man stood back in shock. He couldn't believe it! Then he smiled and took Peter's hand. "You did it. You saved them."

Peter went outside and took each one by the hand, and led them in to meet Old Dick. He was enchanted. "Pleased to meet you. I'm Old Dick. I've heard that you guys are hardened killers, tyrants who prey on small children in the night and tear the hearts out of the strongest of miners." He laughed, and Stumpy and Mo grinned. "It might have even been your mummy, but she saved me from certain death. I'm so glad they saved you."

Stumpy looked at Mo, who just said, "Uncle Steven."

Old Dick had seen the coming and going of so many miners over the years. One of the reasons that he would not get into the ship was that he knew that he would die soon after going home, as *all* of his previous friends had. They had all died from liver cancer, very quickly after their return home, although living healthily for many years on the colony.

"I think your uncle will be ok, he hasn't been here for long enough. The others? Well."

Poor Peter was wondering why his uncle had left them, but when the old man explained about his state of mind, he began to understand. "The whole world will be thinking that he killed the last of the local inhabitants. But here they are."

"Yeah." Peter looked at his two new children who were cuddling Katie, and with a wry smile said, "When they can talk, they've perhaps got some explaining to do." The teenager never dreamt that he would have a ready-made family by the time he was fourteen.

They retired to their tent, leaving Old Dick to ponder over his diminishing clientele. The days of the Shed Bar could soon be coming to an end, especially as the gang almost drank him dry during their leaving party. But he smiled as he closed the doors.

Peter suggested that he clean Katie up, change her nappy and give her her drugs before they worried about the rest of their lives, but she proudly stated, "I can go without a nappy, I think. You'll have to help me though." Peter was so pleased for his little sister. Her brain was so strong, alive, but her body had been her personal prison, but suddenly she was at least now out on remand, controlling her arms, legs and movement, and her talking had simply blossomed.

"Peter."

He looked round at Katie and smiled, and she just smiled back at him. "Well?" he asked.

"Wasn't me." She looked at Mo and chuckled.

Little Mo sat with Stumpy, tight up to his waist, as if they were joined. Peter wondered if they were twins, although Stumpy was so much bigger than his brother. He then began to wonder if they were brothers at all, or maybe sisters, or perhaps they did not have separate sexes. So much for him to find out about his new adopted children!

"Peter." Mo called him again, so he stepped over to them and sat down. Mo looked into Peter's eyes with intense concentration. He wanted to say something, but couldn't, and so he pointed towards the tent flap.

"What's up, Mo?"

He again pointed to the flap, but this time slapped his face afterwards. Then he pointed again and tried to say something. "O…." He could not get his tongue around the word.

"Show me." Peter picked him up and held him to his chest. "Come on, show me." He walked with the baby out of the tent and stopped. "Where now?" Stumpy had followed them. Mo pointed to the shed, and so the three of them went over to Old Dick's shed. "You were trying to say 'Old'."

"Old." At last Mo got it right. He held his hand towards the shed door and tapped it, then looked into Peter's face with concern.

Peter realised that he was trying to tell him something about Old Dick, so he put the child down, and looked around to see if there was any way to see inside. He then knocked hard on the door. "Dick! Are you ok?" There was no reply. "He's gone out. Gone for a walk. We'll see him at tea-time."

Mo and Stumpy began to wheeze, like they did when the ship left, and they were crying. Peter walked them back to the tent.

"Sis, they're scared for Old Dick. Something's wrong, or they think it is."

She pulled herself up. "We should get inside. He could be ill."

Peter put Mo down, and replaced him with Katie. They went over to the shed. Suddenly they were all concerned for Old Dick's well-being, so Peter pushed the door hard. It had been padlocked from the inside; he *must* have been inside.

"I'll have to break in." Peter put Katie down, and went off to the tool tent. He came back with a long crow bar, and forced it behind the door, then jemmied it open.

"Oh no!" They all stood at the door, looking at an old man laying down, motionless, with his arm stretched out and bloody. He had cut his wrist. "He's done himself in," whispered Peter. The children all stepped inside the old shed bar and bowed their heads in respect. "He must have been so scared. Left here to die, *and* he'd run out of whisky." He picked Mo up and asked him, "How did you know?" The little being just smiled and looked up towards the skies. "Yes, he's gone to heaven."

Neither Peter nor Katie had followed a recognised religion, so they decided to cremate him in his shed, right where he lay. The medicine cabinet could be useful so they emptied that out into their tent, and took all the beers and spirits to another tent, just in case they had visitors. They then set light to the shed and watched it burn, until the sun dropped down below the horizon. Mo and Stumpy said some words in their own language, which made Katie laugh, and Peter just said 'goodbye Old Dick'. That seemed to be enough.

That night was stressful for Peter. It was the first night after the ship had left with the miners and his uncle, and the loss of Old Dick had compounded his nightmares of the years to come, with no other human companionship but for his deformed sister. He began to wonder why they had left the comfort of their lives back home, but soon remembered. He thought about being locked up in the school, always fighting everybody else's battles, and about Uncle Steven being locked up in prison, and about Katie's brain and spirit being confined to a useless shell as she lay for years on that mattress, alone.

Katie crawled over and lay with him. "I crawled." She hugged him and grinned, but then became serious. "Thank you for coming with me. I had to come. And we will be ok here."

Peter had heard her apologise several times, but never quite understood them. "You came with *me*, remember? I thank *you*."

She grinned and whispered, "Whatever." She nodded towards the babies. "They will grow to about ten feet tall. Big boys."

"How do you know? We didn't really see their mother."

She screwed her face up at the question. "I just know. They will look after us as we look after them. They are beautiful people; gentle, intelligent, and divinely loyal. They've lost all their people and we are their only living relatives, and we have to understand that. We need to help them all that we can before we go home."

"Go home? I won't hold my breath. Besides, I don't want to go home. I was so unhappy, and what about you? What was it like laying on a mattress for about six years, looking out at people looking in at you. Was it lonely?"

Katie laid her head on his shoulder, "Not so bad, I've been lonelier. That was when I couldn't stop crying, and I've cried for so long now. You know Peter, I've almost stopped crying now. But I won't stop properly 'til I've found her." She sighed. "And when I do I won't cry any more. I've missed her so much and the paintings told me she was here, but she's gone again. Don't know where." She began sobbing. "You know Peter, I thought you were Daddy. You're not. But you're my brother instead, and I love you so much for it. Will you help me to find Mummy? Please?" She looked into his eyes, but they were fast asleep, sound. She whispered, "How much of that did you hear? Not much, I think." She kissed his cheek and allowed him to escape the colony for a few hours. She watched her babies and her big brother sleep, wondering where they were in their dreams and whether they would return in the morning. Old Dick would not. "I'd like to chat more with you one day, Old Dick. You had a lot of love festering inside that lonely old body. You never shared it. What a waste." She stared out of the window at the night and quietly asked, "Are you out there Mummy? Please come home, I miss you so much. I need you, we all need you. I forgive you." She looked over to her babies who slept arm-in-arm and asked, "Do you know who your daddy is? I bet your mummy didn't tell you before she died, did she. Naughty humans doing that to her. But that's my fault, I suppose. But I'll tell you about your daddy, and try to be your mummy. Then I *must* go home, I've so much to do." She chuckled to herself, maybe over some long laid memories. "My mummy helped Old Dick, when he fell down the crack. I know it was her. Her face and hair. You know babies, she's not all bad, just naughty. And now she's lost." Katie shed a few tears while passing the night away, waiting for the others to return home from their dreams or nightmares. She did not sleep.

The morning rose, and the babies awoke. They jumped up and rushed over to Katie and Peter, diving in for cuddles. Peter woke with a screech.

"Ouch, that hurt!" as he held his rib.

The two smiles left the green faces.

Peter calmed. "It's ok. You just made me jump. You're a bit too big to be jumping on us." He pulled all four together for a family morning love-in. The little people laughed and chortled as they rolled around on the floor. "You know what, Sis? They've grown, I'm sure they have." He pulled back to have a proper look at the little monsters. "Stumpy has grown, definitely." Katie just giggled and flopped around.

They spent a little while talking about nothing and playing around, as kids do, and bonding. The little ones were picking up on what was being said, but saying nothing, just staring deep into Mummy and Daddy's eyes as they listened, picking out what they needed, and maybe a lot more. They were learning at an astonishing rate.

Katie chatted and jested with Stumpy for some time, while Mo snuggled up to Peter. The conversation between the little boy and the girl was not clear, and, although Peter strained his ears to hear, he could not understand any of it.

"Are you two in another world?" he jested. "Or another language?"

Katie and Stumpy looked across and grinned. Stumpy said, "Peter." Then they chuckled.

The first day on the colony alone, and they just played around, bonding and learning, and in the case of Stumpy, growing. He was definitely growing, almost by the hour.

"Sis, how long before he is adult?"

She whispered in Stumpy's ear, and then answered, "About thirty."

"Thirty what? Years, months?"

She whispered again in his ear and laughed. "Days. About thirty days." Her head swayed about as she watched Peter's reaction.

"Thirty days?" He was gob-smacked. "Thirty days? How old is he now? No! Don't ask him. I want to ask him." He nervously readied himself. He spoke very slowly. "Err, well, Stumpy. How old are you?" He frowned as he looked into Stumpy's very dark little eyes. "Do you understand?"

"Yes."

Peter gaped in amazement. But did he really understand? "Well. How old?"

Stumpy held out his hands and stuck out all four fingers and the thumb from his left hand and two fingers and a thumb from of the right. Eight.

"Eight days old?" quizzed Peter.

Stumpy smiled and nodded. "Eight." He held his fingers out. They were very slim, but the tips were enlarged and creased and they did not look to be very sensitive. Peter touched the fingers. They were seductively warm but leathery, designed for some rough handling, and the enlarged tips were creased down the centre and had no nails, just a hard, bony end. "Eight days." Stumpy was showing off, and started to laugh and he jumped forward and held Peter around the waist. "Peter. Friend Peter."

The children would grow to manhood in just thirty days, twenty two days hence, amazing, but that meant that they needed to learn enough about life, language, love, companionship and survival in their first month of life. As they stared deep into the eyes of the two humans, it became clear to Peter that they were learning from their thoughts. They did not even need to talk to them to teach them their language; the amazing little creatures just took it all from their new parents' minds. Within a few hours they were talking, with a few problems with the use of their mouths and tongues, but they were talking.

"Katie, this is amazing. They've learned what we would take years to learn."

Katie grinned and joked, "You'll be learning from them soon." They weren't the only ones that were changing so rapidly. Katie was getting better by the hour. It was as if the four of them were networked, drawing all the good from each other, and sharing knowledge, and becoming whole. Katie's distorted frame would never become perfect, but it was beginning to work almost like a normal child's body. She was crawling, controlling her toilet, talking clearly, and laughing and smiling, and not crying. She was having a wonderful time. Perhaps tomorrow she would walk.

Colin Hodgson

6 -- GENESIS

The family wasted the day away playing and bonding. But what a bonding session it turned out to be. They seemed to gel as one, talking, understanding and laughing and they all forgot about the real-life situation which engulfed them; that they were castaways on a distant colony.

But night eventually fell and they got down onto their beds. Katie cuddled up to Peter to keep warm, and the two babies cuddled on their own bed. Peter immediately fell asleep.

"Katie," whispered Stumpy. "Are you awake?"

"I'm always awake." She crawled over to the babies and joined them. "I'm here."

They got themselves comfortable and pulled the blankets right over themselves. "Do you sleep?" asked Katie.

"Yes, but not much. Shall we talk?" asked Stumpy, very quietly. "Don't wake Peter."

Katie whispered, "What shall we talk about? You, or me?" They chuckled below the blankets. "Would you like me to tell you anything about you?"

"But Katie, you are not my mummy, just a friend. How can you tell me anything?"

"I'm a special friend." She hesitated. "I'll tell you who you are. Are you cuddling comfortably. And you Mo?"

They all jiggled to get comfortable, and she began. "You are two little children of the God Edward. You are the only two boys left."

71

"Our daddy is a God?" Stumpy wasn't convinced.

"Yes, honest. You were in the paintings that your daddy showed me. He had died and you were alive. All the people of this place have been killed by the humans, and by disease, and there are none left to carry on the race. Your daddy is God to a world with no subjects. And I don't know what you are going to do."

Poor Stumpy and Mo were confused. "But you haven't told us anything. We're *all* the children of God." Hmm, good point.

"But the other children are his subjects, but *you* are his children. You are God."

"Why tell us this? Besides, how do you know, you're human?" They were not taking too much notice of the little girl's rantings.

"Please believe me, and please trust me."

Stumpy reminded, "If you know anything about us, then you know what happens to people who lie to us? Yes? Well, keep it in mind."

The babies were demonstrating a level of threat which surprised Katie. "Why do you threaten me? I'm more than just your friend. Don't threaten me, ever."

The babies were becoming agitated, and dangerous. Katie decided to close the talks. "I'm going back to my brother. He loves me."

"But he isn't your brother, is he." Stumpy pushed himself up onto his arms, but Mo poked him and he lowered. "Is he your brother?"

Katie thought very carefully. "No, I adopted him. But I love him as my brother and he loves me. That makes him my brother, in my belief. What's your problem with that?"

The babies calmed down and cuddled her. "Can you really love him if he's not your brother?"

"Of course! I love all my people, but some much more than others, especially my brother. I shouldn't, it'll cause problems, it already has, but I do love him. I think I do, anyway."

They lay for a while without talking, but then Stumpy snapped, "You've got somebody to love. We haven't. You've killed everybody here." Stumpy held Katie a little too tightly.

"Let go!" Shouted Katie.

Peter awoke, and rushed over to the bed, pulling back the blankets. The bigger baby had hold of Katie, but was only cuddling, but very tightly.

"Let her go!" snapped Peter. "You're hurting her! Let go, she's only a baby herself and she's delicate." He rolled Stumpy over to release Katie. "Get to sleep, or there's trouble."

They all changed back to their proper sleeping arrangements, and retired. Some of them slept, while others thought, and wondered.

The next morning soon came around. Peter exercised his command.

"Right, we've all got things to do before we start the day. Katie, what're you doing?"

"I want to go to the toilet." She giggled.

"Stumpy?"

"I will help Katie go to the toilet."

"Mo?"

"I want to give Katie her drugs."

"Right, that's sorted. I'll get myself washed and ready to take the world on. Today is the start of the *real* adventure."

None of them knew what Peter meant, not even Peter. But he was determined to do more than just play around on a blanket all day; he had a life to lead.

They left the tent and bowed their heads in respect as they passed the remains of the shed. Their destination was the tool store. As they routed around, the babies kept looking at Katie, sitting in her wheelchair. She looked back. They were exchanging some thoughts.

Then Stumpy spoke up. "Katie, I'm sorry. We thought you were just a nosy kid." He had a giggle. "When I was asleep, somebody told me off. They said you are more than a friend, as you said. I'll never get nasty again." He stood in front of her and she noticed how he had grown, about six inches since they had first met in the cave. He was going to be a stunner.

Peter had found some of the small tools for which he searched, such as a pruning saw, loads of matches and some sharp knives. He was thinking like a boy scout. On the other hand, the children all messed around, without a care in the world. They were thinking like children. Poor Peter looked at them and wondered how he would get by, with protecting them, feeding them, and everything else with them. He was a fourteen year old with baggage!

"Come on, we've got to sort out how we feed. Stop pissing about."

Katie smiled at him and suggested he look in the food store. Silly Peter. The food store was packed with tins and dried stuff, enough for a whole gang of miners for at least six months. He grudgingly put the saw back where he found it. But he kept the knives and matches.

"So, we haven't got to find food, so, what shall we look for?" He stood smiling, waiting for some input from the kids. "Right, Mo. You first"

He screwed his green face up, and then, "Stumpy's scraper."

"Right, that's one thing to look for today, whatever it is. Katie. Your turn."

She screwed her head round towards Mo. "Mummy."

"Hmm, ok. We'll search for Mummy. Stumpy. What do you want to search for?"

He grinned, showing his perfect white teeth from behind his red lips and green face. "Daddy's burial vault." He stood proud, chest puffed out.

"Good. We've got a lot to do today. We've got to find a scraper, a Mummy and a Daddy's vault." Peter suddenly wondered what he was doing with those tiny (getting bigger) kids. "Right, what's a scraper? Mo, tell me and we can begin the search."

Mo said, "Stumpy gave it to Uncle Steven. When he let us free. It's important."

Peter stood wondering how they would find something which had probably been shipped back to old blitey with their uncle.

"So, what do we do with it, if we do manage to find it?"

Stumpy replied, "We stick it in a hole, to let us in. We'll need to find it else we won't find Daddy's vault or Katie's mummy. And I need to find Daddy's vault soon, cos I don't know what to do."

It was beginning to make some sense to Peter, "So it's a key. But how will it help to find Katie's mummy? Or my mummy?" He raised his eyebrows and looked hard into their eyes, hoping to see some of the things that the others seem to see from behind the eyes. He could not see anything. But then Katie spoke to him. *Their daddy will tell me where Mummy is.* She did not talk, but he just heard her.

"Was that you, Katie?"

Then she spoke, "Yes." She sat in her wheelchair grinning. "If he can tell me where Mummy is, we can go home."

Peter was becoming immune to the total confusion which was scrambling around in his head. Just going with the flow, he suggested, "So we need to do the first thing first. We should, then, look for the scraper. What does it look like?"

Mo looked at Stumpy, and Stumpy held his hand out, fingers stretched. "It's a very big one of these."

They all stared at the hand, then suddenly the fold in his forefinger opened and a brilliant silver claw flicked out. They had claws, hidden under the folds in their finger tips.

Peter stood back. "Wow, that's scary. That's what Dick meant when he said they cut them to bits." Peter was impressed, but aware that the fairly large claw, which was razor sharp, would be a *very* large claw when Stumpy reached ten feet tall.

Mo said, "We are looking for one of those."

Where the hell do you begin? It should either be on it's way to home with Uncle Steven, or somewhere in the camp. They had to hope that the second possibility would prove fruitful, as going home to look for it was never an option. The search very sensibly began at home, in their tent. They turned everything over, and emptied every box, can and bin. They shook the bedclothes out, and they went through all the pockets they could find. They went through the chemical toilet, yuk, but only found poo. They had gone through the tent with a fine toothed comb, and found no nits, nor scrapers, nor anything unexpected.

"What's this book?" asked Mo.

"Mine. It's mine, please leave it," begged Katie. "It's my only real possession, and I'm looking after it for somebody." She crawled over to Mo and took the old book. "Thank you Mo. I'll read it to you one day. I promise."

They did not find the scraper.

"Where on earth do we look now?" asked Peter. "I wonder if he went anywhere else that evening, or yesterday morning." They left the tent and looked around the street. "That little tent is still there. Shall we check it?"

Katie turned round and said, "No, it won't be there."

"How do you know?" Peter and Stumpy looked into Katie's face. "How do you know? He could have got pissed up and laid in there all night." Peter wanted an explanation.

She winced and bit her bottom lip. "He could have done. But he *couldn't* have because his bed was slept in when we got home. That's it."

Peter frowned and sang, "Well, *we* didn't notice it, *did* we boys?" The two boys shook their heads in agreement. "You're hiding something, Sis."

Katie leaned forward in her wheelchair and put her hands on her hips, then snarled, "Don't gang up on me." She tried to be mad, but her imperfect body didn't really work. "Leave my tent alone."

The three boys stepped back. "Sis, we're joking. Lighten up a bit." Peter shook his head. "Anyway, what about the tent? It's not yours. Come on, no secrets."

Katie calmed down. She looked at Peter and said, "Sit down here, in front of me." She was worried about something, and needed to get it out into the open. "I ought to tell you some things, but I don't know how to say it." Her blond hair was hanging a bit over her face and her eyes, so Peter gently pushed it aside.

"You can tell us, Sis, whatever it is. Please." Peter leaned forward. "You don't have to keep secrets from us."

She looked at the tent, and then at Peter. The little girl didn't know how to start.

Stumpy suggested, "I can help."

"How?" She frowned.

"I can start you off."

Perhaps foolishly she agreed.

"Right, Peter, she's trying to tell you that she is *not* your sister."

Poor Peter did not flinch, but just stared at Stumpy. His eyes began to water, and he coughed, and then put his head down. "What the fuck you on about?"

Katie managed to push Stumpy's shoulder with her foot, to shut him up. She whispered, "I *am* your sister. Really. Don't cwy." She leaned forward to see if he was crying, but his face was too low down. "Please don't cwy. That's what I do. Please don't you."

Peter jumped up and ran off. He went down the street and into the derelict school. He was a big boy, fourteen, and big boys don't cry, at least, not in front of the children.

The three little ones stayed where they were, the two boys sitting at Katie's feet and watching the school for movement. Peter never came out.

"I think we need to go and get him," squeaked little Mo. "He's really upset. You shouldn't have said that, Stumpy."

"We don't keep secrets, *ever*."

"But you should've let Katie tell. It was her secret to tell." Mo was a bit more intelligent than his ever-growing brother. "We need to go and get him."

They moved down the street with Stumpy pushing, and Mo holding Katie's hand. As they reached the old school, they could hear Peter crying. He was devastated, sobbing his teenage heart out, like the end of his world had arrived. That in turn, started Katie off, and soon there were two children sobbing. The two green babies just let them get on with it.

As Peter caught his breath, he managed to calm down, and the sobbing turned to sniffing. He looked out from the broken walls and called to Katie, "Come here, please, Sis."

Stumpy began to push the chair, but Katie put her hand up to stop him. She had to do this thing by herself. "Stay here." She put both hands on the chair arms, and pushed. She leaned forward and stood up, leaning to one side on her shorter leg, and she made that first step. She did it. She took her hands off the chair, and just stood for a few moments, then, after nervously looking at Mo and Stumpy, she made the next step, then the next. Her slow walk swayed her from side to side on the two odd legs, and her head hung to one side, but she moved forward, towards her brother. Peter saw her coming towards him, and stopped crying, instead began to smile.

"Sis." He slowly walked towards her, and met her halfway. "Sis." He again began to cry, but this time it was from the absolute joy of watching his little sister walk, something he never believed he would ever see. It was like a miracle. Katie reached her brother and flung her arms around his waist, pulling her wobbly head into his chest, and they shared a very special moment. "I don't care who you are. I love you, Sis."

After holding each other for some time, Peter looked over to the two babies and asked them to go back to the tent. He needed some time with his sister. They had to talk. He sat down with her in the sun, in front of one of the school walls. The rays were warming and life-giving, making them both feel charged, ready for the future's uncertainty, and ready for Katie's dark secrets which she felt compelled to tell.

"I'm ready for the truth. You've dropped a lot of hints since we got here, so come on, hit me with it. Please."

Katie held her big brother so tight. "I *will* tell you about me. But first, I'm sorry to have brought you here. I was wrong to be so selfish, but I'll never leave you here. I promise. I really promise. If we have to stay here until you are old and grey, and until you die of old-age, I'll stay with you." She paused, and pointed to the burned out shed. "Old Dick knew a lot about life, and death." She stretched her head up and kissed Peter on the lips and her big grey-green eyes looked into his brown eyes. Her stare was hypnotic, and Peter relaxed, and began smiling. She asked, "Are you ready for just a tiny bit of my story? I've never told any body else before." She took her stare from his eyes. "Right, Brother, my only brother. This is it. I've lost my mummy. She's been gone for a long time, and I need her back. My daddy is also lost, but I really need my mummy, and if I find *her*, I know I will also find my *daddy*, and vice-versa. So when Catherine told me that you might be my daddy, I had to be near to you. You know that your father tried to kill your mum, almost succeeding, but he did succeed in knocking your sister down the stairs. He killed your sister." She held Peter tightly as she broke his heart. "Your sister died. And as she left, I moved into her. Peter, I am your sister's body. I *am* your sister. But your sister's soul went when her brain was killed, and she is now at rest, at peace. Now I'm your sister. Can you handle that?"

Peter never said a word. He was in a daze.

"You *can* love me as your sister, as you did just an hour ago. I'm the same person. But if you can't, then I'll understand. After all, I'm an eight year old cripple, with a billion year old brain. And that's a *British* billion." She bit her bottom lip. "When Catherine let me know about you and how much you are like my daddy, same human age, same beautiful temperament, I actually stopped crying, just for a while, because I had hope. And even though you are not my daddy, you've still given me hope. You've come here with me after I hoodwinked your Uncle's thoughts, and you stayed with me when you might have been able to get home on the ship."

Peter was waking up from his trance. "I could never have made it back in time for the ship, even on my own."

"No, but you didn't know that when you stayed with me, and the boys. You deliberately stayed with me, chose to stay with me, like a good, loving brother would. You sacrificed going home to stay with me. I know you did. I've seen it in you. So, although you're not my daddy, I think I've fallen in love with you as my brother. I don't think I've ever before loved outside of my real family. So please, please still love me as a sister."

The two sat in the sun in silence for several minutes, and then Peter asked, "So did you make Uncle bring us here?"

"I only gave him the idea. He did everything on his own after that. He's a lovely, generous person really. He idolises you. I bet he's killing himself over leaving you here." She took some time out for thought. "Maybe I can let him know that you're ok. Yeah. He'll be fine, and when he arrives back I'll make him happy."

"I still don't really know what you're talking about. I don't know who you are, even."

"I'm so sorry." She put her face into his chest and began to cry. As Peter wiped her tears from her cheek she sucked his wet finger. "I don't know if I can tell you who I am. You'd hate me for it."

"Try me."

Katie pushed herself up from Peter, and suggested that they get back to the children.

"No, they can look after themselves even better than we can. Tell me who you are."

She flopped back down with him. "Well, have you ever wondered who you are? No? Well, you should have done, cos you don't know who you are, do you. If I was to tell you that I'm your mother, what would you think?"

"I'd think you're a crank. My mother died when you were a baby."

"She died apparently from her injuries, but really from a broken heart. She had lost her baby, me. I was just a shell to her. And she was right, her baby *had* died, and she knew it. I hope you don't blame me."

"Course not, Dad killed my real sister. See? I'm starting to talk like I believe it all."

"You *do* believe it and you *know* I'm not eight. Anyway, in a way I am your mother. That's who I am, your mother, and everybody's mother." She asked, "Have you ever wondered why there is life on Earth?"

Peter's teenage face screwed up and was ridged with frowns. "Because God made it that way. I've read the bible loads of times. I've spent so much time on my own in my room, and often it was the only friend I had. And sometimes I had my music." He smiled, "The music makes more sense most of the time." Katie looked up at him with a grin. He asked her, "Shall I tell you about life on Earth? Let's see if that billion year brain can remember back that far." They had a chuckle and he continued, "I'll tell you what I believe about it. It all started off as a black hole, with God's spirit looking in, wondering what to do with it, and then he got himself a plan. So God started his chores, and on his first day, got the earth out of the black hole and into the orbit of the sun, which gave it light, and he called the light day and the dark night. And there was evening and there was morning." He cuddled his little sister and they both giggled. And there was brother and there was sister, the first day.

"But the earth was covered in water and nothing else, so on the second day God decided to create the air and the atmosphere, and so he left the earth covered in water, and created the watery clouds which drop rain down onto the earth, and that part in the middle, the atmosphere, was called heaven. I wonder if the writer thought that the blue sky was water, but I think he probably meant the rain clouds. Not sure." They both shrugged their shoulders, and there was brother and there was sister, the second day.

"I think he had a really good day then. Cos on the third day he raised the hills and mountains and dropped the valleys down so that the water flowed into the seas, and Earth was dry land, which was drained into the seas by the rivers. And he then made the plants and flowers which were all different kinds, and which had to mate with their own kind to reproduce, to keep their form. I think I know what that means, pollination by the same type of plant?" Katie nodded. "And he called the watery bits Seas and the dry bits Earth."

"Well done, Peter." Katie put her thumb in her mouth and snuggled into his chest, and there was brother and there was sister, the third day.

"Hmm, fourth day. I remember. He made the moon and the sun in the expanse of heaven, the moon to rule the night and the sun to rule the day. And they would dictate the years and the seasons. And he put the stars up in the sky." He frowned and thought. "I think that meant that he made the earth spin and then go round the sun. Hmm, maybe. But if there was already evening and morning, the earth must've already been spinning." He pulled his head round to check Katie, who was suspiciously tired. But she was still awake, sucking her thumb, and there was brother and there was sister, the fourth day.

"And on the fifth day, God made the fish and creatures of the sea, and the birds of the heavens, and told them to multiply, but they had to breed only with their own kind. And they swarmed the seas and the heavens, apparently." They both smiled, and there was brother and there was sister, the fifth day.

"Then the sixth day. God made the animals, reptiles and livestock and all the things that creep on the ground. And they had to breed with their own type, and I think he must have meant the insects as well; they creep on the ground. And then he made man and woman in his own image. And he gave all the fish and birds and seed and fruit plants to man to eat and the green vegetation to the other creatures. I think that was it. Oh, and man was told to multiply and have dominion over, and subdue, *all* the other creatures and plants. Man was to be the boss."

He pulled Katie up to his face and he kissed her, and there was brother and there was sister, the sixth day.

Unusually, Katie was almost asleep, but still compo. She whispered, "Hmm, very good. That was a lovely account of the creation of Heaven and Earth. It's quite close to reality, and it's unbelievably creative, as are most of the scientific explanations. The scientists are clever, but boring, and even less believable than the bible's account, which you just described."

Peter was a believer in science, but also a believer in God, if it's possible to be both. "Thanks, Sis. You know, just talking about the bible, and faith, has helped me to accept the shit that we're in right now."

"Silly billie, we're not in the shit. I'll look after you."

"Thanks." He looked down at her blond head and asked, "Are you really billions of years old?"

"Silly billie, that's a daft question." She squeezed his cheek. "Of course I am."

They sat grinning, quietly appreciating the warmth and power of the life-giving sun. It was one of the ingredients without which life could not exist, and it felt so good as it injected both contentment and strength into their delicate bodies.

"The bible has got it a bit mixed up, hasn't it?" asked Peter.

"A bit. But it's fundamentally correct, and let's face it big Bro', a page of writing can hardly do justice to billions of years of development work. And you have to remember that when they wrote about it, they didn't even know that the earth was round, nor that it went around the sun and not the other way round. It's a quite brilliant explanation of how it all began, especially considering their lack of technical knowledge at the time of writing."

Peter asked nervously, "So, is the bible correct?"

"If that's what you believe, then it's correct. And look what it's done just talking about it; given you hope and inner strength. Religion is a powerful controller of people's actions and their determination. And who's to say that your belief is right and anothers wrong." She looked longingly into Peter's eyes, and the love, which had fleetingly waned after Stumpy's blunderbuss, flowed back. "If you like I can tell you the truth about the earth. But first we've got to find the key."

They slowly walked back, hand-in-hand, to the wheelchair, Peter taking some of the weight from those spindly, distorted legs, and Katie giggled all the way.

The four of them sat on the ground in front of their tent, to discuss the way forward.

"Right," said Peter, "I need to know a bit more about the claw. My sister has suggested some questions for me to pursue."

Stumpy stood up. "That's a lie!" he shouted.

"*Now* what are you talking about?"

"It's a *lie*. She is *not* your sister."

Peter looked at his sister and raised his eyebrows. "We are sister and brother. That's what we want."

"But she is *not* your sister, it's a lie. She is your *mother*. She is the mother of *all* humans."

Poor Peter sat with his head in his hands, and desperately needed his sister to look after him. She obliged, grinning as she spoke. "I am the mother of all humans, and so can choose a brother if I wish. *Now shut up!*" Stumpy sat down and shut up.

After a few moments of electrifying silence Peter continued. "The claw. Stumpy, why did you give your claw to Uncle Steven?"

"For him to look after."

"Hmm, but why couldn't you look after it yourself?"

"I don't have any pockets."

Peter smiled to himself. "So did Uncle put it into his pocket?"

"No."

Peter sighed. "Let's go back to the beginning. What happened when Uncle first saw you?"

Stumpy scratched his cheek. "He got his gun up towards us and looked at us. But he didn't fire. He was asking us to stop him, so I did." Several seconds of silence.

"Well? Carry on."

"That's what happened."

Peter was finding it hard work, but realised that the little green folk answered the questions honestly and fully, almost as if they had no imagination. "Ok, next question. How did you stop him shooting you?"

"Mo *shocked* him to the bone. He said 'Uncle Steven'. Uncle shook and Mo said it again. Then Uncle replied 'Peter'. He must have thought you two had turned into us." He chuckled. He had answered the question.

"Right, then what happened?"

"Right, I didn't have any pockets to put my claw into, so I gave it to Uncle to look after."

Peter looked at Katie for some inspiration. Got it! "How did Uncle know that you wanted him to look after it for you? Well?"

"Because I asked him to."

"What did you say to him?"

"Nothing."

"Nothing? You asked him to look after it for you. What did you say?"

Stumpy frowned. "I didn't say anything, just asked him to look after it for me."

"God, Katie. Is it me or is Stumpy going around the bushes?"

Katie giggled and suggested, "Change your own words. He's answering your questions, so ask the right ones."

Peter looked at his feet as he planned his next interrogation route. "Ok, I get it. So you didn't say anything to him, but what did you ask him?"

"I asked him to look after the claw and give it to the old bar tender."

Wowee, getting somewhere at last. "Wish you'd told us sooner. Right, what did he say to you?"

"He didn't say anything, he just thought."

Peter was slowly realising that they could hear thoughts and convey them. He tested them, thinking *what did Uncle think?*'

"He would hand it to Old Dick. That's all."

Katie smiled. "They have a different imagination to us, and things are more black and white when they look at them. It's your fault, you should have asked them sooner!" She looked at Stumpy with a mischievous grin. "So we need to find out where Old Dick put it, if Uncle gave it to him."

They mosied over to the old shed, staring at the ashes. There was a lot of ash to sift through, and some of it was Old Dick's. Peter didn't fancy that. They needed to think very carefully.

Mo asked, "Do you have any ideas?"

Peter looked thoughtfully at him and replied, "Get sifting, I suppose. Anybody else?"

Stumpy shrugged his shoulders and replied, "It's a risky one, but we could gunk it out."

"Not sure what you mean."

"Blast it with the gunk gun. The key will then sit out on it's own. But it'll be in the middle of a contaminated hole, and we wouldn't be able to get to it."

Peter shouted, "Wow! It's izaline? Really?"

Stumpy donned a smug smile, "Of course. Our claws are izaline. Obvious ain't it?"

What a surprise. Peter chuckled, "They've killed all the things that made izaline? What a bunch of dumboes! Wait 'til I tell them."

Mo looked sternly at him. "Don't you *dare* tell anybody. They'll all be back. Fucking humans, all of them!" I wonder whose mind taught him to swear. "But I have a more intelligent idea. Get the bloody detector!"

Yes. They rushed over to the tool store, and routed around for the izaline detector. They searched everywhere, but never found it.

"They must've taken all the electronics with them." They sat dejected, and considering the rotten task of sifting through the ashes, and Old Dick's bones. "Suppose we'd better get started. I bet it was in his pocket. Who's gonna check the body area out." Nobody volunteered, so Peter accepted his lot.

It was a dirty job, and some of the ashes were still quite warm. They had to be careful. Peter cleared the loose ashes from around Old Dick's body, revealing the skeleton. It still had charred pieces of flesh attached to it, but was still fresh. Peter bravely picked away at the body, searching every piece of it, but nothing. It definitely was not on his body. Katie called from her wheelchair, "Maybe he was holding it when he died." But Peter checked his hands and it was not there. What do they do now?

"Right," said Peter, who was black from head to toe, "you two boys will have to help me. We'll get some rakes and forks, and move all the ash from here over to near the little tent."

"No!" shouted Katie, "It might be hot and burn my tent." So they set about raking the ashes to the left of the shed. It took hours, and was threatening to get dark. But they had moved every ounce of ash, and still no claw was found. They were beginning to deflate.

"Sorry Stumpy." Peter could see the frustration on Stumpy's face turning to despair. "We'll have to get cleaned up and try again tomorrow. We'll find it."

Katie was solemn. She quietly spoke, as if to make sure nobody else could hear. "I could break the rules, I suppose. I make the rules, so I suppose I could break them sometimes." The boys looked at her with hope. "I could ask Old Dick for his help." She grinned, and the boys joined her. "He has only been dead for a little while, his spirit will still be strong. And besides, I want to get his story for Catherine."

Peter cuddled her and asked, "Who's Catherine? You've spoke of her before."

"I shouldn't tell you, but she looks after me, and stops me from being bad. And she writes for me." She spoke no more of Catherine. "I'll talk to Old Dick." She refused any help, struggled to her feet and set out towards her little khaki tent. The twenty foot walk seemed to take an endless amount of time, but she arrived and fell to her hands and knees, then crawled into the mysterious tent. The boys stayed clear.

The tiny little blond girl curled up on the floor of the tent and closed her eyes, then began sucking her thumb. There she lay for some time, so long that the sun suddenly dropped over the edge, and the world turned silver under the twin moons. Not very long after, the moons raced down to the other side of the World. Total darkness.

Peter whispered to Stumpy, "I'm scared. I'm gonna get a lamp." He crept off to the tent and soon returned with some light. "Has she moved?" Stumpy shook his head. They waited for about two hours before Peter suggested, "You two go and get some food and rest, and I'll keep a watch over Katie." But Mo refused to go. "Ok, shall me and Stumpy go, and you can keep watch?" He smiled in agreement, so the two bigger boys retired to the tent.

As soon as the boys had gone, Mo crept over to the tent and looked inside. It was empty, as he seemed to have expected. A massive grin crossed the little green face, and he curled up outside the tent flap, and settled down for the long wait. The night was dark, and deadly silent, as Mo turned off the lamp.

Colin Hodgson

7 – ME AND MY FAMILY

The night sped as the exhausted children slept, and soon it was morning. Stumpy shook Peter to wake him as the sun shot into the skies.

"Where's Sis? Is she ok?"

"Don't know. Come on, let's get out there."

The two rushed out to the little khaki tent to see Mo sitting up, giggling and tossing stones into the air.

"Where is she?" Peter was concerned.

"She's just got back. She's resting. Look." He pulled the flap aside, and there she was, still curled up with her thumb in her mouth. "I was going to leave her to rest before waking her. We should leave her as long as she needs."

But almost as they spoke she stirred, and stretched her arms and legs.

"Sis, are you ok?"

She rolled over to look at the boys peering through the flap. Her big eyes opened wide and she grinned. "Had a lovely chat. He was such a lonely man."

"But where's the claw?" asked Peter. He reached into the tent to help Katie out. "You look pleased with yourself. You must know where it is."

She just giggled and pulled herself into the three boys for a morning cuddle. As she laughed she wet herself. "Urgh, it's all down my leg. Ain't done that for days." They all laughed their pants off.

Nobody said a word as they all washed, ready for the new day. They ate, drank and toileted without a word, then, "I know where the claw is," announced Katie. She chuckled quietly. "If I tell you where it is, will you get it for us, Peter?"

"Of course. Where? Come on, and I'll go and get it."

"First I want to tell you some things. I've had a long night." They sat round in a circle. "Uncle Steven is ok, he'll be home soon. And I've asked Catherine to look after him when he needs it. And she's looking out for Mummy for me, and she's found Ninah, and that's brilliant. I thought Catherine would make me stay with her, but I came back to you, and she let me, almost made me. Don't know why." Her face showed some sadness. "Things will work out somehow, and I'm here to look after you." She stopped talking.

"I'm even more confused than ever." They all held each other tightly; they were a team, an isolated, lonely team.

She quietly told Peter, "We need to accept that you will never go home. Unless we can get some *real* help."

Peter almost cried, but held on. "But did you go home last night? How?"

"I went through the tent. But I came back for you. I'm here. I'm your sister, see. I can love, I *can* really love. It's so naughty, but I don't care."

"So take me through the tent. We can go home."

"No, sorry. Even I can't go through the tent now. I'm too tired. Going last night took so much of my spirit. I don't have the strength to go again. And you are alive, so you can't go anyway."

"But, didn't Old Dick go through it, when he was rescued."

She bit her bottom lip. "No, well, not alive. Old Dick died in that cave. I now know that it was Mummy who rescued him, but he was dead. She is such a naughty Mummy, so full of love for Daddy that she can never get anything right, and her vision is constantly blurred by her undying love for Daddy. It's all that matters to her. But she's lost, and I really need her. Luckily when she came home to look for Daddy, she left behind two things, knowing that I would be searching for her. She left me the tent, and she left me an old man to look out for me when I came back. He's done his job, and now he's gone to where he should have gone when he fell down the crack. But at least he's got the claw for us."

"What, Old Dick? Was he dead when we first met him? That's *stupid*."

"Look around at things. What's stupid about it all? You need to accept what we all are and where we all are. These are the children of a God, God Edward. You are a human being, and I am your sister. I will be your sister for as long as you are alive. The others can wait." She bit her bottom lip and frowned. "Is this what love is?" She grabbed Peter around the neck and almost squeezed the life out of him. "I'm only just beginning to understand Mummy."

They loved for some time, forgetting about the claw. It seemed that they had all their lives to find it. But life goes on, and Mo broke the circle by pushing himself away and asking, "So where's the claw? We'll get that and worry about the rest of the millennium afterwards."

So Katie explained to Peter, "It's up his bum. Up Old Dick's bum. The izaline detector doesn't work through flesh! Good Old Dick." She began giggling as his face screwed up. "Go on, get it out of his bum." The two boys edged him on, and the three of them laughed together as they watched him gingerly walk over to the burned out body. He bravely pulled about at the bottom end of the corpse, breaking the cooked meat from the bones, and there it was. It shone like a star as it poked out of Old Dick's bottom.

Peter handed it to Stumpy, and they had a high five, and then a little jig. Something *was* good about that day, after all.

"We've found the first of the three items. Things aren't so bad." Katie thought a little. "Peter, you didn't say what you wanted to search for. What do you want to find?"

He went a little red, and fiddled his thumbs, "I think I've found what I've always wanted." He hugged Katie tightly, and the two boys just sat wondering what it was that they had found. Eventually they all got back to normal.

The day was warm, so they decided to search for the other items another day, and chill out around the camp site. The two little green fellows opted to go for a walk, leaving Peter to spend some prime time with his sister, sitting in front of the derelict school in the soothing rays of the sun. Peter was suddenly relaxed about the rest of his life, on the colony, and just hoped that Katie had done the right thing. At that point he wasn't really sure just what it was that she had done.

"I still don't understand about you. You don't have to tell me, but it might help."

Katie was very thoughtful. "I am a special thing. You know the boys' dad, well he's God Edward. Honestly." She closed her eyes as the sun glistened in her hair. "And I am Gayla. I am a God, and my domain is the Earth. I am your God." The little girl winced as the tears formed. "And I've forsaken my domain to be with you. How could I fall in love with a human? I've broken all my own rules, and for the first time in the existence of the World I've let my emotions rule. Catherine was so mad at me, but not so mad. She's supposed to stop me from doing anything stupid, but she didn't, and I don't know why she didn't." Maybe Catherine knew something that she didn't. "But I've made my decision and I must stand by it. We're together for life."

They sat quietly for some time.

"If you're God, then why can't you just go home?"

"Sounds easy, but I'm so hungry. Mummy and Daddy and Ninah have been missing for about two hundred years, and I haven't fed since then. I've been searching for her for many years now, and I've been so sad, and so angry, but oh, I've been so lonely. I've spent two hundred years crying for my family. I lost my temper once, and almost destroyed our Earth, so ever since I have left Catherine at home to protect the Earth from my anger. And now my spirit is so hungry and weak that I can't get back. But I still came back to you. Why?" She was confused by the human emotions. "I should have left you here with the boys, and carried on with my work. Why didn't Catherine make me?"

"I'm sorry, Sis. What are you going to do?"

"Make the most of it and live it out with you. If we have to stay here we can be happy, do things, have a life, and then I can sort out my business when you have gone." She at last smiled at her big brother. "It's not all lost, though, Mummy could come back looking for me, and that would change things. And I could contact God Edward, if he'll talk to me."

"Are you enemies with the other God? His children seem to love you."

Katie raised her eyebrows. "You remember when you pulled Stumpy off me, well he was angry because of what the humans had done to his people. Killed them all, including their mother. My children have killed nearly all of God Edward's children. Why should he like me? We have been in dispute for millions of years, over the makeup of the children on each of our two planets. They were created in our own images, and my image has won over his, leaving just Stumpy and Mo to prove that their race ever existed. He must hate me. But when Stumpy slept that night, he was told to respect me, so maybe Edward wishes to help me." She crossed her fingers. "Now you know who I am, I can talk about it. I've never done that before, and I think I'm going to enjoy every minute of it. It's not *all* bad to be shipwrecked with somebody you might love." She suddenly had a naughty smile on her face. "What do you want to know?"

"Well, I'd like to know why I'm in this dream."

"That's an easy one. Because I love you. And if you weren't here, it would be a nightmare."

"Smooth talker, little girl."

"You know, bruv, I always end up in a child's body. Spoils my chances with a hunky piece like you." They tickled each other and laughed, like two schoolchildren learning to mate.

Peter suddenly stopped. "Sorry, shouldn't have acted like that." He turned bright red with embarrassment. "Sorry, Sis."

Katie smiled up at the guilt-ridden face and chuckled, "Bet I know what you were thinking." She pulled her cheek into his chest and giggled, "*Naughty* boy." They sat quietly for a while, while his blushes subsided. "You know what, Peter, morals are a human thing. We don't have morals, we don't need them. If I wanted to make love to you, what's the problem? I don't mind if you don't, so why not?"

"Because you are my *sister*. And you are a lot *younger* than me. That's all."

"Well, I'm not so young, and I'm not so innocent, and I'm only sort of your sister. And I've got a little girl, a daughter, so I'm big enough." She had menace in those beautiful grey-green eyes.

Peter twisted his head down in disbelief. He looked into her eyes and, "Really? You, a mum?"

"Yeah, why not? This is just my body, and I've had many others, but I'm always Gayla. That's my real name. My little girl is on Earth, waiting for me and our mummy and daddy. She's beautiful. So true and gentle, like the perfect God, just, fair and a perfect temperament. She is Catan and I am so proud of her."

"I'm struggling to believe all this."

"I know. Just hang on in here and you'll get used to me. My little girl is thirteen. She's always been thirteen. I bet you would love her to bits, and maybe you can meet her when we get home. She's a mysterious princess."

"Why aren't you with her? Why are you with me and not your daughter?"

"She's at work. We have a project going on, and she is a pivotal part of it. She can't walk away from it; it's what she was created for. My little girl will have to hang on in there until I can get back to finalise the project. Hopefully by then I will have found my mummy and daddy." She could sense that her adopted brother was becoming stressed by the circumstances. "Cuddle me, please."

The boys were still away on their walk-about. They were on a bit of a route march towards the hills, pushing their way through the wooded areas and the brambles as their smooth, leathery skin protected them from the thorns. They left the woods, and then moved swiftly across the heath land, heading towards a pre-planned destination.

"There." Mo pointed to a large bank of granite scree, laying up against the cliff. They marched onwards to that destination. When they arrived at the scree they sat on the ground and carefully studied the surroundings, and listened. "It's quiet," whispered Mo. "I think we can go in." The two of them walked up the loose rubble and stopped abruptly. "It's here." They again studied the surroundings and listened before getting to work scraping the granite chips away from a small area. Their tough hands ploughed through the rubble with ease. "There it is," beamed Mo. They had found their fathers burial vault!

Stumpy stood upright and pushed his hand down between his legs, and behind a small flap of skin which was almost unnoticeable in his crotch. He pulled out the izaline claw. He handed it to Mo, who carefully located it into a hole at the bottom of the scrape, and the scree around the scrape began to role and fall into a hole. As the granite stopped rolling, the open entrance invited them into their daddy's burial vault. The door was just large enough for them to climb through, and it was closed behind them, invisible amongst the granite rubble.

Back at base Peter and Katie were enjoying the sunbathing, but his head was still crashing around from the overload of enigma. He couldn't relax.

"What did you say your name was?"

"I'm Gayla. But I am Katie, your sister."

"But your mum and dad, what are they? Same as you?"

Katie had to think about that question. "No, they are not like me. They're alien."

Suddenly Peter burst into laughter. "Alien? Are you the kettle or the pot?" He pushed her away in jest, and they both sat sniggering. "I suppose when you said yesterday that you are my mother, everybody's mother, you also meant that we are now looking for my nanny. This is getting better, and better."

"Oh, you doubter. D'you wanna know some more strange things? I can talk for centuries about me and my family. I could talk you to death." She stood up. "And you know what, Peter, I need a wee! Before I wet my leg again!" She smiled as she hobbled behind the wall. "I'm still walking ok, but I wee a lot more. And I have a bit of a pain in my tummy. Why is that?"

"You must be drinking more."

Katie returned to Peter and plonked herself right down on his lap. "I'll tell you about my mummy and daddy. She is the daughter of God Edward, and my daddy is her twin. When I got friendly with Edward, this planet was quite well developed with life, but mine wasn't. Earth was still cooling, with nothing but gases covering the surface, and I had a lot of work to do. The physical presence in an atmosphere such as this one drains my energy quite quickly, and I need to recharge fairly regularly, maybe every one and a half centuries. So my very good friend Edward gifted me with his only daughter and her twin, to feed me and keep my spirit nourished, but warned me that his daughter was a naughty daughter, obsessed with loving her brother, and totally devoted to him. I didn't see that as a problem, as long as she fed me when I needed, and I felt that she would be really useful to my future projects. She is a feisty girl, not taking any shit, and she can talk. She's been a loved and revered deity on Earth during many periods. But Edward was right, she is a naughty mummy, always leaving her position and duties to chase around to be with daddy. She has caused me so many problems by running off, that I was going to kill her, but Catherine stopped me. Thank God she stopped me."

Peter wasn't liking what he was hearing, and frowned as he questioned her. "You would have killed her? That's sick. How could you want to kill anybody? Especially your mum. Even *just* adopted."

She just smiled and looked into his eyes. She could see the sudden fear beginning to distort his perception of the little blond girl, sweetness herself, who could kill her own mother, just because she was hungry. "Don't think that. I didn't kill her, did I."

"Only cos you haven't found her yet!" He jumped up and Katie almost fell on her face. "If I see her first, I'll tell to run! Cos her pretty little girl is gonna kill her!"

She shouted, "Don't you *dare*! Don't *dare* judge me. I've told you who I am, now *listen*!" Peter froze, so she calmed a little. "Now listen. Please, brother, listen. I can make you understand."

He sat down and Katie pushed herself onto his lap. "Now listen, calmly. I am your God *and* your sister. I have given myself to being your sister until the day you die. I've never given myself to *anybody* before, since time begun. That's what I am right now, your sister. You must believe it. But I am also a God. I am *the* God who made heaven and earth, and man and life, and I am *not* what the humans think I am." She stopped and bit her bottom lip. "My children think that I sit up here somewhere on this glistening throne, looking down and spitting thunder and lightening at the earth, and blowing up tornadoes and tsunamis, and torturing the poor folk with volcanoes and earth-shattering quakes, leaving millions for dead. And cursing man and beast with broken bodies and cancerous growths." She stood up abruptly. "And I need a wee!" She hobbled round to behind the wall. When she returned to Peter, she looked sad. "You know, Peter, I must keep this poor old body going until you are gone. I couldn't bare to leave you on your own here."

"Come here." Peter whispered in her ear. "Sorry if I got mad."

Her head nestled onto his chest, and she put her thumb in her mouth. "I know you didn't mean anything. Anyway, this is why I say things like 'I was going to kill her'. The *definitive* excuse. Ready?" She pulled her face up to rub her nose on Peter's. "Well, we start life as twins, and then make a decision on which way to go before reaching adulthood. The decision that we have to make very early on in life, is whether we should be one apart, or one as one. And it's a decision which we have all been led to believe is written in stone, and would be forever irreversible, for the duration of the universe. It's not true, because we die, eventually. We live for billions and billions of years, but we die. Anyway, Mummy and Daddy chose to be one apart, that is, they kept apart and share their existence as one. They cannot live without each other for much more than a couple of hundred years, feeding each other as they get hungry or weak, and running my plans ragged, just because they are so obsessed with each others love. They are one. But apart."

"How do they feed each other?"

"They eat or drink *anything* that is born of their bodies. They are pure ambrosia. Their blood and flesh, their body fluids, anything which is part of them. And the tears, well, they are *soooo* delicious, like candy. And they enjoy their meals, believe you me." She giggled. "They do enjoy them. Their mealtimes always include some pretty base lovemaking. They are animals and I sometimes wonder in whose image they were made." She pushed up and hugged him around the neck. "I get pretty jealous of them." She just held him and he pulled her body into his. They took some moments to wonder just what it could be like if they were not brother and sister.

"We've only talked about your mummy and daddy so far. What about you? What about the others? Are there others?"

"Yeah. I have cousins. They live as one apart, and one is divinely good and the other is just a prat. Ninah is beautiful, caring, and would make the perfect human. He is the keeper of children's hearts and souls, watching over them and studying their desperate plights. But Kamdar, his twin, is the other part of the identity and he is bad. When they grew up they disputed the course they should take, Ninah wanted to be one together, but Kamdar wanted to be one apart, and by the time they had made their peace with each other it was too late, and Ninah developed a larger share of the good, and Kamdar most of the bad. They became one apart, but stayed apart, the good and the bad. One day I will kill Kamdar and Ninah will be free to be as good as he is able to be. I hope, anyway."

"Still talking about killing."

"Sometimes my job is not as pleasant as people imagine." She stuck her tongue out at Peter and blew him a raspberry, and then had a giggle. "Kamdar's death will prove to me that Ninah *can* live without his twin. That's what I'm hoping." They relaxed for a while as the sun hid behind a small cloud, and the countryside turned grey. "Well, that's my relatives. Suppose you want to know about me." She looked at him for a response. "Well?"

"Don't know. I *might* not love you any more."

"We'll have to take that chance. I'm gonna need your help during this human life, so you must understand me. Right, I am not related to God Edward, nor are my relatives of whom I have already spoken. But we are of similar species, and develop similarly. So like all the others I was born as a twin. We decided that we would live as one together. We became one as we reached adulthood. As did God Edward at a different time."

Peter frowned and asked the question, "How?"

Katie bit her bottom lip. "Well, I was the bad half of the identity and my twin was the good. As with our species, our decision required that we become one, and be balanced as one, with all levels of conscience; good and bad. Only this way, as one together, could we become leaders and creators. Both Edward and I are creative Gods. We make life."

Peter screwed his nose up. "You're like the politicians. It's like Question Time. 'But Mister God, you *still* haven't answered Mister Peter's question!'"

They both smiled, then Katie told him. "I ate my twin!" She rolled over and began laughing. "I had to eat her to take her identity to pair with mine. It was a long time ago, but I still remember it like yesterday. We both got so exited, and then I ate her. Never had a meal like it since. Wowee!"

Peter was beginning to just accept *everything* that Katie told him. It was all too surreal to question, and anyway, even the Sunday Sport couldn't have made this lot up. He held her tightly, waiting patiently for her to get back into her life story, the real story of God. He had to wait for some time.

Then, "I suppose you're thinking I'm a nutter." She sat distorted and crumpled but grinning from ear to ear. "But I'm a lovely nutter who loves her brother. You know, Peter, if you ever get home, you'll be able to tell your grandchildren that you knew God. Their friends will be at school bragging about knowing Harold Wilson, or David Bowie, but your grandkids can brag that 'my granddad fell in love with God'." She stared into his eyes. "And they can brag that 'God made love to my granddad'." She kissed him full on the lips, and then again, but as he began to relax she tensed up. "I need a wee, quick." And when she began to drag her limp leg around the wall it was too late. She peed down her leg. Looking down at the ground she whispered, "Sorry. Couldn't stop."

Something was wrong with Katie. Peter knew that she had controlled her toilet perfectly for the previous few days, but now she was failing, becoming incontinent as before. He stood up and wiped her leg with his shirt sleeve, and then picked the little goddess up. It was time to eat, so they walked slowly back to the tent and set about heating some soup.

Katie lay on her bed linen and sucked her thumb. "I don't want anything to eat." She was not right, and Peter could sense that she knew something. "I must stop eating and drinking so much. This poor body can't handle it. I'm a little bit scared." As she watched Peter working on his food, she called him. "Please, Peter. Take me to the toilet. Quick!"

He rushed over to her and plucked her into his arms. As he sat her on the toilet she had a long wee, and he watched as the blood filled urine turned the toilet water bright red. She was bleeding internally. A fourteen year old lad and a little girl of unknown age sat in the toilet looking at each other, wondering what to do, as she slowly dripped blood into the pan.

"It hurts a bit." She bit her bottom lip. "Can you take a look, please? See where it's coming from."

Reluctantly Peter held her legs up and inspected the region. Katie helped by putting her finger down and pointing to the different parts of her anatomy. "That's my vagina, and just here, below my clitoris is my urethra, where my pee comes out. I *think* it's called the urethra." Peter studied for a couple of minutes, waiting for some blood to appear. It did.

"It's from your vagina."

"Oh no! I must be having my first period!" After a deep sigh she began to giggle and put on a very posh voice as she stated. "I'm turning into a young lady. You can put my legs down now, young man, unless you haven't seen enough yet." God certainly had a naughty streak. Must have taken after her mummy.

Poor Peter turned beetroot red, and swiftly lowered her legs. He never said a word as Katie giggled but just walked out to the stores and collected some more toilet rolls. She cleaned herself and used some tissue as a towel under her knickers.

"What does it all mean?" Peter sat supping his soup. "I don't know about girls."

"It means that I have reached my puberty. I'm a young adult, but it's really early I think. But I've begun to menstruate. That's lay eggs." She suddenly began laughing and could not help but get herself into a fit of giggling. "You know, Peter......" She just rolled onto the ground, totally out of control. Peter didn't even smile, just like he knew what was coming next. "You know, Peter, huh, start again." With a forced, serious face and a deep breath, "You know, Peter, all you have to do is fertilise the egg." She continued chuckling. Peter was *not* amused. "That's if *you've* reached puberty. Have you? Well?" No answer. "Do you wank?"

"That's enough! Stop!" They say that girls grow up faster than boys, and those two were proving the theory. "Leave me alone and mind your own business."

Oh dear. The teenage huff had begun. Peter just finished his soup, cleaned the plate and spoon, and then left the tent to sit outside waiting for the boys to return. His teenage pride had been dented, and it only took one misplaced question. An age of insecurity and self doubt.

The sun was about to fall over the edge. "Where are you? Please come home." He was willing the boys home, with a tear in his eye. "Please." But the sun fell, and the two moons cast their silvery screen across the landscape, and still no boys. Suddenly a hand plonked onto his shoulder, making him jump. He looked around and there was the beautiful face of God, wanting and willing, like a tiny lost puppy.

"Sorry." Her eyes were wide in the silver light, glistening and hypnotic. "I'm sorry."

"Yes." Peter smiled into her mind.

"Yes what?"

He grinned and kissed her on the lips. "Yes, I do wank."

They cuddled for a while, and, as the two moons dived down out of site, they went back inside. The night had set.

8 -- GOD'S BETTER HALF

The morning turned itself on, and the boys were still out. Katie seemed not to worry, but Peter did.

"Where are they? They're lost."

Katie smiled and went into the toilet to clean up while Peter opened a tin of corned beef. "Do you want some breakfast?"

She answered with a no, so he made some corned beef and pickle sandwiches for himself, and a load extra to take with them.

"Where you taking me, big boy?" Our little Goddess was still in a mischievous mood. "Having a picnic?"

"No, taking some food for the boys, if we ever find them. Bet they're lost." Hmm, he was getting worried, but Katie could still only jest.

"Don't worry about me, I'm just hungry for loooove." She winked at Peter, who went the usual red colour. "Perhaps the boys are giving us some space, if you know what I mean."

Peter tried his best to ignore her. He had managed to do just that all night, but she wasn't going to let up, so he snapped, "I'm your brother! I can't shag you!"

"Hmm. Ok, for now, sperm-bag."

Peter had a lot to worry about at the early age of fourteen; two boys who had gone walkabouts and a 'partner' who had gone from little girl to sex-starved woman in just a couple of days. And as his own body changed towards manhood, confusion reigned supreme. But the confusion gave way, just a little, to wonderment and a teenage desire to learn, and experiment, and he looked towards the old God trapped inside the tiny body of his sister, and longed for her love. Maybe when they've found the boys, they can be naughty, him and our God, and discover the joys of sex; the smell, the taste, the feel, the look, and even the unknown. And maybe the commitment? Well, time will tell. But the egg that grows inside his God? It's just waiting for his sperm, expectant of the gift of life, protected from the outside world by the twisted body of a child and by the spirit of God herself, and shouting, and shouting, calling 'come and get me, big boy'. Peter could hear it calling, but his pubic fear was winning the battle, for now.

"Come on. We've got to find the boys. But just behave yourself, and perhaps we can play later." They kissed amorously, and set out in search of their lost children with Katie in her wheelchair, grinning all the way.

They had no idea where to go. The boys had gone their own way, and neither Peter nor Katie took any notice of their direction, so they first went towards the small mountains where they had first met. The sun shone hot that day, hotter than they had previously experienced, but it was not humid, and the air was clean. The woods smelled of ferns as they gazed through the thickets of brambles.

"Look!" screeched Katie. "Some deer. There's deer in the woods. You could eat them." The small deer looked up at them and then carried on grazing. "They're not scared of us. They don't know humans."

They carried on until they reached the heath land, where Peter decided to rest before battling the wheelchair through the long grass. They sat staring towards the mountains, with the sea just visible to the right, and wondering if their children would be over there, panicking and lost. They hadn't thought the trip out. But Peter was at least going to look. If they never saw the little boys again, they would at least have been remembered for trying. It's strange, but with life changing so quickly, and being faced with unbelievable facts and circumstances, Peter was adapting to his life of uncertainty and loss. He desperately wanted to find the boys, but if he didn't………..

Tired and a little despondent they arrived at the cliffs where the cave paintings had been seen, and where they first met the babies. They thought it might be sensible to check the cave, in case there were paintings to guide them to their boys, so Peter carried his sister up the slope to the entrance. It still smelled of toffee apples.

They stood inside the cave, waiting for their eyes to adjust.

They were there, three wall paintings! Peter carefully walked around the mothers hole, and Katie reached up to feel the first painting. It was a crude painting of an air ship of some kind. It was landed, and parked by a shape of a church, with a tower at one end and blotches of colour at the end.

"It's a ship, and it's near a church. Look the tower, and the stained glass, all the colours. There must be a ship here somewhere."

The second painting depicted some bodies without any legs. There was green at the bottom of their bodies and their mouths were just large circles.

"They are screaming. That is a bad picture. It's warning us of something."

The last picture showed two beings in the middle, being watched from a great height by two others. One of the beings was smiling and had like a halo above its head. That was all.

"Somebody is spying on us. Look, it's me with the halo. Edward must have forgiven me, and he is warning us of something. I think we should go."

They took a quick look around the cave in the hope that the boys had turned up seeking a place to sleep, but there was nothing. So they left the cave, and Katie returned to her wheelchair.

"The pictures are worrying me. I don't know what the second or third ones meant." She chewed her bottom lip. "I think we should just scan around here for the boys a bit, then get back to the camp. There might be some records of a church at one of the other old sites."

They did not find the boys, so they made their way home, hurrying to get there before dark. They just made it in time.

"Peter. Are you scared?"

"Not really. I know you'll look after me, and when you can't, then I'll worry about it."

"The pictures were confusing, and the second one was definitely a warning. But I suppose we need to check out the church. Definitely, that gives me hope."

Peter ate, and they sat down to plan the next day. They had accepted that the boys were lost, but could look after themselves, so they would scour the camp for clues of the church, or maps, anything which could lead them in some direction. That was tomorrow's plan. Tonight?

"Still wanna get naughty, big boy? I've behaved myself specially, and you promised." She chuckled as she crept over to him. "What you gonna do to me tonight, then?"

He gently pulled himself away, and Katie's face dropped.

"Don't you want me? Don't you love me?" The slight rejection hit a sensitive spot in the tiny God, and her eyes began to water. "Why? I think love you. Don't you love me?"

Peter pulled her to him and held her tight to his chest. "You're my sister. You keep telling me that you're my sister. It's just not right." He could feel her tears soaking into his shirt, and all he really wanted to do was love her, like a man, but he couldn't. His conscience won over.

"But we're here for the rest of your life. What've you gotta answer to? Nobody will care." She began to tremble, as though she was losing her control, getting angry, and she screwed her face up.

"Calm down. I do love you, but I need some time to get used to you not being just my crippled sister. Give me some time, please, and I'll fight conscience." He could feel that she was calming down. The trembling stopped and she looked up into his face, then breathed deeply. He reassured her, "You're my sister, and very special to me. Just give me some time."

At last she smiled. "I could've got angry then. You stopped me."

Peter wiped her eyes with his sleeve.

She jested, "If you were a real God, you wouldn't have wasted those delicious tears."

"Why have you gone like this? So suddenly. Is it your periods?" Peter kissed the tears on her cheek, and they were sweet, but not ambrosia. He certainly was not a God.

"I'd better tell you a bit more about me. We've got the whole evening to waste, so here goes." She pulled round to face Peter, and grinned, piercing his mind with those eyes. He became relaxed. "Well, you know I said that I ate my twin, to become one as one, and a creator, well I since found out, very recently, that my species is not quite the same as Edward's. He is one with his twin, and always will be. But me, I am better than that, and much stronger. You see, about two hundred years ago my family, the Qeervi royal family, dispersed after an unexpected change in my project plan, and they were lost. I had my little girl, Ca'an, you know, my daughter, on Earth carrying on her work with the project, and laying the land ready for the next project, but all others were lost. Well, Kamdar was there, but he's just a twat. Anyway, after a number of years of isolation and lack of family love I broke. I couldn't stop crying for my mummy and daddy, and I didn't know how to handle the distress. I wanted to die sometimes. But we can't die until our time. I'd never felt like that before, as I'd always had my family. But suddenly I started to replace the endless loneliness with games, angry games, cruel games which hurt people, and I blamed my mummy's desertion for all of it, never accepting that it was all me. And the poor people really suffered. In about 1840 I had a crying session which lasted for over 5 years, non-stop crying for my mummy. The World dried up in many parts of Africa, the cattle died, and the children withered to bone, and were lost forever. Millions died. But that became boring, so I set about playing some more exiting games, and got an undersea volcano to erupt in the South Pacific. A group of islands were washed away by the tidal wave, and I watched for many days as the people, men, women and children, clung onto life in the seas, slipping away one at a time until there was only a handful of them left. They cried for each other as the sharks began to pick them off, and I laughed. I was laughing, and not crying, and I felt so good. And the people were nearly all gone, but one small group clung onto the driftwood until they were in sight of land, and they found just enough spirit to smile at the little girl who was perched on the wood, circled by her surviving family. And I thought to myself 'you're never gonna make it,' and I was going to make sure of it. And as they neared the safety of the beach, their hearts rose to the occasion and they began to sing, and the little girl who was their idol, was helped onto the beach. She sat watching the people help each other from the driftwood, and I was so bitter that I couldn't stand the child's jubilation, and I couldn't understand how a child could be so happy, when I was oh so broken hearted and lonely." Katie had a tear in her eye. "Anyway, I made these salt-water crocodiles come out of the jungle, and two of them fought over the girl, tearing her limb from limb as they contested the sweet meat, and her screams didn't last long. The adults screamed at the sight, as the blood spat all around and the child became dismembered, and eaten by the crocodiles. And I just laughed and laughed."

"Why are you telling me this?"

She sniffed and continued, "Because what then happened makes me different. I seemed to explode, and life disappeared momentarily, and a loud noise cracked through my head, and there she was. Right in front of me. She smiled at me and told me, without moving her lips, to save the poor castaways. And I had to. I couldn't fight her, I just had to do it. So I held off the crocs, so that the people could get onto the beach and seek sanctuary. But they wouldn't. They went back to the driftwood, and they were heartbroken, so they went back out to sea, and one by one, the sharks ate them, and they didn't even fight. When I took away their little girl, I must have taken their spirit. I felt so ashamed, but so jealous of their emotions and love that I decided instantly to blow Yellowstone. Fuck the people, why should they have everything? All that love?" She held Peter tightly. "That's when I changed. Cos she said 'no' and I had to stop. I didn't blow Yellowstone. She wouldn't let me. And I've never been scared like it before." She began sucking her thumb.

"Who was she?"

"My conscience. My twin, Catherine, who I ate billions of years earlier. She moved out. I was the bad, she the good, and I was becoming too strong for her, so she escaped. And she wouldn't go back. She is me, but she will not go back to me, and so wanders the Earth looking out for me, and making sure I don't ever lose it enough to hurt our children. We are now one apart. No other God has been that, whilst also being the creator. I am the ultimate, living as two, but working as one, with Catherine the good keeping Gayla the brilliant from misbehaviour." There were a few seconds silence, then, "Catherine will never allow me to unnecessarily hurt you, nor anybody else. But I'm so hungry, I can barely feel her, she's so distant. I'm scared."

Peter was beginning to understand his sister. He kissed her on the cheek and tried to lighten up the evening a little. "So you came here with us, and forgot to pack your conscience. It could've been worse, you could've forgot your toothbrush."

"Silly Billy." She sucked at her thumb. "I am getting weaker, just a little, but Catherine is losing her control of me. I am the bad half. I don't know what to do."

"Catherine let you come back. She must trust you." They were almost whispering. "She must have had her reasons. It could have been that you needed a holiday. You've been pining the loss of your mum, so she might have meant you to chill for a few years. We can have that break, one apart, if you know what I meant."

Katie wiped her face on his shirt, and grinned, "Oooh, my blue-eyed stallion, are you weakening to our amour? Like a fly, enjoying the fruits of life and wandering just a little too close, as the spider hones her carving knife." She giggled and pulled herself into his face.

"Catherine, help me!"

9 – BIRANGONA (BRAVE WOMEN)

The next morning arrived with a bang. Thunder, lightning and wind. The tent strained on the ropes, and threatened to fly away with the Gods.

"I think we need to get out, Sis!"

Luckily it wasn't raining. They grabbed some clothing and Katie fetched her book and wrapped it in a towel, and then climbed into the wheelchair. "Let's go!"

Peter sped down the street to the derelict school, where they crouched down behind the walls. They felt safer there. As they peered through a window debris began to fly through the camp. They could see their tent, and it was taking the full force of the wind, tugging at the guy chords in an effort to escape its roots. One pulled from its anchor, and then another. And then, like a ghostly executioner, a sheet of corrugated iron was whipped up by the wind. The tent stood in its way but it did not heed, and like a guillotine, it sliced the life from tent. It was through in a flash, leaving the shreds of canvas flapping and cracking like whips in the gale. Their clothes ran off down the street. Peter looked at Katie and raised his eyebrows. He knew that they were just minutes away from decapitation.

The wind continued for about fifteen minutes, and then dead calm. It was as if somebody hand turned it off!

"God, that was close." Peter held his hand on Katie's cheek and caressed her. "You ok?"

She just giggled and raised her arms in the air. "The power of God!"

The street was a mess. They walked back down to their tent, which was the only one to have suffered, and began collecting their belongings. Most of their clothes had been blown away, but the cooking and washing stuff had been spared and quite miraculously her drugs were still intact.

"We haven't lost too much, Sis"

She was clinging onto her book and smiling. She had what she needed.

They walked back to the old school and studied the derelict structure, wondering if they could make a safe bolt-hole in case the winds returned, but the walls were not very safe.

"We were lucky this time. I wonder if it gets much stronger than that. If it does, we'll all go down the road." Peter pulled a fallen section of wooden wall aside. "Hey, what's this?"

Katie struggled over to him, and looked down at the hatch. "A cellar. Let's look down it."

Peter pulled at the handle but the hatch was securely bolted. He slid them back and it lifted easily, revealing the steps leading down into the dark, inviting them to chance it. Giggling with excitement Katie peered down, but her face was hit by a cold brush, and her giggling was halted. "Death. There's death. The spirit just left."

They felt that it would be sensible to collect a lamp before going any further, so Peter went back to their shredded tent and found one of the torches. He wound the charge up, and shone it down into the cellar. They couldn't see anything unusual, just cobwebs, so he took a few steps down. He lifted Katie, who was back giggling. "There's just filing cabinets and chests," whispered Peter.

"No. There's more. Look."

He shone the torch to the left. Katie tried to stop giggling, but she just got worse. "If you don't stop laughing, I'm taking you back up." She stopped. The light fell onto a wooden table, and there were some chairs around it. It was set for dinner. They warily approached the table, which was covered in dust and cobwebs, and Peter brushed some of the cobwebs from the setting.

"Ugh!" He jumped back. "Look!" Through the hole in the cobwebs could be seen a skull, small and human. There was a hole broken into the side of it. He brushed some more cobwebs away, and they suddenly envisioned what had happened. The arms and legs had been removed, and the bones shared around the dinner plates, the flesh stripped off by the diners. There were four plates. "It was being eaten. It's only a child. Poor thing."

Katie whispered, "We need to find the other four. They didn't go anywhere." They walked to the other end of the cellar where it went into an L-shape. The cobwebs were everywhere, and so were the spiders, some quite large, but Katie assured Peter that they were not poisonous, as nothing on the colony was. Around the corner they found the diners. They were cuddled up in a corner, and were just tiny skeletons stripped by time and insects, wearing grey school uniforms. They had all died arm-in-arm, after eating their friend. The last supper must have just prolonged their torture; extended their wait for the inevitable.

"I didn't know people could really eat each other." Peter was upset at the thought of those poor, desperate children. "And they must have killed the child on the table. A bash on the head. How could they do it?"

"I've seen it many times. I *caused* it in Africa, I told you about it, when I was crying and angry. Most of them wait until the person is dead, but not always. And many thousands survived by eating their neighbours and family during the Bengal famine in the late seventeen hundreds. I was there with Mummy and Daddy, and Ca'an. And some of the marauding gangs continued the cannibalism after the famine had subsided. It's only morals that prevents it, and morals are taught. Naturally, desperation and survival take precedence when the shit finally hits."

"I suppose that's one of the good bits of religion. Unless the religion encourages it. S'pose some do?"

"I'd like to walk, please, and search around for some guidance." Katie was lowered onto her feet and she hobbled through to the cabinets. "You can go looking for our clothes while I search, if you like."

Peter took the opportunity to get out of the death hole. He went down the street collecting anything that might be of use.

Katie found a plan chest, and so pulled a dining chair over so that she could see into the top. She carefully inspected the plans and drawings, sliding most over to the far side of the hangers, but pulling out any of interest. That kept her occupied for some time, and by the end she had selected several plans of interest. "Right, something to work with." The little girl brushed her blond hair aside and looked around. The torch was dimming, so she wound it up a bit, but as she did, the room darkened. The hatch had been closed!

"What's he doing, now?" She grinned to herself and whispered. "That'll cost you some dirty fun, big boy." She chuckled to herself as she scrambled down from the chair. She rolled her plans up, collected the torch and waddled her way to the stairway, and with commitment in her eyes she tackled them, stupendous step by stupendous step, plonking her bum on the next step and then pulling her feet up. Eventually she arrived! She placed the torch on the top step and pushed on the hatch. It wouldn't budge. She moved her hands to the opening edge to improve leverage, but it still would not open. Then she banged on the hatch and it rattled against the bolts. It had been locked from the outside! "What you doing? Peter! Peter!"

Peter had collected various items which had been strewn around the camp and deposited them in the equipment store which was a much sturdier tent than the others. It had been designed to bend and bow under the wind, but then return to its desired shape, unless, of course, if a sheet of iron was to strike it! "Great. Let's see if I can find some clothes." He walked further down the street, following the route taken by their clothing, but found only a pair of knickers and a woollen jumper. The rest was well gone. "Might have to become nudists, Sis. Bet she'd love that, 'specially with her naughty head on."

He ambled back towards the old school, kicking stones around in the street, and whistling. He began to sing to himself, All Right Now, in a vague hope that it would convince him that they were, but he soon returned to thinking about the painting, and of them being watched. Maybe not an appropriate song, so he carried on whistling 'It Must be Love'. When he arrived at the school he had a quick search around to see if there was anything they had overlooked, but nothing, not even a cellar hatch. What, no cellar hatch? It's gone!

"Sis! Sis! Where are you?" He stood motionless, listening intently. Some birds were whistling in the trees, trying to mimic 'It Must be Love' and that was all he could hear.

"*Shut up*! Piss off somewhere else and whistle!" He called again, "Sis! Where are you?" His face showed his concern, frowning as he strained to hear. "Sis! Sis!"

Then, a faint reply. It was from beneath a fallen wooden wall, the one which he had already moved earlier. He heard it again, so he pulled the wooden wall away and there was dead grass and brush. The hatch was beneath it. Thank God. "Sis, I'm coming!"

He threw the grass and brush aside, unbolted the hatch and pulled it open.

Poor Katie was curled up on the top steps, sobbing her heart out. Peter leaned down and gently pulled her up into his arms. She wrapped her arms around his neck and almost throttled him as she clutched on, catching her breath as she whimpered in his ear. They walked back to the equipment tent, which Peter had made theirs, and she never stopped crying. They sat down in the tent, surrounded by the abandoned tools and plant.

"What happened?" he whispered.

She just held onto him like there was no tomorrow, so he didn't ask any more. They lay down on their bedding and loved each other, and Peter kissed her tears from her cheek, with a growing appreciation of the sweetness of those celestial drops.

They eventually calmed down.

"What happened, Sis?"

She had a good sniff. "I thought you'd locked me in. I thought you didn't want me any more."

Peter was frowning, and beginning to realise the seriousness of the locked hatch. He hadn't locked it, and neither had Katie. So who did? And why? And why did they attempt to hide it?

She stuttered as she said to him, "I thought I was going to have to leave this body, and leave you. I couldn't bear that; the Earth would have suffered, you'd better believe it. I can hardly feel Catherine now. Please love me, Peter." She began to cry again, so he held her on his shoulder as he pondered the possibilities of other, unfriendly neighbours. They were both fearful of the future.

"Have you lost your conscience completely?" He was becoming oh so wary of what she could be.

"Yeah." She bit her bottom lip. "But I've still got yours. So long as I'm with you, we can be one apart. It's up to you, stud." At last she was smiling again. "We can get back to Earth, somehow. If we don't I fear for my children, and if I lose you, I fear for the whole World. But right now I fear for you. The paintings said we were being watched, so let them watch us. As one apart, we are bigger than all of them. Fuck 'em all." A big grin stretched across her face. She was back to normal.

He suggested, "Let's just remember that somebody is watching us, and carry on as normal, but stay together." Katie agreed with him on that score.

"Ok, and get on with the task of getting back to our children."

"Sis, they're *Your* children."

"Oh yeah, silly me." She bit her bottom lip and suggested, "But I suppose if you are to be the adopted conscience of God almighty, then they're your *adopted* children." She grinned at him, "We must stay together, *really* together, even at night. And since that act of God, I haven't got any pyjamas any more." She winked at him, "Know what I meant, bumbuster?"

He grinned, "I know what you mean. But I'm not that easy." He was sorely tempted. His sister was young, her legs and spine a little distorted, but she was so beautiful. Even if there were other humans on the Planet, she would still have been the most perfect to Peter. He was so sorely tempted. "You know you said about you being the bad and Catherine being the good, yeah? Well does that mean that Catherine is God, and you are the devil?"

She raised her eyebrows and fluttered her lashes at him.

"Was that a yes? You're the devil?"

"Silly, no such thing as the devil. I'm God, and you'd better believe it. And Catherine is me, God. We are one apart, and used to be one as one, but what we are, and always will be, is God. The devil bit is just when the bad in you just gets the better of the good, and takes control. I suppose the devil is a virtual being, just part of our mental structure. But it is dangerous and can be manipulated by other humans, by belief, and by greed. The devil can be created in people by brainwashing, so they believe that the bad they are doing is not bad, but part of God's will. That's when I get mad, when they use my name to corrupt and destroy. That's when my family have to step in."

"I wish everybody else knew what the devil really is."

"The clever ones do, the born leaders. They use God to twist the belief in their subjects, to carry out the word of what is the virtual devil, and they call that virtual devil God. Man worships the devil as much as he worships God. But that's why man is strong, and Edward's children have all but disappeared. Humans use whatever they can control to achieve results, to win, to gain, to learn, to overpower one's enemies, to take, to enjoy and to do anything more than they've already done. Man is *never* satisfied and *always* wants more or better, and that's what distinguishes him from the rest. Man is supreme in the Universe." She paused for breath. "Poor Edward's children never want for anything, and are always satisfied. They just want to live in harmony with everything else, and play around all their lives, and doesn't that sound idyllic? Well it is, until they meet some race which always wants more, like humans. Then they disappear like so many other creatures who cannot survive the battle. My children have destroyed Edward's children. All because they couldn't use them." She suddenly began to giggle, and rolled onto Peter. "Well, that is, they didn't know *how* to use them." She couldn't stop laughing.

"What's so funny?"

"Humans! They're not always as clever as they think. They spent many years mining izaline, a useless metal which looks pretty and is rare, so they spend all that time looking for it, and destroying everything in their way, and all they had to do was ask. They have just about destroyed the most valuable asset they could ever have acquired." She continued with her laughing fit, and Peter just sat, confused. "They killed Edward's children, what a load of stupid prats. And I'm ashamed to say that they are *my* prats, *my* children."

He didn't even ask. Far too much had gone into the teenager's head for one day, and he was tired of trying to work out his little sister. "Let's go for a walk. Expose ourselves to the peeping tom."

They walked slowly down the street, hand in hand, with Katie proudly taking one step at a time. One small step for Peter, one giant step for womankind.

Peter looked past the tents and towards the old school. He was wondering if the cellar was safe to use as a bolt-hole when the wind and rains came back.

"Sis, do you think the children locked you in?"

"They're dead."

He looked around. "Somebody did."

"I know. It's bloody obvious, ain't it." She didn't want to talk about it.

"But not to me. You felt them come out."

"That was just stale, cold air. Nothing else came out."

"How do you know?"

"Because dead things don't come out, from anywhere, unless you pull them out." God was not a believer in ghosts. But she was enjoying the walk, her first for many years. "This is lovely, walking. Some people don't appreciate walking, as they just do it all the time without thinking. And to be walking down our street, hand-in-hand, like newlyweds, well…." She looked up into his eyes, and they willed him on.

Peter just thought, *'You never give up do you.'*

"Are you enjoying our walk, Peter, darling?"

"Yes, honey bunch, it's delightful. And where would my precious like to walk to? End of the street? Next town, where they might have a bar? Or to the church?"

Aha, the church. Katie had pulled out some interesting plans, three in particular, which were prints of aerial views of the colony. They showed all the camp locations, and referenced other detailed drawings of each site. There was a chance that the church could be found, and that could mean that the ship could also be found. Trouble is, they had to hope that there was only one church, as the colony was spread across three different land masses. But New Bury was the one where they found most of the izaline, so it was most probable that the main cultural centre, if it existed, would be there. As long as there is life, there is hope!

"Back to the cellar, we need to set it up ready for the next storm." Peter wasn't thinking of churches, just survival. "But what if we get locked in when we're both down there?"

Katie just grinned at him and said, "Don't worry about that, I have a theory."

And so they went back to the cellar and began cleaning it up a little. The four children were left in the corner, and the one on the menu was placed with them, so that none of them were lonely, and Peter said some prayers to lay their spirits. He was comfortable with them then, and, just maybe, Katie was wrong and their ghosts did live on, so it was best be friends with them. They might even look out for the two adventurers.

Katie was getting about extremely well, and she left Peter working in the cellar, to go into the street by herself. She collected some bits and pieces, such as cans of food and some water containers, and some sanitary stuff, and began to stock the cellar. "It's all for you, amoroso." She winked at him.

Peter had been watching her every move, worrying about her not getting back, but he soon realised that although she was slow, she was able, and so he eventually left her to her own devices. The cellar was soon ready for the next onslaught of the tempest.

Katie was thinking outside of the box. "We need to put the plans back down here, else we'll lose them in the next storm, and my book. We can afford to lose the rest if it happens."

Feeling secure, they went back to their new home, to the equipment tent, and Peter fed. They arranged the bedding and sat together.

"Well, Sis, I think we are ready for the storm. And the cellar is so much closer to this tent."

Katie just smiled, and then pulled over some of the plans. "Have a quick look, and then get them in the cellar."

They combed through the detailed site plans, and just as Katie had guessed, one had a church. But where was it? They referenced it to the aerial maps, and there it was, at the other side of the mountains in which they found the boys, and it didn't look very far on the maps!

"Only nineteen finger strides!" Peter gasped. "I can walk that with my fingers in a few seconds."

"How far by foot, do you think?"

He estimated from the scale that it was only about one hundred and forty miles. His face dropped. "That's an impossible walk for you." He re-stepped it out, this time going around the mountains, and it was then about one hundred and sixty miles. And then there was a river, and that could be impassable. His spirit was low.

As always, Katie giggled her way through the thought process. "You go without me and come back for me."

"Never! Leave you here, alone? There's someone watching us, and they could hurt you."

"I love it when you're the man, hunk."

"Oh, stop it! I'm trying to be bloody serious."

Poor little Katie dropped her head, and her blond hair fell over her face. "Sorry." She was very frail, and some tears began to form.

He pulled her over to him and cuddled her, kissing some of the sweet tears from her cheek. The fourteen year old was having to grow up quickly, and began to realise that handling his God was going to be a bit like handling sweating dynamite. "I didn't mean anything. You just put me off my thinking." He put his hand down to her poorer leg. "You really are getting stronger, and more beautiful. And even more believable." They hugged for some time.

She lightened up and asked in a whisper, "So, do you believe me now? That I am God?" They continued cuddling. "Well?" Peter just smiled and nodded.

"No point in not, is there? You are God. I believe you. Not a very powerful God, to be stranded here with me, and wondering what to do. I thought you would have known all that, and just whisk us back to Earth. But if you can't, then *I'll* have to get us back."

She was back to her grinning self. "You're gonna make a good conscience." Her eyes were wide and shining, and her face suddenly brightened, as if the sun had returned from behind the clouds. "I do know now, why Catherine let me come back. I think she *made* me come back. I so love her."

Peter left her grinning as he walked back to the cellar and put the plans into safe keeping.

When he returned from the short walk, Katie was holding her book to her chest. "You forgot my book." But she didn't offer it up to him, but patted the floor beside her, where he promptly sat. "Would you like to look at my book with me? We can see how the people are treating each other in my absence. I hope they are not too cruel."

Peter frowned, wondering what she meant, but was intrigued by the offer of the mysterious book. "What is that book?"

"It's called 'Unknown India'. Catherine writes it. It helps me to see what our children are doing back home." She placed the book on her lap, and carefully opened it up and then skipped though several pages which did not interest her, arriving at a section entitled 'Birangona'. She glumly said, "There is a situation that has been festering for some time. You know, Tiger, my absence will only add further suffering for the poor people who are to be affected, most of them innocent bystanders. Let's see what's in the book today."

The first page of the section called 'Birangona' showed a picture of several bedraggled young women dressed in eastern styles, who had covered their faces with their hair and cloths, in shame. "You know, Peter, birangona means 'brave women', and something that I had feared has begun. Look, these poor students have been left broken and empty by their torture and group rape in Dhaka. The slaughter has begun.

The poor Bangalees have all gone to Hell." She was very sad. "I'm failing my people at such a critical time."

"Who are they?"

"They are young student girls in Dhaka." She was translating some of the text. "Many have been killed, along with the lecturers and male students from Dhaka University, but these ones have been gang raped, but spared, to be taken to the garrison to continue the gang rape, until they are of no further fancy to the soldiers of the Paki army. Then they'll be killed." A hint of a tear came to her eye. "I can't help them. It's been expected for a little while, but now it's begun."

"Where is Dhaka? Africa?"

"No, it's in East Pakistan. This is the start of the fight for liberation, and the Pakistanis will fight a war against the Bangalee people to the point of annihilation. In the name of God, of course." She was beginning to get boiled up. "Will my conscience allow me to act?"

Peter did not know how to answer, and so asked, "What would Catherine allow?"

"Very clever, Baby Face. She would deny me rage and restrict my actions to ones of encouragement and guidance. But I'm not there to guide, nor influence, and so Hell will reign supreme in East Pakistan, and our children will die in their millions, of all religions and creeds. They are without God. And look at the date of the story, it is the twenty eighth of March, nineteen seventy one. Today. Operation Searchlight has only been running for less than three days and already thousands of civilians have been killed, and as many abused and tortured." She dropped her head. "All I can do is sit here and watch. I am useless."

"No, you're not. We can get back, somehow."

She didn't acknowledge his encouragement, but continued, "They have just suffered one of the worst natural disasters recorded. The Bhola cyclone resulted in nearly half a million lost lives when the Ganges Delta flooded. *That* was an act of God. Yahya Khan's act of *Man* promises to kill six times as many as the cyclone. Man's worst enemy, himself." She slowly turned the page. On the left leaf was a photograph of a shipment of arms being delivered to the Pakistani military, and on the right a cartoon drawing of East Pakistan, overlooked by two large stands, one filled with Chinese, the other with Indians and Russians. They had all turned up in time to watch the game. "The Americans are supplying the killing machine. The others are just watching."

Peter put his arm around her, and she closed the book. He comforted her. "You can't do anything from here, Sis. Don't look at the book any more."

"I have to. It's my responsibility to at least know, even if I can't do anything. If those desperate victims are to be sent through Hell, I have to see and feel their suffering. It will help me to mould the future." She turned the page. Peter was shocked at the pictures of some girls tied spread-eagled, with their breasts cut off, their thighs stripped and pieces of wood pushed into their vaginas. Katie began to boil.

"Sis. Calm down." He held her tightly as she ground her teeth. "Stop!" She responded, calmed down, and then began to cry. "It's not your fault. It's happened."

But she cried fiercely into his neck, and began banging her head on his shoulder, punishing herself for the suffering of the Bangalee people. But she quickly pulled herself together. "The Chi Bantri." She again began grinding her teeth. "My fault. The fucking Chi Bantri. And it hasn't even happened yet. That's tomorrow's date!"

Peter soothed her.

She sobbed, "That's not even happened yet. I could stop it, but I'm here. Why have I deserted them? Help me, Peter." The little girl whimpered as she tried to talk. "My project. The Chi Bantri are there."

He did not want to upset her any more, so deliberately never said anything.

But *she* did. "That is their form of lingchi. It's been their trade mark since Kandy. These are pictures of tomorrow and these girls will tomorrow be gang raped, abused and then slowly killed by the fucking naïve servants of the Chi Bantri. And I can't help them." She was beginning to calm down. "Where's my Mummy?" She looked hard into Peter's eyes. "Hey? Where's my Mummy?" Her stare into his mind was intense. "I need to punish her. She has caused untold suffering through her behaviour. *Catherine* would allow me to punish her." The eyes burned into Peter's head, pushing, forcing, twisting almost until he could take no more. She rubbed her finger across the next photo, which showed the Chinese forces moving across the East Pakistani flag, towards Russian and Indian troops, pushing aside the Americans as they move. The world was at war! And as she shook she continued to burn his mind with her eyes, begging, and begging.

"Stop it! Get out!" He pushed his head away and looked past her, to escape. "Get out!"

She smiled, and got out of his head, leaving him reeling with confusion.

He screamed, "Leave your mum alone! It can't be all her fault!"

She grinned at him and whispered, "Thank you." She closed the book. "You've just changed history."

He frowned, and tried to avoid her stare. "So that hasn't happened?"

"Fraid some of it has, and will. The Pakistani war has begun and those poor girls will still suffer tomorrow, gang-raped, laid out and cut to bits. I can't stop that. But the third world war, that hasn't happened, thank you." She fiddled with Peter's hand. "The whole World, for just a few moments, was going to war, but you stopped it." She raised her eyebrows. "And so the fight for Bangladesh will follow its bloody course alone, until December, with the stands full to the brim with enthused spectators, watching the genocide, but doing nothing." She kissed his lips. "You're a very good conscience. Thank you."

Colin Hodgson

10 -- BACK FROM BEYOND

Peter tossed and turned all night. His mind was elsewhere, heavily influenced by Katie's book, and he violently fought with his conscience, repeatedly asking why. Katie lay watching him suffer his nightmares, occasionally wiping his sweating brow, and licking the sweet fluids from her hand.

As the sun sprang into the sky, the winds began. It was certainly the stormy season. Katie sensed that the wind was not going to be as fierce as the previous morning's, but Peter was not convinced. They moved across the street to the cellar, and took refuge with the little school children.

"Sis, today those poor girls will be tortured and killed."

She shook her head, "Along with many hundreds, even thousands, of others today." She was very matter-of-fact about it all. "We must worry about our own plight, our return to our children. Then I can help them. How are you going to get me back?" She grinned and cocked her head sideways. "Well, you promised yesterday."

He walked to the end of the cellar and looked round the corner, at the skeletons. He studied them carefully, and, avoiding Katie's question, asked, "Why were they locked in here? Any ideas?"

"I bet it was for the same reason as I was." She shrugged her shoulders. "I've a theory, but I'm not saying at the mo." She limped over to him and looked at the children. "I asked you a question. Well?"

"I have a very loose plan, but I need to think it through. I'll tell you later." A bit of tit-for-tat.

The winds whistled through the camp, although they did not reach the ferocity of the previous day's storm. But it did rain, the first they had experienced since arriving at the colony, and it was heavy. However, none of it lasted very long, and the calm suddenly returned. They felt safe enough to leave the cellar and take account of any damage which may have occurred.

"Come on, Sis. Let's see what we've lost."

"Hokey cokey, my little munchkin."

He wound up the torch and they held hands, embarking on the slow climb up the steps. Peter pushed at the hatch.

"Shit! It's locked!" He pushed again, and then began banging at it, and pushing and thumping, and panicking. "Fuck! *We're stuck!*" He grabbed Katie's hand, and looked towards the corner where the children cuddled. "Let us out, you bastard!" They slowly crept down the stairs. Peter stuttered, "I can't stay here, Sis. I can't."

She reached up and stroked his forrid, smiling calmly into his furrowed face. And then she began to giggle.

"Shut up. I'm scared."

"No, *you* shut up. I can get us out."

"Then do it, *now!* And stop giggling." He stared at his little sister, who was taking their imprisonment very lightly. Then he looked towards the children. At least she wouldn't eat him, she never gets hungry. But hang on a minute, she ate her other conscience! Maybe she was the jailor, and he was on the menu. She could build up her strength enough to get home to Earth, by eating her conscience. "*You* locked it!" He pulled her to him, "Why? Why me?"

She stopped giggling and bit her bottom lip, before asking, "What're you talking about?"

"You're gonna eat me!"

Katie's jaw dropped in disbelief, and then she burst into uncontrollable hysterics. Her chattering laughter echoed around the cellar, disturbing the dust from the cobwebs causing Peter to start coughing, which gently melted into laughter. They both sank to the floor, and held each other tightly as the laughter subsided. Suddenly they were quiet, looking into each others tear drenched eyes.

"Yummy, tears of laughter, the sweetest kind." She kissed the tears from his eyes. "I wouldn't eat you, ever, my tender beef steak." She pointed to the hatch. "Come on, let's get out." She climbed to her wobbly feet and toddled over to the plan chest. "This will help." She leaned down to pull a fuel can from behind it. Then she leaned down and grabbed a handle, and then pulled out a chain saw. "And this will *definitely* help." What a darling. Peter looked at his little sister and fell even *more* in love with her. She wasn't just a pretty face. "I thought we might need this, tootles. Come on, *I* can't use it."

He picked up the saw, checked that there was petrol, and pulled the chord. The noise in the confined space was deafening, but the sweet smell of freedom marinated it into an atmosphere of triumph. They were getting out! He offered the screeching blade up to the hatch, and it just ate the wood. He cut the hatch from one side to the other, then pushed it open, and the life giving rays of the sun flowed down into the cellar, and they both cheered. The triumphant freedom fighters scrambled out into the open air. What a feeling.

"Now, you. I want some answers." He lifted her up. "What do you know about all this? None of it bothered you, you must know something."

"Well, for a start, I knew that I'd put the saw behind the chest. Why would I worry?"

He was stumped. A golden duck for young golden bollocks.

"It's a good job one of us has a brain. You must learn to think outside the box, my little pudding-pants! You might just stay alive long enough to get me home."

They wandered back across the street. No damage had been caused by the wind, and the smell of the fresh vegetation, just washed by the rain, was pure sweetness. Everything smelled alive. Then they sat in the tent, amongst the equipment, while Peter ate some breakfast, and Katie studied his face as he chewed, the jaw muscles rippling with every bite. She was tempted.

With a mischievous grin, "Peter, you pussy-packer, if I did eat you, I would have to wonder whether to eat the best bit first, or leave it til last." She chuckled.

"Hmm, I shouldn't ask, but which is the best bit?"

She just grinned.

"Yeah, best you don't tell me."

They fetched the plans to the tent, and studied the route to the church. It was a long way to walk. And they would have to carry enough gear to see through the journey, possibly both ways, so Peter set about his master plan. "I said I would get you home, and I will. But I won't leave you here. We'll stay together, always." He estimated their route more accurately to be about one hundred and sixty five miles. At ten miles a day, it would only take about seventeen days. "That's do-able. But could we do ten miles a day?" He looked at Katie for some help, but all he got was a broad smile. "I don't think we could. Any ideas?"

"I've always got good ideas. I'm God."

"It's no bloody use name dropping, what's your good idea? Come on, we're up against it right now. You couldn't walk ten miles a day, and I couldn't push your wheelchair ten miles a day, not across rough ground."

"No, but *you* could walk ten miles a day, and *I* could stop and wait for you when you get tired. And I could carry all your food and any equipment, and I could take my khaki tent, and another one for us to sleep in. And we could get naughty at night, you know what I mean, Spunky?" Her grey-green eyes were radiant, drawing him into her web. "And we've run out of clean clothes, so we could go all *naked* and *sexy*. What about it, Big Boy? Up for it?" She raised her eyebrows and then winked at him.

"This is not the time."

"God you're hard work at times. I just pray that when you do finally break, you're worth all the effort."

"What d'you mean by that? Come on."

Katie dropped her head as she realised, "Sorry, I keep forgetting that you're a virgin."

He just sat staring at her, completely stumped for words, so she broke the ice.

"I'll teach you how to sort a girl out, and make her *writhe*. Stick with me, Rump-pump, and I'll make you a man." She began to laugh before he could complain. "Right, back to business, babe. We've got to get to the church on time. Hey, we could get married!" She pulled herself over onto her knees and put her hands together in front of her chest. "Please, Peter, will you marry me?"

"Stop it!" He took a great, deep breath to avoid laughing. "Please top. You're my baby sister. Let's be serious."

"Ok." She sensed he was beginning to break, but she would leave the cream until later. "Serious, it is, chuckles. On a serious note, we can't take seventeen days to get there. Do you know why? Well, I'll give you an idea of what time costs. Seventeen days in East Pakistan right now? At eleven thousand killings a day, that's one hundred and eighty seven thousand people killed in seventeen days. *That's* how expensive time is, right now, in East Pakistan. Do you still want to walk?"

He frowned. "What choice do I have? We've got to get to that church, in case the drawings are true. The craft might be there."

"Well……." She decided not to use any of her crass pet names. Serious! "Well, *Peter*, I could ride on that." She pointed at his head. "Behind you!"

He swung round, and there, right behind him, was the motorised truck which the miners carted their tools around on. "Wow. I didn't even notice it. Stupid, or what?"

"Right on, Stupid."

Easy. It would probably have done as much as ten to twelve miles an hour; that was only about three days to get there! They could do it.

"Hey, Pete? We could get there in just thirty three thousand killings. Or in another measure, about three thousand gang rapes. When shall we go?" There is no time like the present. "And I think you could get on it with me and still steer. You could hold the operating handle from up there." The hand-truck was operated by a T-shaped arm which housed the throttle and turned the pivoted front wheels. "I'm sure you can ride it, Cowboy." She chuckled. "And we've run out of clothes, so we can go starkers. Yee ha!"

Fully clothed, they started the truck and manoeuvred it out of the tent. The diesel bowser was already hitched, so they just had to go to the diesel tank by the gunk tanker, and fill up.

"What else do we need? Food, and the tents. And my book. And my drugs. And some tissues, cos I'm still on. What about you, Pete?"

"Yeah, food and hand tools."

There was a small trailer which could hitch to the back of the bowser, and it comfortably held all their provisions and tools, including the khaki tent, and Katie's superior mind suggested that they tie everything down securely, in case the winds came back. There were some small tents in the store, so they just took one of them. "It'll be cosy," chuntered Katie as she pinched his cheek. "Let's get going. Hi ho, *Silver*!"

The train set off along the street towards the mountains. The map was folded to show the marked out route, and an aerial photo print ready to help identify the land-marks. The steering was awkward for Peter with very little lock, but so long as he looked ahead, he could get off and walk it around the tighter bends, and the speed on the straight was good. Three days was very possible!

The route took them across the heath land and past the cliffs which had the paintings. They arrived there in a fraction of the time they took to walk it. So they stopped to check out the cave.

There were still three wall paintings, but they were slightly different to the previous. Katie touched the first one, which still showed a church-shaped building, with colours at one end, and a craft, but it now included a red mark over the top of the craft. "Hmm, don't like that."

The second looked the same, but no, the green had progressed further up their bodies, and the screaming circles, their mouths, were shown as the sad, closed clown's mouths. They had stopped screaming.

And the third still showed the halo'd God and her friend being watched from a great height.

"They're still watching us," sighed Peter.

"But look," she smiled. "The people watching us. They are watching over us, and are now laughing. Look, that one looks like he is clapping, applauding us. And one is big and one is small. And the big one, he has a finger longer than the other fingers, a claw, or a key. I thought so. Edward is not warning us, he is telling us. They are our friends, our boys!"

Peter couldn't help the face-wide grin. "Really? Let's go and get them, the little devils."

"No. Just wait. They are watching over us. Let's let them, and they can protect us; this is their country and their terrain. I'll feel a lot safer while they are stalking us."

Peter didn't say anything, but he was wondering why they tried to kill them in the cellar. Perhaps they were applauding because the prisoners had escaped. Was it just a game to them? Or a test? But the poor children, nobody let *them* out. Anyway, Katie was happy for them to carry on with whatever they were up to.

"We mustn't get into a position where we can be locked in."

As Peter climbed back onto the truck, he pulled Katie up, who exalted, "Oh shit! The spoilers!" Although disappointed, she grinned and said, "I was looking forward to going starkers. Look!"

There was a black plastic bag, full of clothes. The stalkers had gathered up all the wind-swept clothes, and returned them. And there was a note inside which read, 'This is a decent neighbourhood. We don't want Peter flashing his hairy ass around here. Hee, hee.' The boys were on the ball.

The train moved around the mountain range quite comfortably, across the heath lands which swept up towards the rocks, and they made very good time. They stopped to make Peter a tin of soup and potatoes, but kept moving at all other times. The scenery as they looked over from the mountains was flat and boring, just a patchwork of heath and spinney, and it was difficult to identify any landmarks. The only thing that they were sure of was that they needed to move right around the mountain range, to the opposite side. Once there they should be able to see the sea.

"We must be going in the right direction, just straight round the mountains." Peter identified the highest peak from the map. "I think we're about here. Look." They studied the map. "If we're there, we should be able to see that lake, to our left. And the river is not far ahead. If we get there tonight, we're almost half way." That was a result, about eighty miles in one day! He stopped the truck, and stood up, as high as he could. "But I can't see the lake. It could be in a dip." He jumped down from the truck. "I'm just going up there, to see if I can see it." He pointed to a bank of scree. "I'll get better advantage up there."

"Be careful."

He wandered up the slopes, stopping a couple of times to check the view, but then carried on. Katie could see him scrambling up the bank of loose detritus, but then he stopped and sat down, placing his hands on his head.

"Peter.... what's he doing?" She stood up and waved both her arms in the air. "Come back," she tried to shout. "Please come back. I love you, come back." She was whispering. He wouldn't have heard, even if she shouted, but he stood up, and looked around as if he was lost. "Come to me, Peter, please. I need you." She could see that he was confused, and something was distracting him, and looked like he was ducking from a swarm of wasps, but she couldn't see anything near to him. "Look at me, Peter. Here." He looked in her direction, but then returned to ducking, and waving his hands around his head. Katie closed her eyes and concentrated, and then exploded.

"Leave him alone! Leave him!" She was screaming, and turning red. "Let him go, or you'll pay the price! Now! Now! Now! Do it, now!" The screams echoed around the mountains, and the ground shook. As she screamed louder the loose rocks began to fall down the slopes, and lumps of granite split away from the cliffs, but Peter couldn't move, so she screamed ever louder and the quake began to roar. The animals and birds fled away from the rocks to open ground, and they all turned to watch the spectacle. And the mountains shook. But as she screamed again, a figure shot out from hiding and sped towards Peter. It was Stumpy. She stopped screaming, and the shaking subsided, and the roar was replaced by the gaggle of the animals and birds as they screeched at each other in panic. But it soon became quiet, as Stumpy reached Peter, and he hugged the deranged lad. The panic was over, and Katie returned to her normal facial colour, but ground her teeth, and spat. "You fucking idiot."

Stumpy, now taller than Peter, carefully led him down the scree bank, and when at the bottom, picked him up like a small child and moved towards Katie. She was still angry when they reached her.

"What the fuck is he doing? Does he know who I am? Well, answer me before I start again? Now!" Every time she shouted, the creatures joined in, fearing for the worst. "Tell me, Stumpy!"

The poor lad stood with Peter in his arms, and they were both crying. "I don't know. You'll have to ask Mo." He gently placed Peter on his feet, and then gave him a big hug. "Is Peter all right, Mum?"

Stumpy helped Katie down from the truck, and she stood in front of Peter, staring intensely into his eyes. He was empty, devoid of life and soul. She again screamed, "Give it back! " As she shouted into Peter's face, the creatures cried and cowered. "You've got five seconds!" She held her arms in the air, and began counting. "One, two, three, four,........." Then she saw what she wanted. He was back. She desperately grabbed him around the waist and they hugged for a few moments. "Thanks, Stumpy." She was still seething. "Think he needs to sleep now."

Although the day was still bright, they decided to set up camp right where they were. The little tent was not big enough for more than a couple of people, so Stumpy volunteered to sleep outside and keep watch and as the twin moons slipped across the heavens Katie held tightly onto the sleeping Peter. "Nigh night, sleep tight my little dormouse." She rubbed her cheek against his. "I looked after you good, today. I think I scared the silly old prat. Tomorrow you can tell me how you are going to get me home to Earth, like you promised." She kissed his lips and pulled herself to the flap.

Stumpy was sitting outside with Mo. Katie turned the light on.

"Mo. Are you ok?"

He crawled over to her and gave her a hug.

"Yes, Mummy. And you?" His white teeth stood out in the dark. He was no larger than he was when they left, unlike the ever-growing Stumpy.

"I nearly flipped today. It was a close thing." Katie knew how close she had come to doing some serious damage. "What was that all about? Stumpy said you would know."

Stumpy put his thumb up to the two tiny cuddlers. Mo could talk.

"He is a human, and he went close to Daddy's funeral vault. He was very mad."

"But didn't he know who Peter was? Haven't you told him about him?"

Mo looked at Stumpy for support. Stumpy suggested, "Tell Mummy everything. Then it can never be conceived as a lie." They had an ingrown hatred towards lies.

"Yes, we have told Daddy everything. But he said that he would kill the human because he is human."

"Why didn't he kill the other humans? There have been hundreds come through here, and they are the ones that have caused the damage. Well, sort of. They are the ones who have been on the front line."

"He didn't kill them because you didn't care for them. He is jealous. He's never been in love, and now you are."

Katie went scarlet with embarrassment. "Don't be silly. Me, in love? Where did he get that idea?"

"Stumpy told him."

Stumpy jumped, "You didn't have to tell her that!"

"You told me to tell everything! Make your bloody mind up."

"Calm down, you two." She smiled and played with her pyjama sleeve. "Don't know." She was taken back a little with the idea that somebody thought she was in love. "Why do you think I'm in love? Stumpy, am I in love?"

He grinned. His bright red lips shone, and his teeth flashed in the light. "I think so. You get embarrassed when we talk about it. You just did. And you keep trying to shag him."

"What? You been spying?"

"You know we have. All the time. Saw you trying. All the time. Just in case we missed it, have you shagged him yet?" His eyes were wide and waiting for an answer.

"No."

"You'd better not be lying. You know we hate lies."

"On my mummy's life, your auntie's. I want to, but I don't think he likes me enough."

Mo cocked his head to one side. "You are his sister. And only a child. I've seen it in his mind. But he loves you more than anything else in the whole World. He loves you, but doesn't want to shag you. *Weird*. I don't know if you love him, can't see it in your head."

"And you won't. It's private. So don't go poking around in me." She paused for some thinking. "I wish I did love him. But I don't know what love is. It's a human thing. They're so lucky that I gave them love, but they can only have it because they've got hate. I must check my book tomorrow. Hate is big news on Earth right now."

Mo, who was still cuddling Katie, said, "You do love him. I can feel it. And I love you, too. You'll do anything for Peter, never been like that before, has it. And I'll do anything for you. And Daddy is mad about it all. He's going to fight you before you go back."

"Is that a threat? Did he ask you to tell me that? Cos I just let him off the hook, well, Stumpy did, by bravely collecting Peter from your daddy. He's a *lucky* daddy."

"He *did* ask me to tell you. I told him that he is wrong, and we can learn for the future from you and Peter, before we are gone forever. We are almost gone, you know."

"But how will fighting me help you all? I'm dangerous, and he's not, he's weak from imbalance. His conscience is far too strong to survive against me. And there's something that he ought to know. Can you please tell him that I need to speak to him. And can you also please tell him that I am one apart."

Mo whistled in disbelief. "That's not what he told us. He said you are one with twin Catherine."

"I am here alone. Just tell him that. And if he hurts my Peter, he will suffer the uncontrolled wrath of God. Right now, only Peter can hold me back, so without him, well, work it out for yourself."

"If I love you, will you accept my love?" Mo was searching for something. "Stumpy longs to be like Peter, and I love you. Daddy is losing." He looked pleased by that.

"So, do you like hurting your daddy? He loves you both. Well, he's your daddy, I suppose he does."

"We don't really have love. He made us in the wrong image. I really do wish I was one of *your* children."

"But, Mo, my children aren't like you. They're human, not Gods. You can't be like them. There's a big price to pay for their feelings and emotions, like pain, distress, unhappiness, cruelty, and death. They all die, some early and painfully. But you're a God and you'll live forever once you're mature, as one together with Stumpy. That's how you are. And that's why he only makes a few at a time. My children have to reproduce constantly to replace the many thousands who die *every* day. They have sixty years to get good, and have to use that time aggressively to gain and to better themselves and their gangs. You wouldn't like it."

"Me and Stumpy have a plan. None of us has ever done anything like it before, but we are going to do it. We are going to *give*. All we ever do is play around. We don't want for anything, and we don't fight for anything. What's the point? So we are going to learn to give, and love, and help, and move forward, and change our people into something that can survive against others, like the humans. And we think that if we are going to give, we are going to have to learn to take, else we've nothing to give. We are going to be like you and Peter. And if Daddy fights you, we will fight *with* you."

Wow, he was determined to change his World.

Katie held him tightly. She could feel some luck coming her way, so she was careful not to spoil it. "That's a lovely compliment to me and Peter. Thank you. I'll help you as much as I possibly can."

"You just have to point us in the right direction."

"Ok. First. You must learn about death. I know it was good fun, but we cannot dig like you. Please don't play the burying game with us any more, or you'll kill us, well, Peter. We can show you what happens when humans get stuck in confined spaces, when we go back to our camp. You'll be able to practice the *sadness* of death. That's a good place to start."

Stumpy perked up. "It was a good game, though, and you got out really quickly. That was clever."

"Thanks, but next time we might not get out. And you'll lose us, maybe forever."

The boys curled up and had some sleep, while Katie watched the stars, wondering if her own mummy was out there, or if she was lost forever. But she was beginning to feel hope oozing through her body, in the shape of two willing converts. But how would she make their loyalty pay? How would she turn their commitment toward her and Peter into her spirit, which was rapidly diminishing. She soon needed to feed, or float off towards oblivion with her beloved big brother, Peter the human.

11 -- THE CLOUDS OF DEATH

Katie shook Stumpy as the sun rose.

"The wind could be coming. We need to pack up."

They woke Peter, but Mo was gone. The three of them rushed to pack up the tent and secure the load on the trailer and then set off, perched on top of the truck.

"Over that way," instructed Stumpy.

"Hmm, you sure? The map shows this way."

"You calling me a liar?"

Katie stepped in, "Shut up. We'll go Stumpy's way, cos he lives here."

The ever-growing green child really did hate lies, or anything associated, like accusations. Peter looked back to him and smiled, wondering if he was as ferocious as he looked and spoke. But he wasn't going to test him. He was a big lad.

"Sorry, Peter. Just give me a bollicking if I speak out of hand. I just want to be like you."

So by then, even Peter was thinking, *'how can we use this devote following?'* Katie glanced towards him and grinned, but warned him remotely to *'think of England'*.

"Anyway, Peter, we need to go this way because it's the only way over the river." The extra payload was already paying off.

The wind picked up, and they rolled up the plans and stored them away; they continued towards the river by Stumpy's directions, hopefully. But the wind wasn't vicious enough to cause them to stop, and the good going brought the river into sight. It was wide, reeds and bulrushes along the margin, and looked impassable, but Stumpy directed them down to a particular spot. It was about a hundred yards across, and flowing fairly slowly.

He jumped down from the truck. "I'll lead you over. Stay up there." He went over to some bushes, broke off a large, thick stick and stripped the side shoots. "Just don't panic, nor get off the truck. And if you're going to fall in, fall to the left, or you'll get ripped to bits."

He briefly explained that the miners who had made camp further up the river had created a weir, across which he was to lead them. The water which was running over the weir was only about a foot deep, sometimes lower during the dryer periods, and it had been made by the miners to protect their families from the large sea creatures which would venture up the river in search of food. "All the violent, spiteful creatures in our lands are in the sea. You must never venture into the sea, or you'll be torn to pieces. They're *evil* things, the meat eaters." The weir was only about eight feet wide, but was wide enough to prevent the large carnivores from jumping over. "This was one of the good things that the humans did."

He walked down to the river bank, guiding the truck slowly behind him, and then stepped in. As soon as his foot entered the water, the downstream began to swirl. The creatures were there.

"Look!" He pointed to his right, and through the clear water could be seen a massive fish, about as big as a grown man. It gaped its mouth open-and-closed as it breathed the water, flashing its teeth with every gasp. "It could bite your head right off!" Stumpy frowned. "And there's some more." He stood in shallow water and looked up at his two wards. Katie was giggling, while Peter stared at the ferocious hunters. "If the truck starts to go, dive over that side of the weir, or you'll be their dinner." So Katie scrambled back and grabbed hold of her book, Unknown India.

The going was very slow, and the vibration from the engine was attracting meat eaters by the hundreds. The water began to boil. One of them tried to push its way up the slope of the weir, so Stumpy poked it with his stick. It retreated. But another made its lunge. It managed to reach Stumpy's leg, gashing it with its front teeth, and the blood flowed.

"Move over, quick!" Peter climbed down from the truck. "I'll feel for the edge, keep the truck right behind me." He followed the top of the upstream edge of the weir, and Stumpy steered the train's wheels as far upstream as possible, away from the creatures. But his blood flowed into the swarming waters, and more of them arrived, thrashing away as they became high on the taste of Stumpy. They must have selected one their own for dinner, and the waters turned red as they ripped it apart, thrashing the waters with their muscular tails and fins.

The team arrived at the edge of the river. What a relief to be on dry land, and they didn't hang about to watch the bloodbath. They moved swiftly away from the river, until they could no longer hear the carnage.

"Stumpy." Katie pointed to his torn leg. It had a gash which almost split his calf muscle in two, and it was bleeding ferociously. The two humans made him sit down, and Peter fetched a belt from the trailer, pulling it tight around the leg to slow the bleeding. Katie whispered, "We need some algae powder. Is there any about here?"

"Yes." Stumpy pointed downstream to a rocky outbreak. "There's a cave over there. We looked in it a couple of days back. I'll go."

Peter stressed, "You can't walk. I'll go. What we looking for?"

"Take a lamp, it'll be very dark. Go down into the cave, it drops down quite a way, and look for a grey powder deposit. If you see some lichens growing on the lower parts of the walls, there'll be powder beneath them." Stumpy put his hand up for a high five, and grinned. "Go for it, bruv."

He set off towards the rocks.

"Stumpy, I know you do it all the time," said Katie with an enquiring tone, "but what's going on in his head? He hasn't even asked about yesterday."

"He's confused. He had a terrible nightmare last night, or that's what he thinks." He lowered his head. "I'm ashamed."

She held her hand out and held his. "Tell me what it is. I'll listen."

He raised his eyebrows and looked her in the face. "I'm ashamed of my daddy. He killed Peter." He had tears forming in his eyes. "He killed my best mate. Why?"

Katie squeezed his leathery hand. "But he's here. It's Peter and he's just gone into the caves. He isn't dead."

"Not any more. She got him back in time. I didn't even know she was here."

"Who?"

"Your mummy. She got him back. His nightmare was about him laying back, everything fading, and then this bright orange light with the brilliant emerald-green face kissed him, and the skies and the sun came back into his life. And his nightmare ended there. You know, we've all gone against Daddy's wishes and command. He wanted Peter dead, because he is so jealous of your success, and he knows that he himself is a failure. And now he's a God who has lost control. We all went against him." He leaned forward and cuddled Katie. "I don't want to be like him, I want to be like Peter. He's a real boy, and he'll be a real man, and then he'll be a dead man, at peace with his God. He'll be at peace with you, always."

His tears dropped down onto Katie's face. She wiped them with her hand, and then licked the ambrosia. It was wonderful. The tears from a God; life-giving, succulent and addictive. She felt instantly stronger. And her mummy was still on the planet, and as she pondered the many questions as to why, a plan was spawning.

"Right, you two!" It was Peter. "Is this enough?" He had a bagful of grey powder, and proudly presented it to Katie. "I can get some more if we need it."

Stumpy directed the operation. Peter carefully held the wound open, while Katie poured some powder into Stumpy's cupped hands, who then spat into the power, several times, until he had enough spit to knead the mix into a poultice. He carefully pushed the poultice into the wound, as Peter held it open. He then squeezed the wound closed, as Katie wrapped a bandage around the leg.

"There. What a team!" Katie stood up. "Speaking of team, where has Mo gone to?"

"He's with Daddy. He's trying to talk to him. Daddy's been a very miserable old prat just lately." The growing green lad shrugged his shoulders. "Come on, let's find your church."

The three all climbed onto the truck and they set off, with Peter back in the driving seat. Katie looked at him and winked. "Get me to the church on time, Booboo."

As they moved around the mountain range the sea came into sight. They were in spitting distance of their destination.

"Look." Peter pointed towards a low, misty cloud, or smoke. "Somebody must be there." They felt an intimidating excitement creep through their bodies. Somebody there? Who? They decided to move carefully towards the smoke, which looked to be their destination, but to hold up before they went right in. They needed to find out who, or what, was creating the smoke; friend or foe?

"I think we're close enough," whispered Stumpy. "I think we should do a reckie."

They hid the train behind some shrubs, and with Katie piggybacking on Peter, they set off towards a wooded elevation. There were many brambles so Stumpy then carried Katie on his shoulders, above the level of the spiny bows, while Peter struggled through. The woodland floor suddenly dropped steeply downhill, and from their vantage point they could see the remains of the stricken church. It was smoking, with the tower-end almost completely gone, melted into the ground with the rest of the camp. Most of the camp was just a hole in the ground, steaming, and slowly spreading outwards. Almost everything was gone.

Peter sadly stated, "The gunk tanker must've spilled out. It's got everything in its way."

Stumpy whispered, "If we'd got here earlier, we could have been down there. Wonder what caused it."

"Old Dick said that they were unstable, and would all go like that at some point. If we go back to the camp, we need to move right away from *our* old tanker."

They decided to get a little closer. As they moved very slowly down the slope the woodland turned back into heath land, and Katie suggested they sit down for a while, and just look around. The steaming ground was still corroding away, so the accident had not long happened; could have been within just a few hours. And then the quiet was disturbed as the whole roof on the church collapsed into the smoking pit below, throwing dust and debris over the melting pot, sparking as it landed, and then dissolving like a child's ice lolly on the stove. The gunk just ate everything.

"Shhhh." Katie had heard something. There was a whimpering sound from the right. It seemed to be coming from behind some debris by the side of the gunk-hole. Then it became a scream! Loud and painful, full of absolute fear! "The paintings!" shouted Katie. The little girl struggled to her feet and began moving towards the screams.

"Stop!" Stumpy grabbed hold of her. He hugged her tight. "Don't run down there." He made her sit down, and then very carefully walked down the slope, inspecting every piece of ground before moving forward across it. He looked like he was mine clearing. "It's safe to follow me, but only stay in my path." He was looking for gunk spots or splashes.

The screaming became louder as they approached the debris. Stumpy inspected the ground, and then looked round the corner. A man in a white uniform lay screaming. The sound was frightening, and pierced their ears like needles, conveying absolute agony. It was like hell to Peter's ears. The uniformed man shook as he saw Stumpy, and held his hand out, then screwed his face up and again screamed. Peter held his own hands over his ears and closed his eyes, but the screams still got through.

"Stop him!"

But the screaming continued, getting deeper and deeper into Peter's mind with each burst.

"Stop him!"

Stumpy bent down to push his hands over the poor victim's mouth to quiet him, but stopped dead. The man's face and lips were beginning to bubble, oozing out milky green puss, and popping with a puff of steam.

Stumpy shouted over the screams, "He's got gunk into him! He's eating away from inside!"

As Peter panicked he thought of Old Dick's story of the man who had got gunk on his foot. He had screamed for hours before dying. So he pulled a lump of wood from the pile of debris, moved around to the man and held the weapon high above his head. But the man stopped screaming and smiled up at Peter, his lips splitting as the grin stretched his face, and Peter hesitated just momentarily. But the smile waned and the screaming returned. The lad's eyes screwed as he swung the wood. It smashed the skull with a muted thud, and the body writhed.

"Again!" shouted Katie.

He swung the wood onto his skull even harder and it split, splashing blood into the air. The writhing stopped.

Katie breathed out, "He's gone." She stepped over to Peter and held his waist. "Come away. Come up the slope and we can have a good cry." None of them spoke as they returned to their sitting spot, where Peter wept.

After a while, Stumpy suggested that they make a move.

"Where to?" asked Katie.

The green youth grinned, and those bright red lips shone in the sun, and Katie remembered. "The *painting*! The ship had a big red mark over it, just like your lips!" She began to giggle, cuddle Peter, and to just swing about around his shoulders. She sang, "Thank you, Stumpy. I *love* you." Her childish face was brighter and more gleeful than he had ever seen it, so he grabbed her and they began to dance about and shout. Peter pulled out of his shock and joined them. "We can go home. We'll soon be gone! Gone, gone!"

The dancing slowed down and Stumpy, laughing, sang, "We can all go hoome, hoome on the range!" And then the realisation hit. He stopped. "You can go home." Jubilation turned into sadness as they all thought about leaving each other to go their own Godly ways. And then sadness moved into depression.

"Where's the ship, anyway? In the hole?" asked Peter. They all stared at each other. "But that poor man, he must have come from somewhere. But even if he did, we couldn't drive a ship. Wouldn't even know which way to go, if we could." Hmm, cup half empty today. "We're still fucked." Nearly empty. "But wait, he could've had a partner who wasn't killed by the gunk." Cup now half full! "Quick! He might leave without us!" Cup runneth over.

Katie scrambled up onto Stumpy's shoulders, and they set off down the slope.

"This way!" shouted Stumpy. "The man probably came from this way after the accident, and just went too close." They swung around to the right, but the slope hid the land. They began to run, like as if the bus was about to go, and Katie shouted and cheered as Peter went on ahead, and disappeared over the ridge.

"Yeehaaa! It's here. Yeehaaaaaaa!"

Stumpy and Katie were laughing as they mounted the ridge, and there it was. Dirty, rusty, small, but there it was! The ship, the one which would save the World from Godlessness; the one which would answer the prayers of millions of Bangalees, who pray for forgiveness and God's deliverance from their personal hell-on-earth. The ship!

They sat down and looked at it as it nestled down in the slight valley with its door open and the gangplank inviting them in, and silently whispering 'welcome'. But they just stared. They stared at the rust, at the filthy windscreen, and at the union jack which stretched along the fuselage. Their ship.

"We need to take a look. Before he drives off." Peter had broken out of his shock. He had just killed a man, but hey what, Uncle Steven did. They walked towards the ship, half expecting something to happen, or somebody to come running out, but nothing. "I'll take a look." Peter stood at the bottom of the plank, and wondered. "What if somebody's in there?"

Stumpy laughed, "Then he'll welcome you. He's lost his mate."

"No. You know what I mean. What if he's got a gunk gun. He'll shoot you, then go looking for Mo." Stumpy took the cautious warning and walked back towards the scrub and hid.

Peter walked up the plank. He had to bend down to enter the small hatch, but once inside it was quite spacious, but dull and dusty. He had entered what seemed to be the goods section, with boxes and bags stacked all around the walls. To his right were two doors and to his left just one single door in the centre of the wall. He opened one of the doors on the right and peered in. It was a small bedroom, and messy. He checked the other door, and it was the same. Then he checked the one on its own, and it opened up into a room full of equipment. There were two suits and two helmets, and electrical equipment. And there were two guns. There were two large backpacks hanging in a convenient spot and two pairs of silver boots. And there were many hints that this was a two-man craft.

He moved to the opposite door, and carefully opened it. "What!" and he stepped back in surprise, as he stared at the back of the pilot, in the left seat. He didn't say anything, but waited for the pilot to turn, but he didn't. He didn't move. "Good morning, sir." Peter was nervous and his voice shuddered. "Good morning, sir," he said again, but no answer. So he quietly turned around and walked out of the ship.

Katie stood at the bottom of the plank, grinning with expectation. "Well?"

"Don't know. Can you look?" He went down and picked her up. "Will you look for me? I'm scared."

"Course I will, sweet-pea." She put her thumb up to Stumpy, who moved down and joined them. "Let's have a look."

They entered the ship, followed by Stumpy who stayed in the goods section, and then Peter showed her the pilot. He still hadn't moved.

"I think he's dead," Katie whispered.

"How can you tell?" he asked.

"This is how you check." She leaned forward with her mouth close to his ear, then shouted, "Oi, mush!" The pilot never flinched. "See?" she chuckled, "Told you so."

Peter wasn't amused. "*That* was *shit*. What's wrong with you?" He placed her on the ground and walked out of the craft, plonking himself on the grass with his head in his hands. He needed to scream, but his breathing was sporadic, and he couldn't.

"Sorry," she whispered in his ear, but he turned away. "Please, my silver prince. Sorry."

He looked into her begging face. "What's wrong with you? I've just killed one man and found another dead. And you're just laughing about it all. You're sick."

She held her face to his, and then swung round and kissed him on the lips. "Please my darling pinky-tickler, don't be mad at me. I just want you to love me, love this little girl. I can cry if you like. Would that help? I've been crying for over two hundred years. But I can do some more, just for you."

He returned her kiss and smiled. "I don't want you to cry. Not for me." The smile turned to a grin. "Maybe just a bit, for those sensuous-tasting tears."

"You can have more than just my tears, clit-splitter."

"Oi, behave." He was grinning.

"*Not* my fault, pussy-pump. You're my *only* conscience. Control me, if you can."

Peter pushed her back and jumped up, playfully slapping her on the head as he did.

"See, stud, you can do it. Grrrrr, take me home, all the way." She winked.

He just grinned at her and walked up the plank to Stumpy, who patiently waited at the hatch, smiling. They left Katie sitting in the sun, as they moved down to the pilot to investigate. Stumpy carefully pushed himself past the seat, and instantly diagnosed the cause of death. He had slit his left wrist. The blood had dried, but was still red, and so he hadn't been dead for long, and in his right hand he clutched a piece of paper. A note?

"You can read the letter, Peter."

"Ok. It says, 'Sorry friend. So sorry. Please forgive me my sins and errors.' And that's all it says. S'pose we'll never know what he meant." It was a struggle, but they managed to carry the body outside, where they said some prayers and burned it on a pile of brushwood.

"This is now *our* ship," stated a proud Stumpy. "Who's gonna drive?"

The excitement of finding the ship had gone to their heads. With no pilot, the craft was next to useless, and the immediate future looked bleak for God and her adopted conscience. Earth seemed an eternity away. But Katie's spirit, although weak and dying, was still high enough to pull the two youngsters through the depression. She carried on, laughing and giggling, and winding poor Peter up.

"Oh, my little cherub, we can at least sleep in a bed. Our first night in a bed together. What ecstasy do you have on the menu for me tonight?"

Stumpy looked at Peter, who had turned bright red, and laughed. It was bad enough having to suffer her chat-up lines in private, but in front of the children? He said, "Peter, cherub, I bet you'll shag her before you go home."

"Shut up! Both of you." He walked off towards the raised woodland. "Going to get the truck. See you later, perhaps."

It took Peter a little while to go around the woodland, towards the truck, but he arrived back in one piece, just after Mo had turned up. They all high fived, and danced.

"I'm a bit concerned about our safety here." Peter frowned. "When I rode back around the woodland, the pit had gotten even bigger, and it's still eating away everything around it. Where the man laid has all gone now, so it's moving pretty quickly. You know in the cave. Well that was only a tiny bit of gunk and it made a hole right through the rock and into the water. This lot is a *tanker* full. God knows how far it will go before it's spent. Could even reach here." He looked at his sister. "And what's worse is that I stopped and looked for a little while, and that misty haze around it, well it's started to eat at the leaves on the trees. The fumes from it look like they are as corrosive as the gunk."

Nobody spoke for several minutes. Then little Mo suggested, "We could be wiped out if we stay here. I've picked up loads of knowledge to pass onto Stumpy when I go, and I know that when we're at the other camp, we're in the winds which always approach from the sea. They're clean and fresh, and so is the rain. But over this side of the river, the land is swept by the winds which come from the land, where the other camp is. So, all the air movement is from our camp to this area and beyond. And I think Peter has a point that the fumes from the pit over there, are corrosive, and also will get into the clouds and rain, then the rivers. This accident could contaminate a massive area. It could destroy the small amount of land that we have. Nobody could be safe downwind from these fumes, so we need to go back upwind. Very soon."

Katie looked sympathetically at the two local beings, knowing the gunk could all but destroy their planet. The miners had already reduced the intelligent life to only two, but the tankers, spread around the tiny land masses, could finish the rest of the life.

They all agreed that getting back to the other camp was priority.

"Do we need to go now, or in the morning?" asked Katie. "It's almost dark."

Mo pointed in the direction away from the accident area. "We can go that way and then right, along the river to the weir. It will keep us out of the down wind from the camp. We could go in the morning, I think."

That was good. It gave them a chance to rifle through the ship. The ship which was no longer to take them home, nor to relieve the poor souls' plights in East Pakistan, nor to reunite God with her conscience. *That* ship.

Katie looked at Peter with morose eyes. Peter suddenly remembered her as a little girl, laying on her blanket and peeking out onto the world from her carcase through her beautiful grey-green eyes. Beautiful, but sad. She was troubled.

He snuck up to her and gave her a brothers cuddle. "What's wrong?"

She turned her head to look into his eyes. "I'm scared for you. I've completely lost Catherine. It's down to you to save us all from me." A tiny tear formed, and he gently kissed it from her cheek-bone. "Thank you, brother." Brother! It wasn't stud, or big boy, or spunky-pants, but just brother.

"What's happening?"

She grinned. "I'm getting weaker. And I can't bear to look at my book. I can't bear to."

They watched as the sun neared the drop-off point.

"Why are the people in East Pakistan being murdered?" He wasn't sure if she wanted to talk, but, "And why isn't any country doing anything?"

She shrugged her shoulders. "Mostly money. A bit of personal ambitional, two potential prime ministers putting their own goals in front of others safety." She spoke slowly and quietly. "Jobs all going to West Pakistanis, and profits going back to West Pakistan, and all the benefits of success feeding the West Pakistanis, and then the outside influence. The Chi Bantri. They are influencing, from within, *all* gangs, pushing the genocide further, stopping the governments from intervening, and fanning the inferno of hell. They will be profiting from the suffering of the millions."

He thought, and then asked, "So what are you going to do about it when we get home?"

"Well, India must convince Russia that India should break a habit of a lifetime, and go to war as the offender. All they ever do is defend, but they must now offend, before the entire peoples of Northern Bengal are wiped out. Then I must close down the Chi Bantri. That will take a lot longer, maybe forty years. I must get rid of that secret sect which has set itself up as God, in my absence. And I must apologise to the people of the World for their existence. So, as an apology, I'll give them a new God to worship and learn from, the perfect God. That's all I have to do." She grinned.

"So why can't you get Catherine to get rid of the Chi Bantri? Just kill them all, if they're that bad?"

She sighed. "Rules and laws. I made them, and I have to stick by them. When I don't, everybody suffers." She looked in to his human eyes. "Man is man's very worst enemy, and man alone can kill his enemies. *That's* the law."

"Then I'd better get you back. Very soon."

"Ok, my celestial clam-digger." She began to snigger as he tickled her ribs.

"Glad to have you back, Sis." They kissed, and Stumpy and Mo cheered, and the sun finally fell behind the horizon.

12 -- IN GAYLA'S ACCORD

It made a pleasant change to sleep in real beds. But Stumpy and Mo insisted on sleeping outside, leaving the two adventurers the use of the bedrooms.

When the sun rose, Peter stretched as he walked down the gang-plank, watched by a chortling green giant, who by then had reached about seven feet tall.

"Hey man. It's my man Peter. So how was it for you, honey? Did you give her a good sorting?"

Oh no, Peter thought, not him as well. "Just mind your own business." He looked around. "Where's Mo?"

"Gone to talk to Dad about something."

Peter was beginning to think that he might just wake up one day, and be back in his room in the borstal. Maybe one day. Katie hobbled out of the ship, having to hold on tight as she stepped over the lip of the hatch. Peter shot up and picked her up.

"Well, well. Our princess has been at it all night, and can hardly walk." Stumpy tried to wink, but failed miserably.

"Shut up." Katie pointed at Stumpy as she spoke. "If, just if, it's any of your business, Peter insisted on separate rooms. So shut the fuck up." She successfully winked at him.

Mo had loaded some gear onto the trailer before going off to Daddy. So the three had another look around, and decided that there was nothing else that they needed, and they set off away from the ever-growing cloud of gunk. It was by then visibly destroying everything in its path as it wafted down-wind. The trees were first defoliated, and then after a little longer stripped of their bark and the wood began to rot and run down the trunks, like thick treacle. And as the mist fed, it seemed to thicken and multiply.

Stumpy looked back as they moved away, and sighed. "Where will it all end?"

They veered right, to move around the wooded elevation, and were in sight of the river. As they neared the banks, they looked back, and they could then see the full spread of the cloud. It had stretched several miles in the light breeze, and was getting thicker as it moved. Was this the start of the end? Peter began to think so.

At the weir, the fish were boiling over. Perhaps they knew they were going to cross that day.

"Ah, Mo." Little Mo caught them up as they arrived at the crossing-point. He had a large stick with him, with two nails banged through the end, like a spiked club. He carefully approached the water downstream from the weir, and waited. As soon as the fish sensed his presence, they came for him, and one pushed its head right out of the water as it snapped at his legs. He jumped back in time. And then two more approached. He swung the stick, sinking the nails into one of the heads, and then swung it again as the other creature turned, and it ripped into the fish's side. The turmoil began, as the blood spread through the water. The fish swarmed over the injured ones, tearing them apart, and in their feeding frenzy, snapped out at each other, causing more blood, and more frenzy.

By then the truck was slowly moving over the weir, not even noticed by the ravenous monsters from the deep, and this time they arrived at the far bank unharmed. They looked back at the scarlet water flowing downstream, as it attracted ever more of the carnivores. The apocalypse thrived.

Stumpy quietly said to Peter, "With that cloud getting bigger, we may never see those creatures again."

By the time they arrived at the spot where Peter had died, it was time to set up camp. Mo was wary of staying there, but Katie insisted. Perhaps she wanted the fight with Edward.

"This is a good spot. Halfway back to camp." She didn't say anything more about Edward.

The book stayed in its safe storage spot. No news reel that night.

As usual, Stumpy and Mo stayed outside, whilst Peter went to sleep with Katie in his arms. As soon as he was sound, she pulled herself away and sat outside with Mo and Stumpy.

"I want to speak to Edward." She waited for a response from his children. "Well?"

Mo leaned forward and whispered, "He may not want to speak to you."

"Tough!" The little girl crossed her arms and sat bolt upright. "He *needs* to speak to me. He's in trouble."

"And so are you. Be nice to Daddy, he's very down at the moment. He knows what the gunk is doing, and he knows your situation." Mo looked towards Stumpy, who just smiled. Mo then shuffled over to hold Katie around the shoulders. "I'll look after you. Come on."

They set off towards the scree bank, Katie struggling to walk through the long grass, but persevering. They did not take a lamp.

As soon as they were consumed by the darkness Stumpy crawled into the tent, and shook Peter to wake him.

"Pete, Mo has taken Katie to see Dad."

"Why? I thought they hated each other."

"No, not really. They go back a long way. Billions of years, British billions, and they've done a lot of work together. But they fell out because Katie did so much better than Dad, with a completely different approach to intelligent life. Katie made man in her own image, and Dad made us. Do you know what I'm saying?"

Peter frowned, "But he made you and Mo. You're lovely. You're my best friends, and that's not a failure."

If a green lad could turn red, he would've done. "Thanks, Peter, that's lovely. And I'll do anything for you, anything That's why I've got such a *special* gift to give to you. But you can't have it yet."

Peter was confused, but just grinned at Stumpy, wondering what the gift could be.

"And Mo feels the same. And we've got another gift for you to take home when you go. It's for Ninah. Don't let me forget to give it to you before you go."

"You know what. I don't really want to go. That way I won't be disappointed when I don't." The two boys did a high five and grabbed each other. "You gonna get much bigger?" They had a friendly wrestle. "You're not as strong as you look." Peter swung him over and pinned him to the floor. "Got you." Stumpy just lay chuckling, and then rolled him off, and they settled back down.

"But the people at your home are hurting and Katie has got to get back. So you've got to go."

"I don't have to. Just Katie. I can stay here with you."

"She won't go without you. You know, Daddy said that if she was strong enough she could take you home in her tent. But she's not even strong enough take herself home. But he did say that you may not make it through the tent. It could kill you properly."

Peter frowned. "What do you mean, properly?"

"I mean dead, not coming back. Forever!" He raised his hands into the air. "You know what dead is. Anyway, it might be the only chance for your people to get their God back."

Stumpy could see what was on the forefront of Peter's mind.

"Shall we?"

"Don't know if it would be right."

"No, it wouldn't." But Stumpy was tempted. "Let's look at it."

Against their better judgement, they took her book out from the trailer and sat down with it in front of them. Unknown India. What was it all about?

"Katie showed me some pages. They were about East Pakistan. Millions of people are being killed there, even more being abused, and raped, and imprisoned. And nobody is helping them."

"Why?"

"Katie said something about money and personal ambition. I think it's always about money and control and power. Shall we have a look?"

Peter carefully opened the book but every page was blank. They closed it and returned it to the trailer.

In the meantime, little Mo was helping Katie to climb up the bank of granite detritus, to the entry to the vault. He dug the loose granite away from the door, reached into the flap between his legs, and pulled out the izaline claw.

"Be careful. I don't want you to hurt yourself."

They entered the cave, and closed the door behind.

A squeaky voice rang. "Stay there. I'll come out to you."

From around the corner walked a giant Mo. He was about ten feet tall. The flickering lights threw moving shadows around the walls, and across the paintings which filled every surface.

In a rather squeaky voice, he began. "I've been waiting for you, so I was ready with the body." The God held his hand out to Katie. "It's been a long time, Gayla. I haven't looked forward to this moment."

Katie giggled, and replied, "Neither have I. But work is work, so let's sort this lot out. If it has to be once and for all, then so be it."

The God invited Katie to sit opposite him on some wooden benches. Mo sat beside Katie, grinning.

God Edward broke the ice. "My son says that his brother is going to be like Peter. He's mad. What do you have to say about it?"

"Before I answer that, did he tell you that I'm here alone?"

He shuffled his feet and looked down at them. "That is not possible. We all know that."

"But I'm a different species to you. And I've done it. Catherine is at home, looking after our domain. But I am here, and we've lost touch. I have no conscience."

"Then why haven't you killed me? You hate me."

"Because I don't want to. I have no need to and Peter won't let me. Unless, of course, you kill my brother. Again."

"He can't be your brother. He's one of your children."

"A special child, my brother. And I love him. I've fallen in love with him. And I'll do whatever he asks me to do. He's my conscience until I get Catherine back."

"Ridiculous! You are *God*."

"And he is my brother, my adopted conscience, and I love him."

God Edward thought carefully. "But how are you one apart. You became one as one way back when I gave you Maya and her Lamma. That was when I still admired you."

"I think Catherine escaped, rather than me pushing her out, or maybe subconsciously a bit of each. But when I was so desperately lonely and wanted to destroy my Earth, she got out, and stopped me. She was all that stood between life and death for the Earth."

A silence fell. It was chilling, and Mo pulled himself to Katie. And then Edward stood up.

"I've got nothing else to talk to you about." He turned to walk away, but was stopped.

Katie whispered, "I'll help you. I can help you rebuild, if that's what you want. You helped me, and I owe it to you. You gifted me with life, the life which swarms the Earth, and I *will* return that life, for you to rebuild your beautiful colony, in your own image. You are God Edward, strong and righteous. You'll survive, and become strong again."

He slowly turned. As he did, Mo put his thumb up to the offer of help. Edward asked, "Why? Your children have come

162

here, and destroyed my planet. Why send them here, and then try to be nice and pally about it all?" He pointed at her and demanded, "Tell me why!"

"For a start, I did not send my children here, and unlike your minions they are free minds and spirits. They came here to explore, and find out what was here that they could use. They are *not* controlled by me, nor any of my family. We can only influence. The rest is down to them, and *that* is why they are so strong. Your own minions were wiped out thousands of years ago, by your own life forms. You made happy, tender, kind people who wanted for nothing, as with your two children. But they had no ambition, no hatred, and consequently no love or desire, nor greed. They *never* developed, and the emotionless, laid-back minions could not be bothered to do *anything* but play and be happy. They invented nothing, no weapons because they had no use for them, no money because they wanted for nothing, no transport because you made land a tightly knit set of islands, no farms because they ate only vegetation, no clothes because they had no genitals, no shelters because the temperature was constant, no medicine because there was no illness.... You got it wrong. Our cattle are just as prepared for life as your people were. So when you got it wrong, the diseases which you accidentally created, wiped them out, almost over the weekend." She looked hard into his face. "Are you still with me, Edward?"

He just sat back down and grunted.

She continued, "So when my people came here, of their own free will, and due to their own intelligence, their own industry and ambition, they found a land abandoned of normal, intelligent life. Your *real* children would never talk to them, they would never reason with them, and they would never fight them. They were led to believe that your beautiful children were just wild creatures."

"My children didn't *have* to talk to them. They didn't even have to *acknowledge* them!"

"Course not. That's if they didn't mind being killed by the misled and misinformed miners. Why wouldn't they communicate? Why?" She waited. "Come on, why? They are free minds, why didn't any of them talk to the miners?"

He grumbled and then replied, "Because I forbade it."

"So it was *your* fault that your other twelve children were lost. You killed your minions by creating the diseases many years ago, and then you killed your own children by misguided control. You're a selfish control freak."

He was beginning to slump. "I've got it wrong. I've failed. This World is lost, and me with it." He looked at Katie with a forlorn grace. "Will you really help me? Please?"

Katie was winning, and she hadn't even had to threaten him.

She pledged, "I *will* help you. I promise. I know what you want, and I'll do it. But will you help me?"

He began to smile, and in his squeaky voice replied, "Of course. We should help each other. This corrosive cloud is going to destroy just about all life on this planet in time. If I want it, will you help me rebuild a better community? With love. I dream of real love."

Katie chortled, "You don't get love without hate, and you don't get hate without real jealousy nor avarice, and you don't get ecstasy without pain. So I'll help you, if you want to go for it, realistically."

"Will there be wars and crime?"

"Of course. It's part of a free spirit. You must remember, that if the meek were ever to inherit the Earth, they would never hold onto it for long enough to make any difference. The strong have to be rewarded with success." She laughed, "Unless you were to redefine meek. Suppose we could do that as Gods."

The two were jelling, which sent a warm feeling of success into little Katie's cockles. She was winning.

"So," Edward grinned and asked, "What should I do for you?"

"Nothing. And I mean nothing, including controlling your children. But for one thing, get my Mummy away if you make a certain decision. I know she's still here. She saved Peter from you."

"I can't control Maya and her Lamma. They are as good as gone. Lamma has disappeared, and Maya will not rest until she has found her brother, as you know. She is obsessed, and a bad daughter. But when she finds him, you will find her. But you won't eat until you do."

"But you must leave your *sons* to develop in their own way, and make their own decisions, it's their last chance. These two darlings who have become so close to us. No more control, and you will live on in them, and they will help to change your world. They will learn emotion from a most beautiful human being, Peter." She smiled and bit her bottom lip, as if she had just discovered something beautiful. "You know, Edward, I now *definitely* know why Catherine sent me here." She had a glint of tear in her eye. "We're all learning. After so many billions of years, I've discovered something new, and fulfilling. True love."

Little Mo cuddled her tightly. "Will you teach Stumpy? He wants to be like Peter."

"Gayla, I will let you be friends with my sons. They'll do whatever they wish to do, without my ageing, outdated influence. But I want a promise from you, and I've got to believe in you."

Katie grinned, "Name your price."

"When your strength has returned, and when my time has arrived, please do the right thing. You know what I mean. And we'll meet again in a different life." The meeting ended with smiles of discovery.

Before leaving, Katie winked to Edward, and said "I'm here alone, and I'm not even angry. Is that love?"

Edward bowed his old head and returned to his vault.

Mo finally returned Katie to the camp, where Stumpy and Peter sat talking about Earth.

"Peter's been telling me all about Earth. It sounds wonderful. A bit scary, but I think I'll love it." He had convinced himself that he was going 'home' with Peter. "And he told me about the girl who lives near the borstal."

"Oi, that's private."

Katie grinned at Peter and suggested that they retire, so he could get his beauty sleep, and, "Come on captain bubble-blower, fly me to the moon."

Little Mo cuddled up to Stumpy and whispered, "Wonder if they'll rut tonight, bruv."

Morning came too early for the teenager. He was knackered, but he drove quickly towards the old camp. "Can't wait to get back home, you know, our camp."

Katie suggested, "We'll have to take a careful look at the gunk tanker. Probably not as old as the one that spilled, but sometime it's got to go. They all will."

They decided not to go into the cave of paintings.

"Now we are talking again, he can contact me direct."

Peter was curious about any plans that may have been made during the meeting. "What happened last night?"

"We made friends again and we are going to help each other. When this lot has died from the pollution, I'm going to uphold his wishes. I know what that gunk is, and this beautiful planet will never recover, so I'll do what he has asked me to do."

Stumpy asked, "So when will you help him to rebuild life?"

"As we left it, in another life." She looked at Mo, who understood what she meant.

Peter sighed and concentrated on his driving. All the talk of creating life was above his apprehension, and he was not totally convinced that he was even awake. The dream could end at any time.

Katie quietly reported, "But, Peter, Edward did agree to help me. And I have been able to formulate a plan in this pretty blond head. But I can't tell you about it, you wouldn't understand. And I made a sort of promise to teach these boys how to be like you. Ain't that great?"

Mo poked her, "That's not quite right. You promised to teach *Stumpy* to be like Peter. I want to be like you, the intelligent one." He giggled.

"Thanks, mate." Peter gave Mo a slap on the head. "I've got my uses."

"Yeah? Suppose that's true if you mean keeping your celestial bitch, here, all primed up and wet."

"Stop!" Katie was not amused. "If you want to be like me, you'd better learn to be a lady." She managed to hide the smirk.

"I'm just following your lead."

She bit her bottom lip and wondered. Perhaps she had been a little bit crude with her beloved brother. By hey, you only live once, and it's fun. "Ok. Carry on."

They arrived at the camp. Nothing had changed, why would it? Until, of course, after the cloud has made its way full circle around the small planet. Things might just change then. But in the meantime it was all the same.

They sorted out the equipment tent, to allow all four of them to sleep, but with the truck and trailer outside there was plenty of room. An inspection of the tanker was next on the agenda. There was no sign of leakage so they decided to stay in camp for the time being, and hope for the best. But they all knew that the time was fast approaching when they would best be off the planet.

"You're looking very chuffed with yourself, Katie." Peter was a little suspicious. "Are you up to something?"

She grinned and whispered to him, "I am always up to something, my little bosom-warmer. But you just need to stick with me. We'll soon be going home; it might be the hard way, but it'll certainly be one way." She gave him a long kiss on his lips, and then sucked his nose. "Strip me bare, Yogi."

Peter laughed, and they went to bed.

Colin Hodgson

13 -- HOLODOMOR (THE FAMINE)

Next morning arrived with a bang and Peter almost jumped out of his skin. He awoke to find the three others breaking up firewood.

"We're going to have a camp-fire," stressed Stumpy, very excitedly. "And look, we've found a record player."

They rushed around collecting wood, while Peter made some breakfast. "Don't know what the hell they're up to," he mumbled to himself. "And what's in her pretty little head? She's been really nice lately, even without her conscience." He looked out of the tent and Katie was sitting cuddling with Mo, while the big one broke the wood up. But he noticed that, for the third morning running, Katie was weak and struggling to remain upright. Her head swung around. He asked, "Can we have a chat, Sis? A private chat?"

He lifted her up and they went into the tent.

"We're gonna have a party." Her head lay heavy on his shoulder, unsupported by her neck. She was whispering. "Be good, won't it. Sit around the camp fire and tell stories. You got any stories?"

He put his hand on her cheek and stroked her face. She was going back to her bedridden days. "Don't you have your drugs any more? You should have loads left."

"Yeah. Still been taking them. You know I have. But my body ain't responding any more to them, because I'm too weak to make them work. They never did work really. It was my own strength which pushed me forward. Now it's almost gone." She was losing her soul. "Please take me outside, the sun is soothing and I feel so much better with those rays eating into my head."

He carried her out to Mo, who said, "Come here, I can help a bit." Peter lowered her down to sit by Mo, who spat into her face. She grinned and thanked him.

Then Stumpy joined them and they sat looking at the pile of firewood. The record player had been placed on a table, and a generator was waiting to be fired up, and Stumpy had made some sandwiches for Peter.

Peter asked, "What's the celebration?" His voice was shaking. "Is it because you are going to die, Sis?" His eyes were damp, and a couple of tears formed, so Katie managed to pull herself up to his cheeks and kiss them away.

"Soooo beautiful. I'm feeling a bit better now and we can have a jolly good party. We can say goodbye to Mo properly."

It was Mo who was dying. The two green teenagers had reached puberty, and it was the eve of their union, at which time they were to become one together. Stumpy was to become the God and was to take on the knowledge, conscience and spirit of his twin brother.

Mo explained, "We made the decision to be one together when we were conceived, and I am now to be the inner strength of my bigger brother, who will consequently live forever." He gave Peter a loving look. "Stumpy will look after you, Peter. He'll be strong." So he needed Stumpy to look after him? What about Katie? It looked so much like Peter was going to lose his love, his God, and so was his Earth.

"I know what you're thinking, Peter. Don't." Katie could see his thoughts, and so could the boys. "There's nothing you can do."

"But what about the people in East Pakistan? Who's going to help them if you don't get back?"

She may well have been slipping away, but she still knew how to influence, and to win. She was God almighty.

She whispered, "There's a past, and a future, and I have neglected them both. While I've been pining for my Mummy, my people have suffered. The Kingdom of Hell has established itself in my own Kingdom of Heaven, and they have all prayed to God, who hasn't responded. I've just cried right throughout their suffering. And I know that's why Catherine sent me here, to refresh my love for my people. Peter has done that. *He* is *my* God."

She was feeling stronger after Mo's spit and Peter's tears, so she managed to climb to her feet, and shuffle over to the tent. The little girl returned, very slowly, watched by her best mates who respected her efforts by leaving her to achieve the journey under her own steam. She grinned form ear-to-ear as she slumped down with her book, Unknown India.

"Let's see what we have in here."

Stumpy chuckled, "Weren't much the other day, was there Pete?"

He earned himself a look of scolding from Katie. "Well, *that* was the *other* day. Let's see what it has *today*." She opened the book, carefully fingered through the pages, none of them blank, and reached a chapter simply entitled 'Death'.

The first plate was a delicately painted watercolour, of a group of traders in the Kingdom of Kandy. It was the early eighteen hundreds. They were trussed to posts, bloody and mutilated, but their senses were kept alert by a smoking cup on the end of a stick, ensuring their suffering to the very end. Katie read the caption. *"The first of millions. The Chi Bantri members who where executed by the Chi Bantri because they tried to trade equally and peacefully with the Kandyan nobility. The Chi Bantri forecast worthwhile wealth from the wars between the people of Kandy and the British, so they engineered war, in preference to peace. These mutilations set the scene within the Chi Bantri secret cult for the next two hundred years. Toe the line or......."*

Katie explained, "The Chi Bantri are a secret society who work from inside the governments and religions to control both warfare and peace, to ensure maximum profit for their kind."

The next plate showed the ragged people of the Ukraine in 1933. They were like skeletons, and wrapped in dirty cloths, and the two women were being herded by children with sticks towards some soldiers. The caption read, *"The grain-barbers are caught. The children of the Ukraine are exploited to catch the starving peasants who steal grain from their own farms. Often the children turn in their own parents who were just stealing to feed their own children. The children are rewarded with food for each capture. Nearly seven million people were deliberately starved to death by the authorities during collectivisation."*

Katie added, "The authorities didn't just take their grain crops, they also confiscated their other food, and denied any aid from outside. It was plain, deliberate murder. Seven million Ukrainians."

The accompanying photograph showed some of the results of the enforced starvation, a family group huddled around a fire, with meat cooking, and the remains of the body in the background. They had resorted to eating their own. "Some army officers reported that once they had been subjected to the starvation for a while, they changed and became sub-human. Those observations helped to justify the extreme cruelty to which they subjected their own fellow humans."

Peter glibly asked, "Katie, why are you showing us these? They're miserable."

She smiled, and replied, "I'm not. You are seeing them." And just grinned. "Let's just see what's going on today." She turned the pages to the section on East Pakistan. "This is today's news. Would you like to see it?"

The boys looked at each other, and shrugged their shoulders.

She pointed at the first plate, a black and white photograph. It was a striking picture of dead people, beginning to rot, and they were of all ages and with few clothes, piled on top of each other in a ditch. The buildings around were deserted, but for three old women crying over two dead babies, one without arms nor legs. The caption read, *"It seemed that the whole of Dhaka and Chittagong had either been killed or displaced. After less than a week about forty five thousand had been killed, and the rest were on the move, in their millions. Operation Searchlight was moving rapidly onwards, towards Khan's target of three million Bangalees. Where are the rest of the World?"* Katie knew where the Americans were, with the Pakistanis, and China was no place to run, after their recent big leap forward, and their own millions dead. But India, and the Soviets. Their only hopes.

The boys looked desperately to Katie. "What can be done?"

She shook her head, and turned the page. The next plate was a colour photo. "Look, it's Ninah! And Satvinder, and Doctor Hussain!" She smiled. The picture showed refugees, stretching as far they could see, milling towards safety. But the military could be seen up ahead, looking down the trousers of the young men, and pulling out the Hindus for extermination. The caption read, *"Organised evacuations march perilously towards the safety of India. A belief from within is growing that if enough of them can cross into India, enough millions, India will be forced to intervene, to alleviate the chaos caused by the influx. Ninah and I believe that Prime Minister Indira Gandhi will be forced to intervene, with the blessing of her ally, Russia."*

Katie grinned, "This one's not a World broadcast. It's a message to us from Catherine." She chuckled, "At least somebody is trying to change things."

The sun shone down on the group, and all were forlorn. Peter kept thinking about how he could help the people, and all he could come up with was to pray. Pray to God. But God was in love with him, and she wouldn't before go home when she had the chance, because she wouldn't leave him there. If only he had given his life to allow her to go home and do her work, reunited with Catherine. He wondered if it was too late for him to sacrifice himself for his people. Is it too late for Katie to get home without him? His mind was in turmoil, and all Katie could do was smile at him. She was so pleased with him, and she leaned over and gave him a kiss, like she had never kissed him before, a kiss of a lover.

Mo and Stumpy were saying nothing. They studied Peter intensely, breaking from time to time to look at each other and nod. They were fascinated by his thoughts, and his commitment to his family and people back home, and his love for his sister, in fact, fascinated by everything about him. And the more he became het up by his situation the more they dug into his head, and the more they nodded. Katie just giggled quietly, and when the two students began to slow down with their nodding, she stirred them up some more.

"Peter, if you could have a wish, right now, what would you wish for?"

"That's a silly question. You know what it would be."

"But tell me. Tell me what your wish would be."

He frowned and answered, "I wish you could go home, and help to save those poor people, and banish Hell from Earth. I would give anything, even my life."

She leaned forward and held him tight, and kissed him on the ear, whispering, "I know you would. That's why I love you so much. But it wouldn't get me home, would it. It's the wrong life."

His head began spinning again. How could he do it? How would him giving up his life help to get her home? And the boys began nodding again, taking it all in, and becoming more and more embroiled in Peter's thoughts, and regrets. Just giving a life wouldn't be enough, so how could they do it? And why was it the wrong life? "There has to be a way!" he shouted.

"Stop!" Katie still had enough strength to raise her voice. "You boys, stop raping Peter's mind! It's not a nice thing to do, especially if you want to *be* like *Peter*. He doesn't do it to you." She twisted her head round to look into Peter's face, and she winked. "Let's get the records on and dance. We've got to celebrate Mo's passing tomorrow." They all moved to the table with the record player, and Stumpy started the generator.

What a noise the generator made. The record player would have to be turned up flat out to rise above that row, so Stumpy dragged it across the street and went in search of an extension lead.

"While he's away, can I ask you something, Peter?" asked Mo.

Peter shrugged his shoulders and nodded.

"Would you really give your life to help the people of Earth?"

Poor Peter thought about it carefully, but before he could answer, Mo spoke.

"Thank you, Peter. I can see why you are Katie's God. You will be an absolute teacher for my big brother. Thank you."

The teenage boy was confused, but smiled at Mo, and Katie hugged him so tightly and whispered, "Thank you, cutie-pie. When we gonna dance on the ceiling?"

Stumpy returned with a long extension, and the generator was pulled behind the equipment tent.

"Let's party!" shouted Peter. "What music we got?" He checked the two records, turned his nose up, as did Stumpy, and shrugged his shoulders, as did Stumpy. "This'll have to do." He started the turntable, placed the needle onto the record, and waited. Peter stood to attention, Katie with her legs around his waist and perched on his hip, while Stumpy stood to attention, Mo with his legs around his waist and perched on his hip. As the music began, Peter began the only dance steps that he knew. Chris Farlowe sang Handbags and Gladrags, and Peter moved. "One, two together. One, two together." And Stumpy counted out, "One, two together. One, two together."

Katie whispered, "He wants to be like you. He's copying everything about you." They both giggled amongst themselves, as did Stumpy and Mo. She whispered, "Do something that he can't do." So Peter reached down into his pocket and pulled out a penknife. "He can't do that. He hasn't got pockets." But with a smug look, Stumpy put his hand down between his legs. "What's he doing?" And he pushed his hand into the hidden flap between his legs, where the sun doesn't shine, and pulled out the izaline claw. Stumpy winked at Katie. They all laughed and danced for about three minutes, and then the song ended.

"What's the other one?" asked Mo.

"I'll put it on and you'll find out. You ready, Stumpy? Just follow me."

As the song began, Peter let out a scream, and began to twist and turn, with Katie flying around, her head flopping from side to side, and laughing her pants off. And, of course, Stumpy and Mo followed their moves almost to the tee. They Rocked Around the Clock with Bill Haley, and then repeated Chris Farlowe, and then Bill Haley, and Chris Farlowe, until the sun was almost at its drop-zone. They were knackered!

"I'm shagged out!" huffed Peter.

"And I'm the same!" huffed Stumpy.

But the two little ones were even more tired. They were on their way to another dimension, and Peter watched Stumpy cuddling Mo, and could see the life draining out of the tiny being. And Peter was, by that time, having to support Katie's head in his hand. It was to be a heart-wrenching time for them all.

"Come here, Katie," begged Mo. "I want to kiss you." The two boys held them close to each other, and with a bit of help from Peter, Katie leaned out and kissed Mo on the lips. As she did, he breathed out and she took his air into her lungs. "That will help you to last until after I have gone. Consider it a gift from Edward, and his family."

Katie immediately perked up. "Thanks." She didn't need to say any more.

As Stumpy and Mo messed around with some lighting, and the matches to get the camp-fire lit, Katie secretly asked Peter, "You still want to die for me and Earth, don't you?"

He nodded his answer to the strange question, and she grinned.

They all waited for the fire to be lit before saying anything else. The dry wood soon caught and they moved back away from the scorching heat, laughing as the flames leapt high. But it soon settled down to an inviting heap of glowing embers, whisking the night with sporadic bursts of flame.

"We can tell stories," suggested Mo. "But first, I have a special gift for you from Daddy. He would like you to give them to Ninah for safe keeping and for his use, until the time is right to present them to your mummy and her Lamma." He put his hand down between his legs and pushed it into his flap. Out came two beautiful, shining nails, about nine inches long, and made from izaline. "These are a special gift, and they are crafted from Daddy's lower left leg. Ninah can use them to help the children of Catan."

They all stared at the nails as he handed them to Katie. She thanked Mo, and his family, and placed the nails with her treasured book.

"Right, who's going to tell a story first?" Mo's head waved around as he looked at his party guests. "Peter? Will you tell a story for me to take with me when I die?"

He looked around and then said, "I don't know any stories. Somebody else can go."

Mo snapped, "No! You all have to leave me a story to take with me. It's important to me."

Peter was desperate to please Mo, so he thought back to his childhood days, and the fairy tales. "Well, there's this story which I liked as a child. It was about a boy with the same name as me, and my mummy sometimes used to tell it to me when I went to bed. And every time she told it, it was a little bit different. I'll tell one which I can remember." He took a deep breath, and then began. "Peter lived in the dark forests in Germany, the Black Forest, and he had a little sister called Katie. The animals and birds were their friends, and they played with them in front of their house, while the mummies and daddies went about their work, chopping firewood and preparing meals and collecting nuts. The wolves had long been banished from the lands because they kept on eating the children, and so the forests were safe, and everybody was happy. But sad memories of lost children haunted the mummies and daddies and they never relaxed, expecting, one day, the return of the horrible wolves. But Peter was growing up into a mischievous little bugger, and one day thought he would have a laugh with his parents. He shouted '*wolf, wolf!*' And his daddy and mummy ran into the house and came out with their shotguns. 'Where?' asked his daddy, and Peter and Katie just chuckled and chuckled, so their daddy gave them both a smack and sent them to bed. But he didn't smack them hard enough, so the next day they played the same game. '*Wolf, wolf!*' shouted Peter, and their mummy and daddy rushed into the house and came out with their shotguns. 'Where?' asked his daddy, and Peter and Katie just chuckled and chuckled, so their daddy gave them both a much harder smack and sent them to bed. But Peter became annoyed, wondering why he should be smacked for such a funny game, so the next day he shouted '*Wolf, wolf!*' even louder than he had before and their mummy and daddy rushed into the house and came out with their shotguns. 'Where?' asked his daddy, and Peter and Katie just chuckled and chuckled, so their daddy gave them both such a thrashing that they could not even sit down. Their butts were bleeding. But poor Mummy and Daddy felt so bad and cruel that they had thrashed their own children so hard, that they began to cry. And they cried for a week. Katie told her big brother to say sorry to his parents, and he did. And his daddy promised that he would never smack them again. And they were all happy again." He stopped for thought.

"That's a *lovely* story," exclaimed Mo.

"But I still haven't finished. Anyway, one of the wolves which had been banished from the woods went to the Belgian Congo to live. He was happy there, hunting and eating Mbuti pygmies, but life was getting harder for the old wolf because the Bantu tribesmen were eating so many of the pygmies, and also because the pygmy children were being exported to the zoos in Europe and America by the Belgian colonial government. Poor Mr. Wolf was feeling the pinch. So he came home, to the forests of Germany, where the hunting was so much easier. And one day, as he walked his domain, he ventured close to Peter's and Katie's home. '*Wolf, wolf!*' shouted Peter, and his mummy and daddy just chuckled and chuckled, and Mr Wolf, amongst the laughter from mummy and daddy, took little Katie, and ate her."

Stumpy and Mo were devastated. Tears appeared in their eyes, and they felt, for the first time in their lives, a feeling of loss and heartache. They were feeling emotions!

Stumpy sniffed and pulled himself over to Katie. "Did he really eat you?" Then he began to cry.

She put her arms around his neck, and "Silly. It's only a story. He didn't really eat me."

Stumpy pushed her away, and looked over to Mo. His tearful face took on anger. "You saying it's a lie? You two lying to me? You'd better not be."

"No, no!" Katie screeched, "It's *not* a lie. It's a *story!*" She could sense that he had learned more from Peter than they had realised. He had learned temper. She tried to calm him, "Don't you *dare* get nasty with me. Stop it!" She scowled at him.

"He lied to us! I won't have that. *Peter* wouldn't have it, so nor will I." He lurched towards Peter, and held his hand up. Then his nails flicked out! The claws were massive and razor sharp. And as he leaned further towards Peter he caught Katie, and she fell to the ground.

"You bastard!" Peter leapt at him and grabbed him around the neck, pulling him to the ground. "You *fucking* hurt my sister!" The two grappled, Stumpy much larger than Peter. But Peter had the speed, and he got him in a headlock, then Stumpy reached his claws towards the boy's face and Peter screamed in his ear. "You hurt my sister!" But suddenly they stopped. At exactly the same time, they stopped.

Katie growled at them, "Now *get up*, you idiots." But then she began to laugh, and Mo joined her.

The two fighters, still locked together, looked around, and then slowly released each other, sitting up and looking at the two little ones, who were laughing their heads off. Then they looked at each other.

Stumpy grinned, "Did I do good? Did I do what you would do? You did good, worrying about Katie like that. I must be sure to do that as well. You know, Bruv, we'd both do anything for our little sis, and *you've* taught me that. I think we're nearly the same, now." He grinned uncontrollably as he realised how much like Peter he was becoming. "You're a good teacher."

Peter frowned. "One little thing. You can't go trying to kill everybody as soon as they tell a story."

"But it's a lie."

Peter looked to Katie for support, and she just smiled.

"Right, the difference between a story and a lie. Right. Hmm, difficult one. I'm beginning to see your problem with the two. Well, I think it's about intent. If you tell an untrue story which you intent the listener to believe is true, for your own gain, then it's a lie. You know, like trying to deceive them. But if you tell an untrue story which you don't try to deceive with, you know, don't try to make out it's true, then it's a story. So an untrue story which is intended to entertain, or to educate by demonstrating a point of view, would be a story, a tale, but not a lie. Understand?"

"Sort of. But it made us cry. That's not very entertaining."

"But a lot of people like being made to cry with stories."

"Weird, but I'll get the hang of it. So it's all about intent."

Peter looked to Katie and Mo, and shrugged his shoulders. He was beginning to feel something big brewing. Katie and Mo were so content, and considering that they were both at the point of death, it wasn't quite cricket.

"Stumpy's story," stated Mo. "Come on, before I'm dead."

They gathered around the fire and Stumpy composed himself.

"I've got a story. I've thought about the intent and it's the absolute truth, so it's not a lie and I'm not going to try to make out it's a lie." He frowned a little. "Not sure if I quite got that. Anyway, many billions of years ago our daddy was asleep on his bed outside, and he'd forgotten about the volcano which was scheduled, so he carried on dreaming. While he floated around the heavens with his daughter, Maya, and her twin brother, the Lamma, the volcano blew. It created these islands on which we are living now, and gave him the dry land on which to develop his children. But when he had finished wasting time with the twins he returned to his body to find that he was entombed in granite. As he lay there he wondered what he should do, and came up with a brilliant idea, which was to just stay there until the weather had worn the mountain down to a plateau, when he would be able to sit up and look around, before walking off into his domain. So he waited for *over* two hundred million years, and eventually his patience was rewarded. One stormy, dark night, when the wind was stirring sharp, abrasive sand into the air, a glint of light appeared in his eye; it was moonlight. But what he hadn't bargained for, the silly idiot, was that the colony of bacteria which he had produced before the volcano, had done their job and eaten *all* the detritus, and had then become hungry. So for just *under* two hundred million years they organised themselves, waiting for God Edward's body to become exposed, so that they could eat it. They had organised their lives so that they had six queues lined up, homing in on the buried God, and as they had a baby, the baby went to the back of the queue to wait, and the one at the front was eaten by the one in second place. So the queues remained constant length, for just under two hundred million years. They appointed policemen to count the length of each queue, to make sure that it never varied from three thousand and ninety, and to make sure that they only ate the one at the front when there was a new baby at the back. And so life went on for the bacteria, self sufficient, organised and happy, and first in, first out, and the perfect example of communism. But one bacteria thought he might not want to be eaten. He was enjoying life up the front, so he developed a contraceptive to stop the births, and passed it all the way back down the queue, and they all partied and shagged till their hearts content. What a life! And he boosted his pension fund by selling his contraception to the other queues, and so they all started shagging and partying, *and having no babies*. But the three thousand and ninety bacteria in each queue started to get too old to have babies, and they were seriously hungry, so the one in second place said to the one at the front 'can I eat you?' But the one at the front said, 'only when there's another baby born. The rules, you know.' So the one in second place thought, 'rules? Contraception is against the rules.' So the bacteria formed a committee to discuss the issue of eating, and deemed that, due to the shortage of babies caused by the contraception, they could eat the one in the front of the queue, even if a baby wasn't born. So the second one ate the first one, and so became the first one, and the second one ate the first one, and so became the first one, and this continued until there was only the last one left in each line. And he was now the first one, *and* the last one. And the remaining first one from each of the six queues got together and decided to create a committee to decide on whether the first one could be eaten by the other first ones, and a sub committee was also formed to work out which first one was first. And all through that millennium while the committee was discussing and voting and reconvening, the tomb was eroded away, enough for God Edward, our daddy, to sit up and look around his domain. But as he did, the bacteria had such a bril' idea; they would be like humans, and one would be appointed as leader to make fast, interactive decisions, and he would take the pretty bacteria from queue three who he fancied and they would have wild sex, and their children would go forth and multiply, and build civilisations, with schools and hospitals, and factories, and they would feed on God Edward, not each other, and they would be called the human wace. But God Edward had finished stretching and yawning and he proudly climbed out of the tomb, and without ever knowing it he stood on the committee, squashing them all dead. He destroyed the human wace, and didn't even know."

Stumpy chuckled and sat proudly waiting for some sort of applause.

"Is that it?" asked Peter. "That was even worse than mine."

"Don't be a prat, I haven't finished yet! The best bit's to come." He recomposed himself. "Right, Daddy just wiped his feet, and went in search of a proper burial tomb. He found one, and that's where his skeleton lies right now, to this very day, under the mountain where he killed Peter. *The end.*" Stumpy sat chortling at his own story.

"Killed me?" Peter huffed.

Katie whispered, "It's a long story, one for another day. But just take in the moral of Stumpy's story." She winked at Peter.

"Well? Did you like it?" Stumpy asked.

Peter smiled at Stumpy. "It was beautiful. A real twist at the end."

"And it's all true. I made it up myself."

"What? You made it up yourself, and yet it's all true?"

Stumpy nodded, so to avoid the fracas which they had before, Peter held his hand out and they shook. Best of mates, and ever more like twins.

Mo reminded them, "Not all of Daddy's skeleton sits in his burial vault. You have part of his lower left leg, Katie. To give to Ninah for his use and safe keeping, while you wait for your mummy to return."

The two nails that Mo had given to Katie were izaline. Peter raised his eyebrows and was suddenly recalling how Katie had laughed at the stupidity of the humans when they killed all of Edward's children. They were walking izaline deposits. But they can't be, they dissolve completely with the gunk. "Are you saying that your skeletons are izaline, like your claws?"

Mo answered. "Yes, no, well they will be. When the skeleton is exposed to the air it oxidises with the caskin and hardens into the izaline that the miners searched for. While it is our bones, it is soft and pliable."

No wonder Katie had laughed. They gunked the source of the izaline, and each one of Stumpy must have been worth millions. She was right, they are stupid.

Peter looked past Katie's pretty face, and could see a most contented Mo, as if his boat had come in. He was looking forward to his union with his bigger brother.

Mo said, "When I am moved you must take my skeleton to be with Daddy's. It's important." His good mates all nodded their promises.

14 -- SAINT NINAH

Mo looked to Peter and asked, "Got any more stories?"

Peter looked sadly at Stumpy's brother, Mo. "But I don't *know* any more stories. You know I don't." He had begun to think a little more deeply about Stumpy's tale about the communist bacteria and how they had finally been wiped from the face of the planet, never to return. He looked down at Katie, and she grinned, and then nodded in agreement. "I do have a story. And it's a true story, if you're interested." He was thinking of England.

"Why are you thinking of England?" asked Stumpy, his head cocking sideways.

"To stop you raping my mind. If you want to be like me, don't do it to your friends." Peter was beginning to understand where things were all leading.

Stumpy stressed, "I *do* want to be like you. I'll do anything. Just lead me and I'll follow."

"Right, leave my mind alone, and follow my words. That's an order." He cuddled Katie. "Once upon a time, there was this little colony, many miles from anywhere, and the human beings who found it discovered that there was something on the planet that they really wanted; izaline. Now, through their ingenious ability to plan, create, invent and conquer they found this gunk which dissolved everything except for izaline and lead, so they went in search. And the local beings wouldn't talk to them, so they developed their own misguided understanding of the locals, and mistrusted them to the point where they thought they were anti-god, and should be destroyed. They honestly had no idea just how close to God the local beings really were. But over the years, because the miners didn't know where the izaline actually came from, they ran out of deposits, and have long gone home, leaving just a God and his two sons, and Katie's mummy and daddy who are lost. But they didn't know what to do with the gunk, so they just left it there. And after a certain amount of time the containers broke down, leaking the gunk into the atmosphere, and eventually spilling out to release a devastating, self propagating cloud of corrosive gas. The gas dispersed with the winds, and strengthened as it fed on the substance of the planet, and it engulfed the entire colony until there was nothing left for it to eat. The colony was dead."

Stumpy snarled, "Yes, *fucking* human beings. They will soon have destroyed our planet *and* our civilisation."

"Yes, just like when your *daddy* finally destroyed the civilisation of the communist bacteria, the human wace! Just the same. An accident, caused through ignorance."

Stumpy and Mo just looked at each other, having realised that Peter was right in what he was saying. And Stumpy tried to read Peter's mind, but all he got was England.

"So," said Peter, "Being a human being is not a crime, and we are no different to you. We make mistakes. But we also do good and help others, often to our own cost."

Stumpy frowned, and asked, "Then why does Katie only give us bad news from her book?"

Peter looked at Katie, but he didn't get any help, just a smile. He continued, "Well, big news is always bad. Good news is not interesting enough to be so big. An example, Kahn and Rahman will cause three million people to die in East Pakistan. That's bad news, and big news. But Queen Elizabeth will *not* have three million people killed in England. Very good news, but not very interesting, and so very, very small news. And good news never lasts so long as bad news, and it usually has a balancer. For example, five years ago, we won the football World cup which was very good news for England, but kind of bad news for Germany, because they lost it. So news is all about imagination, and about what that news sparks off in the mind. If it doesn't really spark the imagination, it is soon forgotten, as is most of the good news. Bad news always leaves devastation, suffering, long-term consequences, and so we keep on going over the news and looking in ever smaller detail at the badness of it. It leaves a lot of long-term memories, and nightmares, and retribution. Bad is big, in news terms."

Wow, Katie gave him a round of applause.

He continues, "And as we all know, when things are good, people don't need any help. So Catherine doesn't try to contact Katie through the book, only when the people need her." He was struggling a little, but luckily Katie had read his mind all the way through. She prompted him in the right direction. "And maybe we should stay here, anyway, because you are the ones who are needing help right now. Your planet is in melt-down."

Stumpy became concerned. "But what can you do by staying here? What we really need is to get away."

But Peter was one step ahead. "*We* can't get away. Me and you are going to die with this planet. But if it can get Katie back to her work, then it will be life well spent. But how can she get enough strength to get back?" He stopped thinking of England.

Stumpy had a deep breath. "Would you do that for Katie?" He was back looking into Peter's head, but this time, Peter was prepared for it. Stumpy whispered, "Would you really give your life to get Katie home?"

"Of course. I love her dearly."

Hmm, Stumpy was becoming very thoughtful. He looked at little Mo with a frown, communicating. They both pulled together, and Mo developed a tear in his eye, but smiled while clinging around Stumpy's muscular, green neck. They both then looked hard and long at little Sis, their dark eyes burning into her mind.

As the four of them kept themselves warm around the camp fire, the colony slept. They all knew that the corrosive gas was wafting its way around the globe, destroying everything in its way and propagating, and when it had travelled full circle around the planet, it would all be over. A sombre mood had fallen on the camp with Stumpy's and Mo's black eyes fixed on Peter's little sister. She looked back at them with a distorted grin which seemed to ask 'what the hell are you two looking at?' and then she twisted her head a little so that she can look up at Peter as he cuddled her.

"Can you get my book, please, big-boy?"

Peter reached over and set the book in front of her. She opened it and fingered through to a section titled 'Saint Ninah'. It was blank and she forced a look of fear. "There's no story to tell." Her mood was morose. "I'll have to make up a story, just for you, Mo." And she put her mouth to Peter's ear and whispered. "Peter can tell my story."

As she whispered he began. "This is little Sis's story. It's all about a time when God went missing." His sister just whispered, and whispered. Peter continued. "Sometimes, God has to leave his throne and his children, and go out in search. And we suffer."

But Little Mo interrupted, pushed himself away from Stumpy's neck and kissed Katie on the lips. He held one of his spindly hands on her forrid and stroked it with his razor-like nails. "I'll give you, when the time comes," he gasped, struggling for breath.

She knew what he meant and she answered with a loving smile.

Looking into her face Mo slowly said, "Tell us your story, Sis, before I die." Little Mo's breathing was strained as he pulled himself back around Stumpy's neck.

Stumpy enquired, "Is it a long story?"

Peter looked at the book. The pages were suddenly populated with pictures and narrative, and Katie twisted herself around and gave him a big kiss on the lips and whispered, "It is now."

"Yes," replied Peter, "very long." He could not stop grinning.

Stumpy continued, "Then, Peter, I'd better tell you what we've agreed. Mo is going to give himself to your sister when he goes, not to me. We've agreed, and so has our daddy, so, no arguing. Now, brother, you can begin."

Peter was shaking with the promise of Stumpy's gift. Peter had been unwittingly drafted by Katie into her subtle brainwashing of the gentle green giant, but he had no regrets or bad conscience. He would have done exactly the same, if it would have done any good. And so, to be *exactly* like Peter, Stumpy was to give up his life as a God, by giving Katie his inner strength and knowledge, by giving her his twin brother, little Mo. Katie was to go home.

With the book perched on his knees and Katie whispering constantly in his ear, he begins the story of Saint Ninah.

"The story of the missing God, the return of the Qeervis. Now listen carefully.

"Back in the seventeen hundreds God worked with her earthly project team, the Qeervi Royal Family, to study man's ability to be good to each other. A secret society was formed, and it set about its business helping others. The benevolent society began to spread throughout the trading world. But their plans changed when a certain naughty God's mummy decided that she wanted to go home with her Lamma, and so the Qeervi family were ceremoniously murdered by a scholarly sect from Nepal, the Chi Bantri. Nobody knows why but the family dispersed, as God went back to her throne, and the others went elsewhere. They were lost, and God was alone, and very, very lonely. But the daughter of God, Princess Catan, showed her undisputable strength and refused to die, and after a few years the Chi Bantri saw the light and stopped trying to torture the poor girl to death, but rather began to worship her spirit. So she became the foundation of the sect, guiding them towards the good and charitable, in the name of the formidable Queen Maya, the naughty mother of God. But one terrible day, the new Monsignor met with his inner court and they changed direction, murdering their own members in Kandy to begin their two hundred year reign of terror. They became the malevolent society which today influences all the governments and powers into acting in the interests of the Chi Bantri. Every act of genocide has had the Chi Bantri behind it, reaping the benefits of inhumanity. Anyway, the poor Catan, her eyes blinded by the torture, kept the tabs on the vile sect by her spiritual influence, knowing that one day her family would return and they would, as God's earthly project team, destroy the monster which they had created. And they would record their project results; man *still* cannot handle absolute power without becoming corrupt."

He stopped for a while as he studied the next couple of pages.

"One of the barbaric events which arose from their beliefs and superstitions was the annual Festival of Life. In the early years they would smoke the poppy and fuck the children from the district, but one horrific day, they tried to have sex with Princess Catan, and so, with the help of God's conscience, she ferociously killed all those who tried. As punishment they ate Catan's six best friends at the next festival, and they deemed that it brought them very good fortune and wealth. As a result, they believed that their spirit could be fed by eating the children of Catan, and from then on she was required to raise six new children each year, to be cooked alive and eaten at the annual Festival of Life. They were slow-cooked over a coal fire, still alive, and it was believed that the longer they stayed alive, the more powerful the spirit. The screams rang around the whole district of Anglia. It was the sound of hell. The project could not be closed because God had taken time out from her work to search for her beloved, but naughty, mummy, and after nearly two hundred years of crying, poor God went missing, searching. Her conscience, Catherine, was left to keep a cursory eye on events on Earth, and on Catan, but one fine day Catherine had a result: she actually found the wandering Ninah. So God's most loyal servant had returned from a two hundred year absence from his work, but, alas, the children of the festival almost broke his angelic heart. He *screamed* with them, and accompanied their spirits to the heavens to ensure that the Chi Bantri did not lay claim to them before they had chance to disperse. In the meantime the murderous Operation Searchlight had begun, so Ninah set about doing what he does best, and had taken up arms with two good human friends in East Pakistan, Satvinder and Doctor Hussain, in an effort to draw the Indian Forces into the fray, and in a hope that the massacres could be stopped. He organised, with Satvinder and the Doctor, a mass exodus across the Indian/East Pakistani borders, to cause chaos and crisis in the Indian areas of Bengal. More than ten million Bangalees crossed the border, forcing Indira Gandhi's government to break a habit of a lifetime, and go on the offensive. They moved in in December 1971 and the carnage eventually ended. But only after almost three million had died and several more millions had been left mentally broken, all in just about nine months."

He turned the pages, and Katie whispered, and Stumpy and Mo sat with mouths agape.

"So after the war Ninah, with many of the refugees from East Pakistan, moved to the Anglia region of Bengal, into the slums, and he met up with God. *Gayla* had returned! A little impish Indian girl who never stopped laughing and giggling, who was considered a friend of the people, but a witch. Along with Ninah she gained acceptance in the Anglian Fort, to be with Princess Catan, and the Chi Bantri. Gayla became her daughter's little sister and Ninah became the Chi Bantri's carpenter, maintaining and operating the cooking equipment used at the Festival of Life. With the izaline nails that Gayla had given him from God Edward, he pinned the children's heads up, through the neck, to be proud and alive while they were being cooked over the coals. But he pinched the nerves in the neck with the izaline, and they became completely anaesthetised, totally numb, and felt no pain. The Chi Bantri never knew, but just thought that the nails stopped the vocal chords from screaming. The children's suffering was curtailed."

Stumpy and Mo had moved over to cuddle up to Katie as the story unfolded.

"After many years of planning, the time was right for the demise of the vile Chi Bantri. And Catherine had at last found God's mummy and daddy, and so the Qeervi family was back, back in charge. They could not just destroy the secret sect, but, because of the laws laid down by God and her conscience, they had to influence the *World* into killing them off. Now, that very year in the early twenty first century there were six little eight-year-olds being primed by the Princess for the Festival of Life. They were to be ceremoniously eaten by the Chi Bantri members, feeding the sect's spirit and greed. But the children had a dream, to help to bring the World's disgust and anger upon the sect. They wanted to die for God, and not for the Chi Bantri, so they asked Ninah, their protector, to cut their throats. He was horrified, but obedient. He cut their throats and they died in a surging millpond of blood. And poor Ninah cried. He was crucified for his crime, by the Chi Bantri, amongst his friends from the Anglian slums, but the people could not accept his guilt, and so many, many victims of the Chi Bantri regime at last came forward. The World was told of the barbaric and inhumane society which had taken on the mantle of God, and they at last knew what the Chi Bantri was. The World thanked the spirit of Ninah for his killing of the six children, God's Six Catalysts. He became recognised as Saint Ninah, the protector of the children. And his spirit lives on."

Peter closed the book.

Stumpy held little Mo tightly as the tot's strength waned, and said to Peter, "That was a lovely story, Peter. And Mo has managed to hold on right 'til the end. Thank you. But when did all this happen?"

Little Sis whispered to Peter, who then replied, "Thanks to your family's love for my little sister, Gayla and Katie, it will all be happening soon. It will be happening very, very soon."

Stumpy said with pride, "Tomorrow, God will eat my brother, and she will be strong again, and I will be like Peter, mortal. We'll fight and die together."

He put his hand in the air, Peter high-fived him and the two green brothers stood up and slowly walked into the darkness. They went off to spend their last few hours together.

Katie put her mouth back to Peter's ear and whispered, "Well, beautiful, you know what this means?"

Peter wasn't sure whether to laugh or cry. "I've been part of a terrible scam. I've been turned into something which you needed Stumpy to be. And now you'll get what you want."

Katie frowned and just said, "Sorry." They pulled each other together. "But he's got what he wants. He's now your twin. He loves you."

Peter pulled away a little, enough to see her full in the face. "Do *you* love me? Or am a just an object? After all, you're going home through the tent, and I'm staying here with Stumpy. You'll never see me again."

She pulled her hand up and pinched his cheek, and then winked at him. In a low, husky voice, the little girl uttered, "God works in mysterious ways. So don't fret, my angel, and for once just *take*. Take *me*, before Mo's spirit brings Catherine back to me. I want to fly the universe, with you."

The morning came and Katie lay in Peter's arms, looking at his sleeping face. The sun was up, and she could hear some movement outside.

"Katie!" shouted Stumpy. "Quick!"

She couldn't get up by herself, but Peter awoke from the calls, and picked her up.

"Quick, it's Mo."

They went across the street and Mo was lying by the khaki tent. He was wheezing very heavily. Peter leaned down to offer Katie to Mo's face, and he kissed her, and while their mouths were together he breathed out. She took the breath into her lungs and she felt life eddying through her body, as little Mo went. He gave her the last of his life, enough to give her the strength to devour his flesh, which was to return her to her former strength, and the three of them wept.

They stood for some time, just looking at their beloved Mo. He was peaceful and smiling.

"I need to prepare his flesh for you," stuttered Stumpy. "You get ready to eat. It'll rot very quickly."

He picked up the limp body and carried it over to the table where the record player has sat. He had no tools. "You get ready, you've got to eat him soon after death."

Peter took Katie back into the equipment tent, and sat his little God on the floor. They waited. She was excited, but nervous, and she bit her bottom lip as she looked towards the flap.

Stumpy put his hand between his legs and from his pouch pulled out his daddy's claw. It was razor sharp, and with surpising skill and dexterity Stumpy used it to cut through the leg muscles like they were butter. He filled a plate, all from Mo's legs.

"Here it is." Stumpy was smiling. "You've got to eat it all. It'll make you big and strong."

Katie was feeling stronger after receiving the last of Mo's life, so she refused Peter's help, and picked up a piece of the meat. She made a start. It was tender, and she loved it, greedily getting as much into her mouth as she could, with Stumpy and Mo laughing at the gruesome act. "It's beautiful," she said, through her bloody cheeks, "Just beautiful." The feast lasted about ten minutes, and she was almost full, but wanted more. The plate was cleared, but she had to lick every bit of Mo's blood from the crockery. "Is there any more?" She held her plate out to Stumpy, like a well known Dickens character.

"*More?* You want *more?*" Stumpy grinned and went outside, and then returned with another plateful.

Katie got stuck in, blood dribbling down her front and on her clothes as she tore the flesh apart with her teeth, and she looked hungrily at Peter. He remembered what she had said about her mummy and the Lamma feeding, and having wild sex as part of the ritual and he could see some fire in her eyes, so he stepped outside while she finished. He stood looking at the partly stripped body of his little friend Mo, and wondered when he would wake up from the dream.

"Peter, she's had enough. She wants to speak to you alone."

He turned back towards the tent, and his hands shook. What does she want? He nervously entered the tent, and Stumpy very politely went for a walk.

"Peter, come here!" She burst into tears. Peter hugged her and she whimpered. "Sorry. Don't hate me." They didn't say anything for while, as she calmed down, and then she stuttered, "Sorry. I didn't answer yesterday. I do love you. I haven't ever before, but I do. I do. I'll never stop loving you, through everything, I'll love you." He wiped her running nose, and then kissed her tears from her cheeks.

"Just when I'm getting the taste. You're going."

They walked slowly around the camp, Peter still carrying his tiny God in his arms, and they stopped to look at Old Dick's scorched earth.

Peter carefully picked his words. "He met your mother when he died. So did I." He sighed. "This was all a set-up. Don't suppose I'll ever know why."

Katie laid her head on his shoulder and whispered, "Catherine. She's trying to teach me something. And she's selected you to be my teacher."

God most certainly works in mysterious ways. And the two common denominators in all the scheming were Catherine and her mother. God's missing mother. Missing, or hiding? Who was Edward warning them of, in the painting of the peeping toms? Stumpy and Mo, or Maya and her Lamma? The whole thing was hanging heavy over Peter and Katie, even though Katie was already feeling her strength building up.

Katie pulled her head up straight, and grinned. "I'm feeling so good. Love me, please. That's all we have left, human love." Catherine had achieved what she had set out to achieve, instilling a cold, heartless and divinely powerful God with feelings. "I know exactly why Catherine got me here. And it's worked."

Peter frowned. "She's made you love me?"

"She has. Now all we have to do is to work with what we've got. Fuck the teacher, she can swivel." She chuckled, and then bit Peter's nose. "We'll make our combined love get me home. I'm not going in the tent on my own. Are you with me, richard-edward, my little potato-face?"

He laughed, "Cheeky mare. Do I have any choice?"

"None, just do as you're told. Her indoors has spoken." They jigged about in the sun, not really knowing what they were celebrating, but they were becoming delirious with success.

"What we laughing about?" asked a bemused Stumpy as he joined them in the dancing.

"We're in love!" shouted Katie. "Gayla loves Peter, and Peter loves Stumpy!" They danced and laughed. Not sure what at. "We're all in this boat, we'll all pull the paddles. Together!"

Eventually, a confused Stumpy stopped them. "Stop, now! We've got to burn the rest of Mo. Before he rots. The bacteria here are kings, and nothing hangs about for long after death, not even his soft skeleton if we let them at it." So they settled down, for a while, and made a fire up ready for the cremation. The body burned very quickly, and, amazingly, left a most beautiful izaline skeleton. As promised, they carefully laid it onto the motorised truck, and drove quickly towards Edward's burial vault, where it was to be deposited, to lay beside his daddy's.

The day was still long, and they hoped to get back before dark, so they never pissed about, just sang, and laughed all the way. But as they reached the scree where the burial vault was located, they could see across the river!

Stumpy began to cry. The gunk and its ever increasing cloud of gases had done its job, as far as the eye could see. There was not a thing left, just black, cratered nothing. The Colony was almost dead.

"That'll be coming around the globe soon," sobbed Stumpy. "It'll go that way until it has caught up with us, from behind."

Stumpy took the skeleton of his little twin to his father.

"Katie, we celebrated earlier. Why?" Peter was as confused as ever.

"Because we are together. Me and you, as one."

"But I don't understand. You need to go back to our people. Your children. We can't go together."

She twisted her face a bit. "You may die if I take you through the tent. And Stumpy couldn't come. So let's not go."

"But you've got to go home. For the others."

"I won't go without you. And Stumpy couldn't really go. They'd just kill him, or put him in a zoo, or eat him. So he can't go, and so *we* can't go. That's what Catherine has taught me." She swung her arms in the air, with her renewed strength. "And I've cut my Catherine out, in case she gets through to me and tells me to come home. I don't want to go without you, so she'll have to hold the fort for a bit longer. This is *our* time, sugar-plum." She thought a little, "But we'll have to be careful. I'm getting back to my full divine strength, and if I cut my Catherine out, it's up to you to be my conscience. Don't make me mad."

Stumpy returned, with a big smile. "Daddy's pleased with what has happened. He has blessed your commitment to me." He looked at the dead lands over the river. "You won't have to be committed to me for much longer."

They sped home, not wanting to waste any more time away from the camp. As they sped, Stumpy smiled and observed, "The last piece of the planet to be eaten by the gunk will be Daddy's funeral vault. It's right close to the river, and will live to the very last. We'll die before him, I'm pleased."

The three of them were being very philosophical about their imminent gunking. Katie just smiled, and laughed, and tickled Peter as he drove, and was behaving very dangerously, from Peter's point of view. "As long as I can keep Catherine out, we have a free reign, tiger-pants." She fidgeted in her seat, "I feel fantastic, but I could do with a poo."

"Katie!" snapped Stumpy, "don't waste your poo. You'll need it when you go back home."

The other two looked at him with disgust.

"No, I'll show you when you've had a poo." Weird, but true! "And when you discover what our final gift to you is, you'll understand." He grinned from ear-to-ear. "We've really learned how to give. Just like you, Peter. And this one was brilliant. Make sure it doesn't go to waste. High-five, man." And they did.

15 -- THE FINAL GIFT, BYE-BYE

All through the night Katie suffered. She had been to the toilet four times, and each time it got harder and harder to pass. Green giants clearly weren't the most suitable staple diet for a little God. But she remembered Stumpy's words, and so she did it all in separate plastic bags. They stunk like rotten cabbage. Poor Peter struggled to sleep through the straining and the stench, but he didn't nag her. "You ok?" They cuddled between poos.

"Katie! Peter! Katie! Quick, get out here! There's something coming over the sea! Quick!"

The gunk cloud! Katie pulled Peter up with her renewed strength, and they rushed outside. This could be their end.

"Get your book, and your nails, and your poo. Quick!" Stumpy rushed them back inside, and helped a panicking Peter put the poobags into a strong, waterproof carrier. "And your book, and nails!" They ran around like headless chickens.

"But where're we gonna go?" Peter screeched. "Where?"

"Where do you think? Idiot!" Stumpy snapped.

They rushed outside to see how close the cloud had reached. No cloud in sight.

"Where? Where's the cloud?"

"What cloud?" Stumpy was laughing amidst his panic. "No cloud, just our last present to you."

The two stood in bewilderment as the nine-foot giant grinned and pointed to the horizon. "I can hear it." He began to dance up and down like a pogo stick, and grabbed Peter. "I love you, and I'll miss you." Then he took Katie from her feet and swung her around in glee. "Please look after my twin brother. Both of them."

Then they could hear it. It droned, but they couldn't see anything. But suddenly a spec, then a larger spec, then a ship! It was a ship! They were going home! It slowed quickly as it approached and stopped overhead, engines screaming, looking for a best landing spot, and then it dropped like a stone to the ground. The large legs dampened the impact, and the noise dropped.

Peter and Katie stood gasping, in disbelief, as a union-jacked transport ship sat by the woodlands. And the hatch opened quickly, with four white uniformed men running down the plank and then the cargo doors lowered below the massive tail of the ship.

Katie giggled, and looked round for Stumpy. But he was gone.

"Half an hour!" shouted the Captain to the three airmen. They rushed past the children, straight into the equipment tent, but the Captain walked directly to Peter and Katie. He saluted God and her partner. "Good morning. Glad to see you alive, but why the hell are you still here?" It was the kindly Captain who had brought them to the colony, and who had advised them to go straight back home. "We were shocked to receive the signal, but we couldn't ignore it. You are *very* lucky."

Peter pulled Katie to him. "What signal, sir?"

"The distress signal. It's coming from that tent."

How much *more* beautiful could those children of God Edward become. Before giving himself to Katie, Mo had loaded onto the truck, and ignited, the distress transmitters from the small ship that they had found. Both of them!

"There's two," said the Captain, smiling. "My men will take them with them, along with some maps and plans which the company has asked us to retrieve. If we can find them."

Katie grinned. "They are under the old school, with some children." She pointed to the cellar, down the street. "But the children don't want to go with you." She had a little chuckle.

"Where is the ship? We expected a reconnaissance ship to be with the transmitters."

Peter sighed, "They got caught up in the gunk leak. They're gone, I'm afraid."

The Captain bowed his head, and went off to speak to his men.

"Stumpy has gone." Katie spoke quietly. "This is the other gift which he spoke about. Mo must have planned this entire episode, even to the point of taking the distress transmitters from the little ship. He was such an intelligence." She looked into Peter's eyes. "But if he knew the ship would come, why did he give himself to me?" Even God didn't know everything. "We must leave Stumpy here, with his daddy. That's what he wants."

Peter was upset, but clear thinking. "I want to stay with him."

"No, never. The twins have done this for us, for you. They always intended to get you home with me, else they would have encouraged me through the tent. Don't let them down. Please."

He was suddenly feeling, for the first time, that this was a nightmare. The young man with whom he had twinned was to be left behind, to die in the mist with the rest of the colony, lost forever. "How can we leave him? I could stay with him. And die with him. That's what he would do for me."

"No. He's so much like you, and *you* wouldn't let *him* stay if the roles were changed. He's given himself to you, and to me." She wiped a tear from his cheek. "Come on, let's get in the ship." She got to the ground and the little girl led him to the gangplank, where they were met by the air stewardess, who marvelled at Katie's walking and talking skills. She asked if they still had the wheelchair, and Katie smiled as she nodded towards the equipment tent.

The cargo doors were closed, after many items of equipment and information had been loaded, including the wheelchair.

"We must leave," reported the Captain over the tannoy. "There is death approaching for this small planet, and we must be away before it reaches us. Please find your seats, and I wish you a pleasant journey home."

Peter sat looking through the window, hoping to see, for the last time, his adopted twin. But he never spotted him. He sank into a tearful depression as they pulled away from the colony, as he surveyed the grey waste laid by the clouds of gunk. The sea was boiling, and the lands smoking, and death prevailed.

"He won't die in the cloud, I promise. Go to sleep, darling." Katie stroked his forrid. "Go to sleep, and we'll soon be home." As the passengers drank their coffee, they fell into deep coma. But Katie never slept. She looked out of the ship at the planet from which the earth was originally populated with life, and felt grief. The destructive cloud had not yet reached God Edward's vault, but it was imminent, with most of the planet already melting into oblivion. "I hope you have kept your promise, Edward. Mummy had better be gone, or I will deal with you in the next life." She smiled. "But I trust you, so I'll keep my promise to you. And if you *are* listening, Stumpy, our bestest friend, thank you. We'll never forget you."

She suddenly realised why Stumpy had given his twin to her. It was not for her trip through the tent; they knew the ship would come. It was for her strength, to be able honour their fathers request for help.

She took a deep breath and stared at the smouldering planet, which was getting visually smaller as they moved through the expanse of space. "I'll now honour your request, Edward, before I let Catherine back; you know how good she is, she'd probably stop me." She chuckled to herself, and then concentrated fully on the planet. She strained her unrelenting will towards the colony, and it began to show signs of lightning, which was splitting the scorched islands apart, and then the lightning spread, and the whole surface of the planet was alight with eruptions. Then in a flash, it imploded, sending shockwaves to the ship. It was gone. If you'd had a long blink you would have missed it, but it was definitely gone. "Goodbye Edward, and Stumpy. You've taught me a great lesson in love. Now I'll join Catherine, and I expect she'll tell me off for all my newfound human traits."

The tiny God grinned and exhumed a dirty laugh to herself as she looked at Peter. "But before I go back with Catherine, I'm gonna snog my man." She leaned over to Peter, stroked his cheek and then kissed him, long and hard. She licked his lips, pushed her tongue into his mouth, and then bit his nose. "If only, moon-dreamer." She let her spiritual defence drop and whispered, "Hey, I've made it back. Where are you, Catherine?" She laid back and waited.

The ship sped across the universe, passing all the dead planets and stars, towards the one which thronged with life and emotion, her beloved earth. And there it was, way up ahead, with its brilliant blues, browns and gold shining in the light of our life-force, the sun.

"Home," she whispered to herself. "The end of a beautiful holiday." She grinned into Peter's face, who was just beginning to wake. "I wonder if you'll still love me when you meet all the other little girls back home. They'll be flocking to bed you, and wow, what tales you've got for them in between shags." She began giggling, and couldn't stop. "I wonder how many different names I've called you since we got to the colony. I think I'll call you Peter from now on. Is that ok shag-puss?" She screeched, "Woops, I've done it again. Just can't help myself, can I throb-knob?" She just laughed to herself as Peter stirred. "And I've made my mind up. I'm not gonna cry any more until my next feed. Two hundred years of tears is enough, even for God, and I'm not going to take anything out on my children, ever again." She chattered quietly, "Unless they cry wolf once too often." She snuggled up to Peter. *'Are you with me yet, or aren't we talking?'* she thought. *'Come on, Catherine.'*

She bit her bottom lip, but then *'Of course we are. We're bleedin' one apart, I've got to bloody talk to you, ain't I.'*

No more said, and they were back together. God was reunited with herself.

Across the tannoy came, "This is your Captain speaking. Time to wake up. I hope you have had an eventless journey."

The few passengers awoke, and Peter cast a confused look into Katie's eyes. "Where are we?"

"Home, sweetheart. Home, where the heart is. You ok?"

He suddenly realised, and looked out of the window to see the shape of the UK. They were just minutes away from his home. He could almost smell the old approved school, the Homestead, and he shivered. "I hope, Katie."

She looked up into his eyes, and replied, "So do I."

The arrival home was a real mix of anti-climax and bullshit. The lovely Captain and his stewardess met the home-comers at the bottom of the gangplank, and so did the press, dozens of them. They flashed constantly at the two kids, the children of the wild colonial boy, the hero who had killed the last of the New Bury monsters. Even good news is sometimes distasteful!

"Please allow the children to past through!" Shouted the Captain, "They've had a long journey. Please let them pass. I don't know how you even got onto the airfield. Let them through!"

Then a Royal Air Force truck pulled up, and the children were helped aboard. They were driven across the grass towards the control tower, leaving the pressmen running after them, but never catching them, until they reached some guardhouses which controlled the entrance to the airfield. An Air Force officer met them.

"Good morning," he said as he saluted them. "I am Sergeant Michaels. We just need to check you for contamination, before we hand you over to your guardian." They were led through into the checkpoint, and stood very still and silently as the sergeant's men checked them for radiation. Once they had scanned them with their crackling handsets they declared, "All clear. We just need to see what you've brought back with you." The Sergeant asked Peter what he had in his pockets.

"Just a penknife and a hanky." He emptied his pockets.

"And in the bag, sir?"

He carefully put the plastic bag on the desk, and grinned. "I have four bags of poo. From my sister, who wants to keep them." The children began to giggle, bringing a wry smile from the sergeant.

"Why?" he asked.

"Because it's a memento from our old friends, little Mo and Stumpy. Check it out if you like."

The sergeant nodded to one of his men, who gingerly opened the top of the outer bag, and could see the three bags inside. They were well sealed, and none had leaked. He put his nose to the bag, and instantly threw his head back. He could smell the contents. He then poked his finger into the squidgy mass, and, turning his nose up, he declared, "I think it's shit, Serge. Really."

"Strange, but true!" joked the sergeant. "What's in your little bag, Katie?"

"Oh, it's just my book. Would you like to see it?" The little girl reached up and placed it onto the table, and opened it. It was all blank. "It's my only possession. Honest, Gov'." Her big, wide grin enchanted the mystified sergeant.

By the time they had convinced the sergeant that they were just a couple of nutters, the other passengers had arrived at the guardhouse.

"Good to have you back in one piece," smiled the sergeant, "You can now go off with your guardian, who's waiting outside." He politely walked them out of the airfield.

"Uncle!" They both rushed over to a frail old man, Uncle Steven. He had not been well, and had seriously aged. They all huddled together, while Uncle and Peter had a few tears.

"I thought you were dead!" he exclaimed. "I'm sorry."

"Uncle, it was great. What an adventure!" Peter was so pleased to see his only living relative, but could sense how ill he had been. "This is Katie, and she's walking. Remember the little snail's shell, who lived on a blanket. It's *really* her!"

They spent several minutes cuddling and looking at each other, and then moved over to the old Ford Anglia. "Got meself a car. Can't really afford it, but hey, what the hell. Jump in. And I've got a council flat as well. It's in Boxted."

"That's a bit close to that fucking borstal!" Peter forced a scowl. "Am I going back there?"

Uncle looked sternly at him. "If you can behave, you can stay with me. I've got two bedrooms. So it's up to you to earn your freedom."

"And Katie? What about Katie? She can't go back to the unit. She's well."

"I know, and I don't believe it. It's like a miracle. God's been good to you."

They didn't say much as they drove back to village of Boxted, to the flat. It was very rural, in a block of four flats, two ground floor, and two first, and Uncle's was on the ground. The nineteen fifties council flat sat in the centre of the newer part of Boxted, on a junction with Dedham Road and overlooking a small green. On the opposite side of the side road was open farmland, and the hedge along the road featured a few very large, stately elm trees. Peter and Katie looked up and down the street as they got out of the car, and thought about the street in the colony. A group of teenagers playing on their bikes reminded them of some of the benefits of Earth, friends.

"They'll never replace Stumpy and Mo. Ever." Peter was taking the loss of his friends very well, which confused Katie a little. She hugged him around the waist as they waited for Uncle to unlock the door. "We'll have to stick together, Sis. Or will you be too busy?"

It was mid April, 1971, and next door were listening to their radio. "I've got to get a radio, Sis. It'll help me to survive." The radio played Lola, by the Kinks, as they watched out of their window, where a man was walking his two greyhounds. "We could sell the nails. They're izaline."

"Never! I would have to eat you if you did that." She dug him in the ribs.

"Careful. Or I might have to put you over my knee."

Hmm, Katie didn't respond in her usual suggestive manner. "Catherine wouldn't like that, she's a nice girl." Well, she had got her conscience back. "Brother and sister can play, but…"

Uncle Steven had made some fish fingers and chips for lunch, and they sat on the settee, with their food on their knees.

"Are you ok, Uncle?" asked Peter. "You've aged."

His look was morose. "I've been quite bad, but ok now. I've really worried about you two. I thought I had lost you both, to those monsters." He coughed. "Had the press after me for a few days; that wore me down." He grinned, "But somebody told me you were ok, and that helped. She said you would be back soon. She just told me that, and went. You know, Katie, I thought she was you when I first saw her. But I can't even remember where I met her."

Catherine! *She promised to let him know and keep an eye on him'.* She turned to Uncle and asked, "Did she say anything else?"

He shook his head, "No she just giggled and wished me well. Then she was gone. You know, I still can't remember where I met her." He frowned, and carried on eating.

"Have you got any money, Uncle?" asked Peter. "Did you get your bonus for killing the monsters?"

He shook his head and grumbled, "We only got about half what we expected. They've promised to pay the other half in September next year. Hell knows why." The company knew that the miners would all be dead by September 1972. "I seriously thought about telling them the truth."

Peter grinned, "We have some izaline. Don't know how much."

"*Oy!*" Katie kicked his shin. "We don't have any, it belongs to Ninah. He's got to have it for the *children*!" She scowled at him. "*What* do you think you are *doing*?"

"Nothing. Uncle's one of us."

"But we don't have any izaline for him. It's Ninah's. And, where is it anyway? You had it!"

Peter put his hands in the air and surrendered. "Don't shoot, I've got it safe." Then he winked at his sister. "If I tell you where it is, will you fetch it for me? You know, like the claw?" He jumped up and took his and Katie's trays to the kitchen.

"If it's in your bum, you can get it yourself," she snapped.

Uncle sat grinning, but bewildered.

"Not in me bum, worse than that. Will you get it?"

She grudgingly smiled and nodded.

"Well, it's in…." His face suddenly dropped. Hell! "It's in the poo." He was rapidly falling into tearful mode, realising what he had just said. He repeated very slowly, "It's in the poo." Poor Peter had just recalled. "The poo." He sat down beside Katie, and put his head on her shoulder, and began to cry, in absolute disappointment.

"What is it, popples? You can tell us." Katie kissed his head. "Please, and then we can help." She looked over to Uncle who was concerned.

Peter sniffed and caught his breath. "In the poo. He said it was in the poo, in the bags. I thought it was real." He sighed. "It must have just been a dream. It's the nails in the poo, that's all." He closed his eyes. "I thought it was him. But just a dream." He looked up into Katie's eyes. "Did Stumpy visit us in the ship?"

Katie slowly shook her head. "Sorry. I didn't see him. And you were asleep."

He looked blankly out of the window. "So it was just a dream. Stumpy's gone, really. He said the poo had izaline in. But it's just the nails."

Katie pulled up to hold him. "But that's good, nothing to cry about. The nails will help the children of the Festival and Ninah will be waiting for them." She stroked Peter's forrid. "The holiday's over. We're back on Earth, in Boxted, where we have work to do. Please don't lose me now."

Uncle asked, "So what was the dream about, Peter? Might help to talk about it."

He breathed deeply. "Yeah. You never know." He had a good sniff, and then got his hanky out for a blow. His voice was weak. "I was just sitting watching the colony disappear, and my friend said it was now all gone. Daddy was moved. And he needed to get to be with him very soon, so he didn't lose him. He said I should use the izaline from the poo to look after you two, because everything on Earth had a price-tag. And what's left after all that, do the right thing with. He said that you and Catherine would work out what to do with it. And to please do it for him and Mo."

"You talking about Stumpy?"

"Yeah, poor old Stumpy. I thought he was with us, on the ship." So that's why he had taken their departure from Stumpy so well. He thought he was coming with them. "Has he really gone?"

Katie nodded, and bit her lip. "It's just us. The three of us, and, of course, Catherine and Ninah. And I almost forgot my little girl, Ca'an, the little princess." She chuckled, "More of us than I thought. But Stumpy is here in our hearts, and Mo is here in my tummy."

He looked at the ground, and wondered. "What has it all achieved? You know, our time on the colony."

"It's been a very selfish move on the part of God Almighty." The little girl brushed her blond hair from her face. "I was so desperate, I know, and dangerous, threatening to take all my hang-ups out on the world. After all these billions of years, I knew so little about my own children, nor about myself. I think that's why she sent me off with you. You are beautiful. The perfect model, from which I could learn, and I've learned so much from you. Thank you." She leaned over and kissed him on the lips, while Steven looked on in total confusion. She started to smile as she whispered, "I should have made man in *your* image, not mine. We would be a better civilisation."

Uncle Steven asked, "Did I miss something while you were away?" He grinned.

Katie answered, with a contented air, "Loads. We fell madly in love, and were the perfect team. The Earth owes Peter; he is the maker of God, the new, improved model. I wonder how they'll pay him." She grinned at Peter, "And getting back to the poo, even if it was a dream, it may have meant something."

"What d'you mean?"

"The izaline in the poo." She started giggling. "I suppose I've got to get it out. Suppose we had a deal."

The three of them rushed around to open all the windows and the front and back doors. "This is gonna stink!" shouted Peter. "I had to put up with it when she *did* it!" He got the plastic bag from the bedroom and placed it on the draining board. A bemused Uncle looked on. Standing on a dining chair, Katie opened the top of the bag, and carefully picked out one of the poo-packs.

"This one first," as she screwed her nose up. She took the bowl out from the sink, and then carefully un-knotted the top of the bag. The smell was atrocious. She tipped the semi-solid mass onto the drainer and gingerly poked her finger into the faeces. She couldn't help but giggle. "There's something solid." She picked out one of the nails, and then put it under the tap to rinse. "We've got one of them. Phew!"

Poor Steven was beginning to retch, so he made a sensible move, and stood in the living room.

Katie pushed the poo into the sink, then turned on the tap to wash it away. "Phew, Petie-baby. That is shit!" The next bag came out, and she poked around for the nail, but it wasn't there. She pushed the contents into the sink, and run the tap. "Oy. You gonna help me? The sink's blocked. Poke your finger down it."

"No way! This is *your* job." He began to laugh as the little girl pushed her hand right down into her excrement. She then began to giggle even more. He laughed, "You enjoying this?"

"You would be if you could feel what I can feel." She lifted her hand from the poo, and with it came an object. It was about the size of a small marble, and as she washed it it began to look like a malteser, without the chocolate, sort of honeycomb texture. Katie started to laugh and toss her head around. "It's him!" she screamed. "He's such a darling, he really is!"

Peter had to ask, "Who?"

"Mo! This is Mo, look." The two boys gathered round, becoming accustomed to the stench. "Look, it's hard, but soft and pliable. It's got *my* thumbs up, cos Mo's bone structure has been passed by the Management. Yee haaah!" She almost fell off her chair with laughter, and Peter joined her but Uncle just watched. "Let's see if there's any more." This time Peter helped his sister to route around in the poo, and they pulled out nine of the balls. "No wonder it bloody hurt when I crapped!" she shouted. "Let's do the others." They tipped the third bag onto the drainer, pulled out the second nail, and then pushed the contents into the sink, tap running. Unbelievable! They found another thirteen balls. Then the last bag came up with another seven! "We just need to dry them out and let them oxidise, like his skeleton did. Should've been enough caskin in my poo to oxidise them."

Bang, bang! The next door neighbour had turned up. "What's going on here? And that fucking stink!"

"Sorry, it'll be sorted," apologised Uncle.

"Fucking wanna be. Shit, we've gotta live next door to this."

Peter rushed forward, and said, "sorry," and then slammed the door. The man smashed the gate shut as he went out of the garden.

The three family members cleaned up the draining board, and the sink, but the plughole was blocked so Steven grudgingly climbed below the sink, and dismantled the waste. "It's bunged solid. Look." The bend was full of muck. He pushed it all out onto the sink. "Hey, it's more of those balls. Little ones." They carefully cleaned them all up and put the sink back together. "There are loads."

They all sat silently considering, until Steven broke the ice.

"So, what is that stuff?" Poor Uncle Steven was just dragging along behind.

Katie grinned and explained, "This is izaline. Honest. It's part of the monsters that you killed. And I passed it in my poo. And I don't think I should expand on that, but their bones are made up of this, and you destroyed it all when you gunked them, because it doesn't harden off and turn to izaline until it oxidises with the caskin. So you actually destroyed the izaline which you were searching for. Ironic?"

He didn't laugh at the irony. "I only killed one. I couldn't kill the little ones." He put his head down in shame.

"We know. You're our hero. And the two little ones loved you for it."

Steven looked up. "You mean you saw it?"

Katie chuckled, "No, they told us. They became our best friends, and much more. They're lovely creatures, never hurting anybody." Katie moved onto Steven's knee. "They looked after us, and they even got us home. You are our hero. And thank you for leaving the claw with Old Dick. Mo was able to get in to see his daddy with it."

Steven, broken and depressed, managed a confused smile of relief and cuddled Katie.

Peter suggested, "We should go to bed soon and get up early to check our izaline. There must be millions of pounds worth there. What we gonna do?"

The three of them looked blankly at each other. And then Uncle Steven came up with a brilliant idea. "Let's first check out the local pubs."

Colin Hodgson

16 -- IZALINE, WHAT IZALINE?

They climbed in to their old Anglia which had been parked on the small green, in front of the flat. The unfriendly neighbour stared hard at them as they drove off, but Steven's jailbird experiences told him that he was all mouth and trousers. Nothing to concern them. The village was predominantly council housing, some built in the nineteen thirties, some in the fifties, and with a small bungalow shop in the main street, but the first pub they came to was much older. The Cross stood on the Cross Corner, opposite some old barns. A low wall swung around the bend to the pub, enclosing the sparse gardens.

Steven parked right in front of the bar entrance. His was the only car at the front of the pub. "I'll go and see if you can sit inside with me."

He entered the pub and approached the bar on the right. "Evening. Can I bring my children in while I get a drink?"

The Irish landlord simply answered, "No, but they can play in the garden. There's a door to the off-sales round there where they can come to if they need you. But tell them to stay off the wall."

"I'll speak to the kids. Thanks." He went back to the car. "We'll try the other one. He doesn't want you inside. Fair enough."

They drove further down the road, and started out along the Boxted Straight Road, past the post office, and soon arrived at the Wig and Fidgett. It stood on its own, but looked like it was closed. Steven went in through the front door to find the landlady welcoming him into the dull surroundings. There was nobody else at the bar, which was small, about eight feet long, and the green lino complimented the old scrubbed and bleached pine tables.

"So long as they behave, they can sit up the other end." The pub was divided in two by an open fireplace and chimney. "We've just had that end opened up, and the toilets built. We've got inside toilets. The Cross hasn't." She proudly grinned.

The two kids sat the other side of the fire, and looked out of the window as the occasional vehicle passed along Straight Road. "This isn't what we're used to, is it, Sis." Life was not looking very promising to the young adventurer. "I wish Stumpy had made it with us. You know, Sis, I was convinced that he was with us in the ship. Just a bloody dream."

"He's in here." She pushed her hand onto his chest.

"Yeah. All that faith and belief is ok, but it ain't the real thing, is it. I've got this feeling that things are not ever going to be the same, ever again. Even *you've* change since we got back."

"What d'you mean?"

"You were God in New Bury. You're Katie here. Don't get me wrong, I love Katie." He paused. "But God….."

She sat closer to him. "I know what you mean, thank you. But I need to work. I spoke to Catherine, and Ninah is getting some encouraging results in East Pakistan. So I can stay with you for a bit and make sure you're ok. But I do need to get some work done."

"You're talking like you're leading into a farewell speech. I think I know what's going to happen."

"Don't be sad. I'll always be with you, and I'll always love you, so don't be sad. What about that girl that Stumpy mentioned, from near your school? You could see her."

"Trying to get rid of me now?" He was beginning to sulk.

"No I'm not. But you've got it all back to front. In New Bury, I was Katie. Back *here* I'm God. I wish we were back in New Bury, and everything was ok, but it isn't. Do you even know what happened to the colony?"

"Of course. I watched it implode. You destroyed it."

She frowned and questioned his knowledge. "How do you know that? You were asleep for the entire journey. I know you were."

He just shrugged his shoulders, but then, "I watched it with Stumpy, out of the porthole. We both cried."

"That dream again." She thought. "Hang on to your dreams, treasure them. Keep that memory of Stumpy close to your heart, and it'll help you through life."

At the bar, Steven had been joined by the landlord, Paddy. He worked through the daytime while his wife held the fort, and they ran the pub together in the evenings. Steven asked the kids, "Would you two like a drink? I forgot to ask earlier. I'm having one more before we go." He bought them each a lemonade and a bag of Golden Wonder crisps. "Paddy says that tomorrow night there'll probably be a pianist here. And a sing-song. Fancy that?" The kids nodded.

"I wonder how much he'll have before he goes." Peter sighed. He had seen it all before.

"He said he'll have one more." Katie had faith in her Uncle.

"Nugget of izaline says he'll go when he's pissed." Grinning from ear-to-ear, they shook on it. Over an hour later, in walked a bunch of drivers from the local transport company. They got their drinks, and sat down for a game of cards, brag.

"Like to join in old mate?" an Irish chap asked Steven.

Steven looked along to the kids, and then nodded. "I'm Steve. I've just moved down the road."

"He's playing cards now," whispered Katie. "I think I owe you a nugget." She looked very small and angelic as the April light was slowly dying into the evening. "We need to do something with the izaline. We can help the children with leprosy. Catherine says that I have to go to India to be with Ca'an, and while there I should steal food for the leper colony in the Anglia slums, and be my little girl's eyes. As I said before, I think I did, anyway, Ca'an is totally blind, due to the torturing that she endured at the end of the seventeen hundreds, and she has led a solitary, private life, just with her six Festival children to keep her proper company. But she has controlled the spirit of the Chi Bantri sect, in preparation for our return. And now I should be her eyes, and she my big sister. It's all part of the plan." She grinned. "But you know all this, you told the story to the boys."

Peter was still feeling dejected. "Was I all part of the plan?"

"Not mine. Don't be silly, we've had a great time. Everything has to end at some point. Apart from me, of course. And of course Catherine. And the rest of the family." She smiled. "Catherine says there is this Catholic Nun, only young, who has given her life up as well as the church, to tend and care for the leper children in Anglia. She's called Saint Catherine. Coincidence, ain't it. You could help me steal for them."

"Will you take me with you to India, then?"

She leaned over to lay her head on his chest. "Against my better judgement, yes. I'll right it with Catherine."

"Why don't you just tell her? You're God, aren't you?"

"Yes, but so is she. I'm the creator and she is the conscience. We are God, one apart. So everything we do is one."

Life for Peter never seemed to get any easier but he grudgingly began to believe again. "Ok. Let's go to India. What's there? Apart from your daughter and the saint?"

"Well, there's a slum area, which was built up in the fifties by the local administration from the Anglia Fort, in Bengal. The Anglia Fort is the headquarters of the Chi Bantri and it was built in the late seventeen hundreds as a sister to Fort

William, which Clive had built on the banks of the Hooghly River. It was gifted, by the British East India Company, to the Chi Bantri when they executed my family, which was when we all became split up, and I began crying for my mummy and inflicting pain and terror on my own subjects. That's when Catherine left me to be one apart, to protect our children, and I eventually ended up with you. You were my medicine, my cure, my God." She smiled up at her God. "And before the end of 1971 Ninah will be successful in his movement of over ten million refugees into India, and the Indians will have to intervene and stop the slaughter and rape, in order to end the turmoil caused by the influx from East Pakistan. And many evacuees will settle with Ninah in the Anglian slums, around the Anglia Fort and around the Chi Bantri. And their collective spirit will be strong to contain the enemy, the Chi Bantri, in the Anglia Fort. And the people will recognise the Hell which the vile sect has fuelled during the Pakistani conflict, amongst others, and they will also recognise what the sect has put their sons, daughters, mothers, and fathers through; the murder, rape, mutilation, degradation and displacement." She spoke very deliberately. "They will contain and they will wait. They will await the return of their mythical Queen and Mother of God, Maya, who will lead them to retribution. The death of the Chi Bantri."

"Wow." Peter sniggered, "That was some sermon. Now, if Stumpy was here, he'd want to know if that was the truth or a lie, or I could even wrestle with him to prove it's a story."

"You know it's true. Or it will be, when it's become the past." She began to laugh. "And you know, Pete, Catherine has found Mummy, the mythical Queen and Mother of God, Maya, and Daddy."

"Really? That's great."

"But I can't talk to them yet, they're not ready. They're only our age." She giggled. "We might meet them, they both live near here, that's why we're here."

Peter gaped in shock. "Here? Where?"

"Can't say. But they come into this pub. Daddy's fifteen. Started drinking beer already. And Mummy's only little, like me. She's got striking ginger hair, real ginger, and she's Tracy."

"What if we bump into them?"

"We probably wouldn't even know them. We can't associate with them until Daddy's over fifty. It's just because, and we'll have to leave it at that."

Uncle Steven crept past the chimney breast. "Caught you! Glad you're keeping occupied. Want another drink?"

They both nodded, and he bought them another lemonade each. "I've just got to get a bit of my money back, then we can go."

Peter was a clear winner; Uncle would not be leaving until he was totally pissed, and probably broke. "Sis, you know more than me about some things. Should Uncle be drinking like that? He's not been well."

She looked sympathetically at her brother, her God. "He can drink. It won't harm him."

Peter suddenly realised what she meant. Uncle wouldn't be collecting his bonus in September 1972, he would be with the other miners.

Peter suggested, "Shall we walk home? He's gonna be all night, and perhaps it's what he needs. He's enjoying himself." Katie agreed, and they stood up. But as they did, a lady entered the pub, seemingly on a mission. She stomped over to the card school and grabbed one of the players by the arm, put her mouth to his ear, and he then stood up. His face was distraught as she marched him out of the pub.

"Wait," whispered Peter.

They waited to see what was going to happen, but the players just talked amongst themselves, laughing. Another player joined, filling the empty seat, and said, "Don't know if I want this seat."

"Come on." Peter waved to Uncle, who responded by walking, or rolling, up the pub to them. "Uncle, we're going home. You can stay, but we need the key."

He said, "On a bad run at the moment. I need to get some of it back. Poor old Sid just got nabbed by his missus, and he's lost all his week's wages. He's right in the shit."

Peter frowned, "That's awful. Aren't they all friends?"

"Not when it comes to cards. But I'll get mine back."

"How much you losing?"

"I'm about a hundred quid down."

"Wow, I didn't even know you had that much money. And you've lost it to that lot? That's fucking pathetic."

"That's enough!" He looked at the floor. "I'll get it back. Anyway, we've got all that stuff at home. We'll have to cash some of that in."

Poor Peter and Katie waved to everybody as they left the pub. They were worried about their uncle, who didn't understand what was going on. He was also pissed.

They slowly walked along the Straight Road, back towards the village, and it was just getting dark. The Post Office Stores had closed, but a bit further on, the old nissen hut, the British Legion club, was just opening. Katie stopped to look, as a group of teenagers were going in through the front doors of the converted nissen hut. She studied them intensely.

"You can't meet him. You said you can't. Anyway, you wouldn't know who he is."

So they moved on towards home. A little way up from the Legion, Len Turner was working in his bike shed, repairing somebody's pushbike. They looked in, and Katie asked Mr Turner if many young boys come into the shop. But he was occupied, and he never heard her ask, so they moved on.

"Come on. You can't meet him, so why are you punishing yourself." He picked Katie up and cuddled her. "Let's just go home. You keep saying that you've got work to do, so let's get going." He walked a bit with her in his arms, but she wanted to walk herself and as they approached the Cross

Corner, she became a little agitated again. Sitting on the wall which ran around the bend from the pub, were two teenagers. Katie asked them, "Do you drink? You know, beer?"

They both looked at her and smiled. "Wotcha. Who're you?"

"I'm Katie. This is Peter and we've just moved here from a long way off." She grinned at the boys. "My brother wants to get a drink sometime, where can he go for beer?"

One of the lads jumped down from the wall. "Not here. He won't serve you. But the Wig's ok if you behave. Old Paddy'll serve you. And if the right person is on the bar at the legion, you'll get served."

"Thanks, mate. Might see you out sometime."

"Hope so." He looked her up and down. "What's wrong with your leg?"

"Oh, I'm a spastic. Born like it."

Just as the lad was about to speak to Peter, another teenager pulled up on his bike. "The police're up here. Coming?" They all sped off to see what the coppers were up to, leaving Peter and Katie standing on the Cross Corner, alone.

They walked slowly, at Katie's pace, hand-in-hand back home. But they soon realised that the police were very close to their flat, so Peter picked Katie up, and hurried towards them. And they then soon realised that they were *at* their flat. They were in the back garden!

"What's happening?" Peter asked the policemen who was walking out of their gate.

"Do you live here, lad?"

"We've just moved in, today. Uncle is at the pub. What's up?"

"You've been burgled. Can we go inside?"

They went into the living room, and the policeman asked them to sit on the settee. "I don't think anything has been taken. But could you look around and confirm that?"

Katie jumped up and grabbed her book from the floor beside the settee and Peter went to the kitchen, and looked inside the crockery cupboard. The bag of izaline marbles was still on the shelf, and he peered inside at the balls, which were turning dark grey. They all looked intact. "Katie, come here." She limped to the kitchen. "Is this everything?" He had a worried frown as he put the open bag in front of her, and she checked. She smiled at him and nodded her head. She was happy.

"It looks like everything is here, sir."

The policeman stood up. "Right. The neighbour saw somebody in the back garden, and accosted him. The person ran off. I don't expect we'll find anybody, but if you find that anything is missing, give us a call. We're at the Dedham station."

Peter was feeling a bit dazed by the events. "Sir, where is the phone box around here?"

Katie answered for him. "We passed it, across from the shop."

The policeman went.

"Katie. Where the hell are the nails? They're not in there!"

"I know. I hid them, just in case something terrible happened. We could lose the balls, they're just money, kind of, but the nails are special." She went back into the kitchen and twisted her deformed body under the sink. She had hidden them in the loose gap around the overflow, and they were still there. What a relief!

The spare bed was just a single, but Katie insisted that they both sleep in the one bed. Peter went to sleep, with Steven still at the pub.

The next morning came around, and they left their Uncle in bed, to sleep off his drinking session. After eating, Peter and Katie decided to go for a walk, so they could talk about their immediate plans, and India, and the izaline. As she hobbled down the New Road, securely attached to Peter by her little hand, she stated, "We must get rid of the izaline. It's no financial value to us, we can't sell it. It'd be like selling the crown jewels from Windsor, so rare that the entire world would know about it."

"I don't know if you're right. Why can't we sell it? It's ours, and we haven't stolen it. So why can't we?" They walked a bit further. "We could try selling just one very tiny ball, and keep the rest hidden. If there's a problem, they can have the tiny ball, and we'll just walk away."

"But why do we need to sell it? You know, it's Mo. Have you thought about that? That's all we have left of our bestest mates. It's the remains of a God, and should be revered, not valued. What we ought to do is give it a lovely burial, and leave him in peace."

The dilemma carried on. Peter remarked, "Uncle Steven could do with some money, to last him his life. And if we're going to India, we'll need money to get there. I'll have to get us some passports, and flights."

"But even the very *smallest* ball must be worth enough to get us around the world many times. And still have enough to keep Uncle. He only needs to be kept for a few months."

Peter was surprised. "Don't say that so glibly. It's sad that he's dying."

"Sorry. But I've seen billions and billions of deaths, and life still goes on. It's the way."

They walked through the cut to the garages, back onto the Dedham Road and then over to the playing fields. The April sun was warm, so they sat under the poplar trees and watched the younger children playing on the swings and slide, over by the pavilion.

"This is like the colony. The warmth of the sun, injecting life into everything. It's my most important tool." Katie rolled sideways to lay against Peter and changed her subject. "We could only sell the izaline on the black market. I think there's a restriction on Gold ownership in Britain. Could be same for izaline."

"Naah, it's not common enough to be a commodity."

"Oooh, listen to you, platinum-bollocks. Give me a kiss and I'll show you my strong-box." She tickled him.

"Careful. Catherine's watching, little sister."

"Spoil-sport." She playfully pushed him away. "S'pose we should get back to see if Uncle's still alive, after his pissup."

So they took a slow walk back to the flat. Wowee! Parked beside their tiny Ford Anglia was a beautiful, grand, white car, with the roof down, showing off its beige leather seats and interior. And the chrome shone like izaline!

"What's that?" Peter gasped.

The grey uniformed man standing by it replied, "It's a Rolls Royce Corniche, young man. Lovely, isn't it?"

Katie stood back as Peter was joined by two other lads. They walked around and around the car, and then ventured closer to look inside. It was certainly a big boy's toy, a very big one.

"Is one of you Peter?" Peter raised his hand. "I've been asked to send you indoors if I see you. My boss is in there waiting for you."

Peter took Katie by the hand and they went in through the back door, where they found Uncle and another gentleman waiting. The grey-haired visitor stood up and held his hand out to Peter, and they shook.

"Hi." He was very well spoken. "I'm John Hutney, and I own the Golden Circle Mining Company. Do you know of us?"

Peter sat in the armchair and Katie squeezed on with him. They both shook their heads to the question.

"Well you should have done. You stayed in one of our mining colonies. Your uncle worked for us, and has gained himself the reputation as the wild colonial boy, who killed the last monsters. Have you heard of us now?"

"We didn't know your name. And why haven't you paid him?"

John just shrugged that one off and sat down beside Uncle and asked, "Do you like the car? One of the first off the line.

Got it before anybody else, because of who I am. Bet you'd like to take a drive in it."

Peter grinned, "I can't drive."

"Very funny. But my driver could take you for a spin later, if we still like each other by then. But first I have some issues to discuss with you two. Katie, have you ever seen izaline?"

She smiled at him. "Why?"

"Hmm. I need to know. You see, we own all the mineral rights to New Bury, and last night a young man was caught burgling one of the big houses in Church Street. He was caught red-handed, and we believe he tried to burgle this flat before he went on to Church Street. But your uncle was quite surprised when I told him of your burglary here."

"So?" Katie wasn't giving anything away. "Uncle was pissed up and we were in bed by the time he got home. And we went out before he got up." She nodded her head at John.

"Fair enough. Peter?"

"I'm with her."

"Right. This is the issue. The young man was released on bail this morning, but when he retrieved his belongings the desk sergeant noticed a fantastic silver marble in the bag. They had overlooked it when he was arrested, and the thief didn't know what it was, so they kept him in custody until they had checked out the marble. Any idea what it turned out to be?"

Peter and Katie both shrugged their shoulders.

"Well, although the thief didn't know what it was, he knew where he got it from. This very flat. He said it was on the kitchen floor. Still don't know what it is?"

Katie pulled a face and responded, "We're just a couple of stupid kids. We sometimes play marbles."

"With special marbles?"

"Of course they're special." She had her face screwed up. "They're *ours*."

John stood up and leaned over the two children. "The marble is made of izaline. Understand?"

Katie shook her head as she asked, "Understand what? You're talking shit."

"Katie!" Uncle tutted and waved his finger.

"No, Uncle! He's not saying any sense to us. So he's found a marble made of some shit." She began giggling, and Peter joined her. "It's all a load of shit!" Uncle joined in with the private joke, and laughed with them.

"I think you're taking this a little too lightly for your own good." John was becoming frustrated. "Do you want to hear the gritty bits? Well, I'm going to tell you anyway. We own the mineral rights on that colony, which means we own the minerals which come out of it. If you can't talk to me sensibly, then I'll have to take legal action." He spelled it out. "Do you have any izaline?"

Uncle Steven stood up, went to the kitchen cupboard, and returned with the bag. "Is this what you're talking about?" He opened it under John's nose. The man's eyes almost popped out of their sockets.

"I've never seen this much izaline in one place at one time. Thank you." He reached up to take the bag from Steven, but it was snatched away. John snapped, "*That* belongs to my company. I have the mineral rights."

Katie shouted at John, "But *only* the mineral rights!" She snarled at the intruder. "You have the right to mine the useful and valuable minerals contained *in* the ground, but not the living creatures and plants which live *on* the ground. And *not* biogenic substances, such as bone." The little girl was seething. "If you even knew what izaline is, you wouldn't be quoting fucking mineral rights."

John stamped his feet like a spoiled little child. "I don't deal with children!"

Katie sneered, "But you behave like one!"

The room was silent. The ageing John Hutney was boiling over, his blood pressure high and he resembled a beetroot with eyes and nose. Uncle Steven, after grinning at Katie, took the man's arm and sat him down. They all sat down.

Peter restarted the discussions. "Sir, if my sister is right, you don't own any of the izaline. It's not a naturally occurring mineral. *We* know what it is, and we've seen five hundred times that amount in just one lot. Your company never even found the real deposits."

John calmed down, and raised his eyebrows. "By God." He looked down at his feet, and suggested, "You've really seen that much? You could show us where it is."

Peter ruffled Katie's hair as he chuckled. "You tell him, Sis. Or was it just a dream?"

"No. If he doesn't know, then let him wallow." She had no pity for this man who had led the way to the total destruction of another life-supporting world. "He can swivel. And he'd better speak to his directors to find out why they've kept him in the dark." She suddenly behaved like the eight year-old that she was, and stuck her tongue out at him. "Goodbye Mister Hutney. We don't want that ride in your car."

17 -- A MUCH BETTER GAME

The following morning, Katie woke Peter very early. The April sun shone, and so did her face. She was exited, but agitated.

"We've got to fight today. Whatever happens, me and Catherine will always be with you."

Peter rubbed his sleepy eyes and shook his head. "What you on about?"

"Mister John Hutney, that's what. He's a spoiled brat, with big connections and he came here, on his own, to see us because he's running scared, for some reason." She put her coat on. "Come on, we've got to get you out of here."

"Why?" He was totally lost.

"Because we are standing between him and his millions. He's as good as bankrupt, but his executives haven't even told him about New Bury, or more to the point, the *lack* of New Bury. You know, you saw it in your dream; its disappearance. *But*, big but, *he* didn't. He thinks it's still there, and he believes we know where the big izaline deposits are." She smiled at him. "I've been talking all night with Catherine. We have a plan, but I'll tell you about it when we're out of here. We'll leave Uncle a note." The little girl scribbled a note.

But as they went through the front door, disaster struck.

"Stop!" Two policemen stood at the gate. "Peter and Katie Knaseby?"

They nodded and so the policemen asked them to go inside with them, to answer some questions.

The sergeant looked hard at Peter. "Now, Peter. I am making enquiries about a burglary. Any idea what I might be talking about?"

"Yes, sir, Mr Hutney came round last night and told us about it, in Church Street. Or do you mean our one?"

"Hmm, no, neither. The Ipswich offices of the Golden Circle Mining Company. I'm afraid we have witness accounts placing you at the scene, seven days ago. A bag of valuable metals was taken. Recall anything now?"

Peter nodded. "Yes, sir. I recall that seven days ago Katie and myself were on the ship on our way back from the New Bury colony. That's what I recall."

Katie was not grinning, unusually. She cuddled up to Peter, and quietly asked, "Would it be better to interview us on the record, not off it? We're children. We must have a responsible adult, and probably even a solicitor. And I notice that you haven't cautioned us."

The sergeant smiled. "How old are you?"

"I'm eight years old. Just eight." She bit her bottom lip. "How old do you think I am?"

The sergeant did not answer her question, but suggested, "Your uncle. He's your guardian? We need him to join us."

Peter went to his bedroom door and knocked.

Katie snapped, "Oh, sorry, Pete, I almost forgot. He went in to town on the quarter past eight bus. Won't be home until the quarter past four one."

Peter frowned at her and then sat down, but the PC stood up. He went to the bedroom door, and looked inside. "He's not here, Serge."

"Right. We'll take you down the station, and you can wait there in custody until we have the adult, your Uncle. But before we go we need to make a full search of the property."

Peter held Katie tightly, and whispered, "What's going on?" She just looked at him and winked.

She asked the sergeant, "Which station will you take us to? To that nice policeman's from yesterday? Or will you take us to a different one?"

"Shut up."

"Are you real policemen?" She stretched her head to look out of the window, at the Ford Granada police car which was by then surrounded by inquisitive children. There was another policeman in the driving seat. "Are you going to kill us?" She chuckled.

The air was instantly electrified. The PC raised his eyebrows at his sergeant as if to ask, 'are we?' and his sergeant just frowned. He suggested, "Let's get on with the search."

They turned everything inside-out. They found nothing but a bag of marbles. *Real* glass marbles. The two men were not amused.

"Not gonna get your bits if we're dead."

The sergeant almost struck her, but for the PC jumping forward. He then sighed and apologised. "I'm sorry miss, but you are a cheeky little devil. Please try to hold your tongue. Regarding your earlier question, yes we are real policemen, and we are stationed at the Colchester station, not at Dedham with PC West, who you met the other day. That's where we'll be taking you, to Colchester. You needn't worry, we'll look after you."

Katie was back giggling again, to the annoyance of Peter. "So, Bruv, they *are* real policemen. But you always have to check, don't you."

The PC was left to wait at the flat for Uncle to return, and the two children taken out to the car. Katie laughed and shouted to the onlookers, "We're off to Colchester police station! What a laugh, hey!" And then the aggressive neighbour came out and spoke to the Sergeant.

"Wilf, you're taking the kids to Colchester? I can let the uncle know when he gets back." He nodded to Peter. He obviously was not the obnoxious person that he first made himself out to be. "I'll talk to your Uncle when he gets off the bus." And that also confirmed that the policemen were genuine.

But the sergeant assured the neighbour, "It's ok, Ray. I've left the constable in the flat. He'll sort it."

Once inside the police station, the children were placed in an interview room to wait for their Uncle. It was dingy and grey with the only natural light squeezing through some glass bricks, and it felt very cold so the desk sergeant organised some hot drinks. He was kindly, and tried to stop Peter from fretting, by talking about the possibility of Sir Matt Busby staying on as the Manchester United manager, or not, and whether their local team, Colchester United, would make it into the third division. It didn't work, Peter never relaxed..

"Sir, we're being set up," stressed Peter. But the desk sergeant was not going to talk about it, instead just confirmed that the duty solicitor was on his way. And when the duty solicitor arrived, he advised them that he was on the case, but would need to wait for their uncle to arrive before talking to them. Shame they couldn't just phone their uncle, but mobile phones were still a long way into the future! But Katie kept her happy face on, as one would expect from our God.

Then, at last, the PC and Uncle were picked up from the flat, and driven to the station.

The solicitor, Uncle Steven and the two children sat around the table in the interview room, and looked at the case from all directions.

The solicitor explained, "You haven't been charged with anything at this point in time. But it looks almost certain that you will be, Peter. I don't think they'll charge you, Katie, but we have to be prepared for it if you are. Now, at around about nine thirty in the evening, the offices in Ipswich were broken into by one single individual. A bag of precious objects were taken, and.."

"Stop!" Katie put her finger into the air, "*Allegedly* taken."

"Thank you, Katie. Allegedly taken. But we must be careful here not to look as though we are treading water, by making suggestions such as 'allegedly'. Why would they make it up?"

"Because," whispered Katie, "of what they are. You don't know what they're accusing us of, do you? Do the police know what it is that we are being accused of taking?"

"Yes. You are accused of taking a bag of samples which originated from below the surface of the New Bury colony. Apparently quite valuable, although we haven't been given a value."

Katie laughed, and bit her lip. "So the police don't even know what we're supposed to have taken?" She stood up. "I'm gonna tell them what John Hutney is after, and what this is all about. Do you think I should?" The solicitor looked at Peter and Steven, and raised his eyebrows. "Right, I will. I'll tell you. The bag that Hutney wants from us had twenty two marble sized balls of izaline, and about fifty smaller ones. Do you know what izaline is?" The solicitor closed his eyes in disbelief, and then nodded. "Don't know what they're worth, probably four or five million. They're worth a lot more now than they would've been just a couple of weeks back."

The solicitor asked why.

Katie suddenly realised that the world did not know about the implosion of the planet. Man doesn't know everything! So, it was back to the drawing board for Katie and Catherine. She looked hard at Peter, and he could sense that she was saying that they needed to talk.

He took the hint and requested, "Sir, could we have a little time alone. We have some personal issues to sort out, regarding our defence."

"I wouldn't advise keeping things from me. If the suspected crime really has that level of value, they'll put a lot of resources into this case."

Katie assured him, "And so will we."

The solicitor, set aback by the children's confidence and intellect, agreed to give them some space. "Half an hour?"

Katie stressed to Peter, "I have work to do, but I don't need to do it until the spring. But this Hutney bloke is powerful, and so is his company. So, I'm gonna get it sorted." She held her tiny hand on Peter's. "My children are misbehaving, as they always do, but this time it's threatening to hurt my own personal God. That's not gonna happen."

"Please don't do anything stupid. Not for me."

"I'll do what Hutney's doing, that's all. Just stick with me and we'll be ok." She grinned at Uncle. "And I'll get you the money he owes you, Uncle. That'll keep you going for a while." She closed her eyes and relaxed.

The solicitor returned after the thirty minutes.

"Right, hope you've sorted your issues. I've got the full rundown on the accusations. Peter, where were you on April tenth, between eight and ten pm?"

"I was asleep, on the ship back from the colony."

"I've checked with the shipping company, and there is no record of that."

"What about the guard house records, when we got in? They can confirm that we got off the ship."

"They also have no records of your arrival. That puts them in a strong position, wouldn't you say?"

"No, not really. Even if they lie their way through, and you all believe them, I still haven't stolen anything. What have I stolen?"

"Katie said, marbles of izaline."

Katie grinned at Peter, and he responded, "She *never* said that. Who's side are you on? She said that Hutney is *after* a bag of izaline marbles. She never said that I *took* it." He huffed, "So, are you on our side?"

He smiled, "Of course. Right, why is he after the marbles?"

Peter continued, "I think, because he is broke, and also because he is a shit-head and liar. Uncle Steven showed him the bag of izaline last night when he was at ours. That's why he's after it, because he knows that we have it. And, you need to ask the police where our other marble is, the one they took off the burglar. It must be returned to us, as it was stolen from us."

"I'll check that one out. So you think Hutney is lying? Why should anybody believe that? He is one of the most respected businessmen in the country."

"I bet he's almost broke. Do you know how he's made his money? By stealing and cheating. He still owes Uncle half his money from the mining work. Get him his money, now, and we might just talk a bit more about the izaline on the colony."

The solicitor grudgingly left the room to contact John Hutney, and eventually returned with a smile. "I have got through to him, and, to show that I am on your side, told him to bring cash for your uncle. And he is on his way, personally. He's only coming from Ipswich, so he'll not be long. Now, if you did not steal the marbles, how did you come by them? I take it you still have them."

Peter looked to Katie, who nodded. He answered, "We were gifted them, whilst on the colony. One of the so-called monsters gave them to Katie."

"But your uncle is celebrated. He killed the last of the monsters."

"No. He killed the mother of the last monsters but was not able to kill her children. They became good friends to us, after the ship came home and so leaving us on our own. Mo gave them to Katie." He realised, "Don't tell anybody that Uncle couldn't kill the children, not until he's got his bonus from Hutney."

The solicitor raised his eyebrows at Steven, who then suggested, "Believe *everything* the children tell you, or go!"

Peter continued, "Mo was to be one as one with Stumpy, but they gave their lives and heritage to my little sister, because they loved her and believed in her. So Katie had Mo and she became strong again. And then the ship picked up on the distress signals. They picked us up."

"What do you mean, Katie had Mo?"

"Once his life had drained, she ate him."

"Do you expect me to believe all this, and stand up in a magistrate's court and repeat it?"

Peter promptly replied. "Yes, otherwise, as Uncle has suggested, go. Make your mind up now because I want to clear my name with the truth. My twin would never forgive me for lying."

"I'm sorry. I will try to understand what you've been through." He thought for a few seconds. "How did you eat him, Katie? Was it Mo you ate?"

She answered, "Yes, I ate Mo. Stumpy, his twin brother, butchered the body, and Peter and Stumpy helped me to sit up so I could eat him. It was fantastic." She giggled a bit. "What I really wanted afterwards, was some wild sex with my space-man. But the time wasn't right for him." She winked at Peter, who went bright red. "But that's not for the record."

The solicitor coughed and cleared his throat. "Ok. For the record, who is your twin brother, Peter?"

"It's Stumpy. He's like adopted as my twin. We are very alike. Sorry, we were. He's dead now."

"And how did he die?"

Peter looked at Katie for support. "Can you answer that, Sis?"

She obliged. "When I removed the dying planet, as I had promised God Edward, he died. Everything died, that which hadn't already been killed by Hutney. Stumpy died, and Edward moved."

Peter raised his eyebrows in question.

With a sarcastic tinge, the solicitor asked, "And how did you remove the planet?"

"I made the core, which was predominantly caskin, vibrate, and it over-heated very quickly. The unbelievably intense heat caused the molecular mass of the core to alter, and the increased pull of the gravity, which resulted, prevented expansion of the core outwards, so it reacted by expanding inwards. It disappeared. Understand?"

The solicitor fiddled with his pen. Then he stood up. "I don't understand." He walked out of the room.

"He'll be back," chuckled Katie. "He's a good man."

They waited and waited. Poor Peter, who had the patience of a fourteen year old, began to grumble. "He'll be back? I don't reckon."

But then the door opened. He was back!

"I'm sorry about that. I had to have a fight with my conscience." He respectfully bowed his head to Katie. "I have enquired about the marble which was found with the burglar. There was no marble. And there was no burglary. *But* when I phoned my friend at the vicarage, he confirmed that there *was* a burglary." He sighed, and sat down. "Your outrageous explanations of what has happened are beginning to intrigue me. So let's go a bit deeper into the subject of New Bury."

Katie grinned and suggested, "Let's all give Stumpy the respect that he deserves, and tell the truth, the whole truth, and nothing but. Now where were we?"

The solicitor continued, "Apparently you never went to the colony with your uncle. You disappeared, and the social services are interested in returning you to the school. What have you to say about that, Steven?"

Steven sighed heavily. "Something terrible is going on here. Surely the staff on the ship will remember the children. They even loaned us a wheelchair for Katie."

"Yes," jumped Peter, "And took it back when they picked us up. They'll all remember us."

"I can make further investigations, but so far, everybody claims that you never went to the colony with your uncle."

Katie grinned at Peter, "Perhaps Old Dick would vouch for us." She then began to giggle. "But, I know, you want to do this the honest way. Carry on, mister solicitor."

After faltering a little, the solicitor restarted. "Katie, you say that you made the planet disappear. Where was Peter at the time?"

"He was asleep. But he says that he watched it with Stumpy. Is that right, Bruv?"

Peter turned his nose up, but nodded. He wasn't too sure.

"But, Katie, the planet is still there. That's what the Company claims."

"It's almost impossible to detect the planet from Earth, it's the other side of their sun. When they next go in that direction, they'll notice it by its absence. It's gone, never to return."

"But if I have to stand in court and tell the bench that you made an entire planet disappear, they'll put me in the cell next to you. It just isn't realistic."

Katie put her hand on her head. "I'll say this as much for Peter as for his defence. Right, the Planet disappeared, from sight. It didn't change into nothing, it just moved inside itself, as its ever increasing gravity put its own structure into implosion mode. The constantly changing molecular mass was pulling everything into the centre and there was no other way to relieve the inward pressure except to move further inwards. It sort of went next door, squeezing into another vacant space, in another universe. And everything living will be gone, but the basic ingredients will still be there. I will, as promised to Edward, help him to rebuild his planet, and to develop the life forms that he so desires."

The solicitor just stared at Katie. He wanted to laugh, but couldn't, so he just stared.

Katie tried to pull him back to ground. "They won't believe a word of it, will they. So, *don't* tell them any of it. Let them find out the hard way, and let's keep all of Peter's defence in line with the accusations. That is, Peter's theft from the Golden Circle Mining Company. We were at the colony, and we brought back some izaline, which was gifted to us by the owner. That's all we need to concentrate on. And if you can't get justice to prevail, then I will. Peter will *not* be framed by John Hutney. Got that?" The wrath of an eight year-old child, beware!

The solicitor eventually nodded his acceptance, and left the room to make further enquiries, but he returned after just a few minutes, with John Hutney. Peter, Katie and Steven looked sternly at the man who was trying to frame the lad.

"Good evening. I came as quickly as I could, with Steven's cash. I don't know what went wrong with his payment, but please accept my apologies. There's an extra five hundred in there, as a sign of good will between us. After all, you *are* a hero." He was an accomplished liar and con-man.

"Thank you." Uncle Steven swooned over the extra money, but kept his cool. "The other things you need to apologise for, are your obnoxious lies about my nephew. But you'll have a fight; we won't lie down."

"We'll see. If, for some fluke, you are not found guilty of theft, you will still have to return my property. I have all the mineral rights to the colony of New Bury."

Katie butted in. "We know all that. We mentioned it last night, remember? And izaline is *not* a naturally occurring mineral on New Bury; indeed it's not even a mineral. It's a biogenic material, and forms the endoskeleton of certain creatures on the colony, and you have been destroying the living form of the izaline ever since you first began mining for it. It occurs only where the skeleton has died and reacted with the caskin in the atmosphere, or where the creatures have had a poo, and the excretia is exposed to the caskin. Varying amounts of izaline are found in their poo, and it quite quickly liquefies, as their skeletons do, and becomes a liquid which is so hard and so beautiful that materialistic creatures such as yourself resort to extreme measures just to own it. Your mineral rights do not extend to the creatures who roam the lands." She looked hard, to make sure he was taking it all in but he was a clever man, and he was missing nothing. Katie continued, "In fact, Peter and I watched some ferocious creatures of the sea, some of which have izaline skeletons, but the dead are never left in the atmosphere for long enough for their skeletons to form into the stable form of izaline, you know, the pretty stuff. As things die on New Bury they are consumed very quickly by the bacteria, seldom having time to oxidise with the caskin in the air. We had to burn our friend's skeleton to make sure the bacteria couldn't attack it before it oxidised. It became a complete skeleton made of pure izaline. A beautiful sight. And there are millions of the sea creatures on the colony, with izaline skeletons. Millions."

John Hutney gasped. Greed was taking over.

"So, despite what you think, izaline on the colony is *very* common. Or potentially it is. But if it's not exposed to the caskin soon enough, it is very quickly disposed of by the many bacteria on the colony. Edward always kept a clean and tidy world, and he is one of the leading experts in bacteriology. He's even better than me!"

Well, how about that? The solicitor was scribbling notes like there was no tomorrow, and Hutney was swooning in the trough of greed.

"So, why don't you leave my brother alone, and go off to get that mineral rights lease checked out. Because you don't legally own *any* of the izaline."

He thought very seriously, pacing up and down and scratching his chin, and then, "So if we brought some of these fish back here and bred them, we could create izaline from their skeletons?"

"I could. *You* probably couldn't."

"Who else?"

Katie grinned at Peter, and winked. "Nobody else outside of this room knows anything about izaline. Honest, guv. And we don't even need the fish. I could create the raw material from some of the very soft hardwood timbers, which are genetically quite close to the skeletons of the New Bury creatures." She began to laugh.

"Hope you're not taking the piss, child. I'm not a good loser."

That made her really chuckle. "You'd better start practicing then. Cos if you take me on, you'll lose." She moved around the table to Peter, and gave him a big kiss on the lips. "Come on, let's go. Mister solicitor, we're going, and this bloke's not gonna try to stop us. If you need us, we'll be back in Boxted. Toodle-loo!"

They left a shocked solicitor and John Hutney in the room, but the desk sergeant snapped, "Where are you three going?"

Katie held one of Peter's hands, and one of Steven's. She snarled, "You should all be ashamed of yourselves. Letting a wanker like him control you." She turned her nose up. "But we're going home, now." And before the desk sergeant could say anything. "Phone your chief constable! My friend has recently spoken to him."

He did exactly that. He walked them to the exit. "I'm very sorry about the misunderstanding. I'll get a car to take you home."

Peter and Steven were both relieved to get home.

"Why did everything change so quickly?" asked Steven.

"Catherine contacted Ca'an, who got the Chi Bantri to sort it."

Peter asked, "Why? We were getting to him, and the solicitor. And you said the Chi Bantri are vile, and dangerous, and are your enemies. Why?"

"They are vile, and dangerous, and the most powerful society ever known, but they're *not* my enemies. They're my children. You all are." Tired and deflated, they all went to bed.

Katie, as always, stayed awake as the rest of the world slept.

She thought, *'what am I doing? This isn't in my plans.'*

An east London thought came back in response, *'you're lookin' after yer boyfriend'.* It was Catherine. *'He's all you've gotta worry about at the mo'. Ninah and Cat' are doing good, so you don't have to get to Anglia til the spring. Chill out.'*

Katie grinned to herself, and then walked over to the front window. There were three cars parked on the greensward; a pretentious white Rolls Royce convertible, and two Triumph

2000s with press badges on the doors. *'Catherine, do you think they'll kill Peter? They're starting to turn up, as I thought they would. There's three cars outside; press, and one with Hutney and his mates inside.'* She bit her bottom lip, and asked, *'should I kill them?'*

'No. But we'll have to get rid of them. D'you know why Stumpy told you to bring the flippin' izaline here? Seems a pointless source of stress, cos those bleedin' lot outside are only after you for the izaline.'

Katie chuckled, *'I think it was something like you sending me to the colony. It's a learning curve. He wanted to be like Peter, and Peter would give everything if he had to. Stumpy thought he would be giving us a wonderful life, by making us rich, but he's simply started a war. That's one theory. The other is that he actually wanted that war, goading me to carry out his retribution against the people who destroyed his home. Can't blame him, he's as daft as I was before Peter taught me about real beauty.'*

'Just fought he might 'ave a motive. And I fink the second feory is looking favourite, can't blame 'im for wanting revenge. Perhaps it makes things easier.' Catherine stopped momentarily. *'There's a communications man who works for the Golden Circle Mining Company. Ca'an wants him in her team. He's brilliant, but has a conscience, and no uncontrollable greed, and he's young enough to see the project through. He'll definitely fit the bill for the satellite development. 'fraid the other bloke we spoke about last night has turned 'is toes up.''* Then there was another noticeable silence. *'And Hutney's 'ad that solicitor done. He was crushed to death as he walked out of the kop station. We'll 'ave to watch Peter and Steven. I know what you'll end up like if they do Peter.'*

Katie shrugged her shoulders. *'If it comes to it, the Chi Bantri can do a bit more for their revered Princess Ca'an. We'll get Ca'an to sort it, if it comes down to a physical fight.* She laid back into the armchair. *'I'm ok now. I'm not gonna cry again for a long time. I love you for being my conscience, and for sending me on leave with such an accomplished teacher. He taught me about human emotions. I didn't know they could be so tender, so loyal.''* A tear began to grow from the corner of her eye.

'Not for a long time,' reminded Catherine. She logged off, leaving Katie staring at their potential assassins.

The sun arose, and Peter climbed out of bed. "Hi Katie. Want some toast?" She shook her head. As she did the morning sun reflected off one of the car windscreens into her flowing blond hair, momentarily shining like a halo around her smile. It reminded Peter of who she was. "I'm scared, Sis. Cuddle me?" She almost jumped into his arms. He kissed her cheek, and shakily uttered, "It's all right for you, you're God."

She sighed and looked into his face. "And so are you. *My* God."

They remained in a loving embrace for many minutes, until they were disturbed from their union by the door. It was banging!

Peter asked, "Should I answer it? Will it go away if I don't answer it?"

She shook her head.

"Better do it, then. What they gonna do to me?"

"Nothing. They want me. Me and Catherine have spoken, and we have made some provisions. Some yesterday, but we had to make a few adjustments overnight." She stroked his cheek. "If I have to go against Catherine, to help you, I will. She knows that. And it's *all* her fault, for sending me off with you. You know, Pete, you almost made me human, my little cavity-former." Her giggling softened the blow. "Pity, ain't it? Real pity."

Uncle eventually emerged from his cocoon to answer the door. It was Hutney and two of his men. "Morning, Steven. Can we come in?"

He looked at Katie, and then with a dignified smile, replied, "No. You're not welcome here. Fuck off."

"That's not sensible." He pushed his foot against the door. "It would be *fucking* stupid."

"Let the old shitter in, Uncle," sighed Peter, who suspected that Katie was in control. "We'll sort him out. He's nobody."

Hutney entered, but left his two men outside. "You're not playing our game, little girl."

Katie hugged her God, and stressed, "*My* game. It's all *my* game. D'you wanna know the rules before we start?" She started to laugh, which annoyed him. She huffed, "But those reporters outside had better come in before we start. The press *love* all this sort of shit."

Hutney was becoming agitated, and he beckoned in one of his own men. "This man will sort it if I need him to. He'll be heading the project."

"Sort what?" Katie struggled to her feet, standing slightly twisted with her deformed legs and spine and then stepped over to Hutney's man. She looked up into his eyes and found something. "Do you know who I am, sir?" she very politely asked. "I can see some good in you. You should use it. If you don't, then you'll be sentenced to death, just like this prat. He's already sentenced to death, for his part in the killing of the New Bury colony, and for his murder of Mr Bradshaw, our solicitor. Did you know that he killed Mr Bradshaw?" She raised her eyebrows, and pierced his eyes.

He looked at Hutney, and then back to Katie. "Are you really?" The big man seemed very gentle. "Can you prove it?"

"If I needed to prove who I am, then I wouldn't be Him." She said no more.

John Hutney got the topic back on line. "Right, child, we need to work together on this." Hutney was too far up his own arsehole to realise what was going on. "If we can get some of those fish back here, would you work with me to create the izaline? Like partners?"

She sneered, "Fuck off. Don't you understand?"

He looked at his man, and asked him, "What's she on about, now?"

He frowned. "I don't think you've been listening to this little girl. She says that you've been sentenced to death."

Hutney was lost for words, but managed to find some desperate ones. "Then sort it. Earn your fucking wages for once."

The man didn't move a muscle, but just stared at his boss, wondering what was to come next. He then looked at Peter and Katie, and then Steven, bowed his head and left the flat.

Katie grinned at Hutney. "He's gone. He's not as evil as you, so he's gone, exactly as he was told to. Now, about this izaline, I'll give you a choice between working for the good of the unfortunate children in East Pakistan and Vietnam, who have lost everything, including their parents and family, or you can die slowly and painfully. It's a good offer. One which you wouldn't normally get, but because my lovely Peter wills it, I'm prepared to be a humanitarian. I think you should just die, but he thinks you should repay mankind for your greed. You know Hutney, me and my darling make a strong couple, you know, like little and large, the good and the evil, the scales of justice, like prosecution and defence, like chalk and cheese, like give and take, like ...."

"Shut it! You're nutters!" He went to the front door, and called his other man in. "Brown's gone mad and walked off. Now, explain to this girl what we're going to do, and how she *will* help us."

The man looked nervous and reminded Hutney, "Sir, the press are outside. *We* can't do anything, and *they* can't be bought." The two cars belonged to the Orb Alliance News group, one of the global concerns which are influenced by the Chi Bantri sect. They were bound to look out for their revered princess's 'little sister'. And they didn't even know it.

Katie hugged Peter. "I'm tired of this. My real plan is soon to be back on line." She beckoned Hutney to sit down while they waited, and for his man to leave the building.

"What are we waiting for?"

She smiled. "We're waiting for the police and the social services. Peter has partly won and we're doing some of it his way, and some of it my way. Which way do you want to go? Death, or repayment to mankind."

The bumptious man just smiled at her.

"Would you like a mint?" She offered over a bag of strong mints, and he took one. She spoke very slowly and deliberately. "You know Hutney, for a man who has built a reputation for spontaneity, bold decisions and risk-taking, you pondered dangerously. You took so long to make a decision on your future, that you've lost the options. You've defaulted to death." She began to grin. "As you already know, all the miners who came back from the colony died from rotten livers, poisoned by caskin, quite quickly. It's an unpleasant way to die, much worse than your crushing murder of poor Mr Bradshaw. And you knew that the miners would all die from it, but you still sent them out there without warning. You knew that you were killing them. All of them."

He shrugged, "Everybody goes to work, and we all face work related dangers. So get to your bloody point."

"Well, because you've never had a sleepless night over it, I'll not have any either." She fidgeted in Peter's arms. "While we're on our own, I'll explain why Stumpy gave me the izaline. I've worked it out, and it's been a really good game, Stumpy, if you're listening." She laughed as she settled down into Peter's arms. "The boys really loved a good game. It was all they did. Anyway, he sent me back with the izaline knowing that its value would start a war. And he was right. He also knew that I would never lose such a petty war. And he was right. He also knew that the izaline would be hidden so well that nobody would ever find it. And he was right. He also knew that another option was to create the izaline right here on Earth, but then it would be so common that it would be worthless. And he was right. He also knew that Old Dick's tablets of caskin are so dangerous that a human would never recover from the affects of ingesting one. And he was right. And he knew that, after all this, no humans would go in search of izaline, ever again. And he was right. And he knew that the tablets of caskin taste ever so much like strong mints. And he was right, wasn't he, Hutney?" She wriggled about. "Do they taste good? Hey? Do they? Hey?" Her head was by then swaying around as she grinned at the shocked man. "Do you like the taste of caskin? Stumpy's revenge! Lovely, hey Pete?" She giggled as Peter began to smile. "It's a much better game than the burying one, and usually has the same ending. Good old Stumpy!" She dropped her smile, momentarily. "Probably get a bollicking from Catherine for that. But what the hell." Her head flopped down onto Peter's shoulder, as she watched a shocked John Hutney slowly walk out of the flat, and as the lovely sparkling Rolls Royce screeched away, probably to the Essex County Hospital emergency ward. Katie sank a little lower, contented.

Peter could feel her sinking lower. Uncle asked what was happening.

"It's all right, boys. We just need to go back into hiding for a while, until I can get over to Anglia with Ninah and Ca'an. Hope you can come, Pete, in the spring. But now I'm going back into hibernation."

The police arrived, asking after John Hutney, who was required for questioning for some reason or other, and then the social services arrived, asking after Peter. The police looked around the property, asked the reporters some questions, and then went off in search of the dying man, while the social services let themselves into the flat.

One of the middle-aged ladies sat down like on old frump, and stated, "Steven Knaseby, you took your nephew out of his reform school under the pretence that you were taking him to a better place. You went off without him, leaving him to fend for himself and for his sister. We need to ask why."

Poor Steven put his head in his hands, and said nothing.

"May I answer on Uncle's behalf?" asked Peter. "He's been under tremendous stress, and is not well." The frump nodded. "Well, he got onto the ship, waiting for us to arrive by cab, but we never turned up. And the plank suddenly raised, without us on board. Well, we were stuck in the traffic, and couldn't let Uncle know, but when the plank was raised it was too late for him to leave. And it was too late for us to get on. The ship left without us. Please don't blame him." He had such pitiful look as he tried to suck the iron-faced social worker in. "He's a hero, you know. Killed the last of the terrible monsters, all on his own and almost certainly saved the lives of his brave miner pals, so please don't treat him like a 'nam war veteran."

The woman was made of iron, but empty. "I've got no interest in what he did on that colony, just that he left his wards, you two, alone. Whatever his excuse….."

"We weren't alone!" Katie snapped. "Our bestest friend Stumpy has been watching over us for all this time. God has watched over us."

The woman smirked, "Doesn't look like God has done too bad a job." She looked at Steven. "I'm going to have to take Peter back into the care of the school, until he's sixteen. Mr Knaseby, I suspect you may need some help with your niece. I'll arrange for you to visit her old clinic. See how she is."

Peter packed a bag, and shed a tear for his sister and uncle. "I'll get to see you as often as I can, Sis. Please look after Uncle. And your book."

Peter and Katie held each other tightly as the boy cried, but she smiled at him. "You know, my little God, I'll always be with you. Come and see me on my blanket, and let me know how the boys are getting. Cos I know you'll dream of them, often."

"Don't get bedsores on the blanket, and look out of your shell *every* day."

They sniffled together, but before she would let him go, she had to pluck his sweet tears with her lips, "Yummy. Pure ambrosia."

18 -- THE BIG LEAP FORWARD

Katie quickly slipped back into her shell, her body becoming uncontrollable and weak. She was taken back to the clinic to spend some time on her blanket. *'Hey, Catherine, I'm back at the clinic. I'll stay here until I go to join Ca'an and Ninah.'* Catherine returned, *'That's cushty, we've got a forty year project to get planned. I'll keep me eye on Peter an' Steven. An' Ninah is getting well down near the Indian border with the refugees. Somefink will soon 'ave to break. Good job, as they've used the American's scorched earf policy near Chittagong, and there's a Captain Plassey causing big shit, an' guess who he is. He's tipped as the next Monsignor at the Anglian Fort. We'll all just follow 'im all the way down there.'* They both giggled together, from a distance. God had finally returned, as one apart.

Peter went back to the approved school, and much of life seemed lost to him. He was back where he was, and so was his sister, but at least he finally understood her, and that love that they had shared in the colony would live on forever. He lay on his bed, thinking, *'I'm glad I did it all. If I do nothing else, those couple of months have given me something that most other people never find. Not sure what it is, but I've found it.'*

He was summoned to the headmaster's office. As he walked past the other boys he felt an uncomfortable air, one of fear, or expectation, and as he passed the four bullies, including Jonesy, he could sense a virtual cauldron of blood and despair. It reminded him of the sea creatures as they tore each other apart in a frenzy of feeding. He was probably letting his mind wander a little too far.

"Sit down Peter. I would say that it's lovely to have you back, but I doubt that somewhat. I need to keep tabs on you, so let's start as we mean to carry on. I am the Head, and you are in here because the courts sent you here. When you are sixteen you can leave, and that's about eighteen months away. So, eighteen months of good behaviour. Got it?"

Peter frowned at the Head. He had had a reasonable relationship with him before going away. The occasional fight. But that was always in defence of his little pal Stuart. "What's changed, Sir? Has Hutney got to you?"

The Head grinned. "I've read about him. He's going to jail, it seems."

Peter thought about it, but kept his quiet.

"No, I know you've been accused of something which I for one would never believe, but no." He suddenly looked uncomfortable, playing with his pen. "Stuart isn't here anymore."

Peter looked towards the window. "Why?"

"Well." He coughed. "I'm afraid he committed suicide. He hung himself."

Peter just shook his head. He tried to speak, but just whimpered, and his eyes became flooded with grief. He put his elbows on his knees and his head in his hands, and cried. Everything was slipping away, everything. Eventually he asked, "Why did you let him? Why?"

"How could I stop him? I wish I could, but…."

"*Bollocks*! You said you'd look after him. You'd stop them bullying. *Why* didn't you?" He stood up and ran out of the office. "Fucking bastards! Come here! I'm gonna fucking kill you all!" He ran around the school grounds screeching and threatening, and came to a halt at the front gates. He never crossed the boundary line, but just flopped down and cried his heart out. Then he suddenly screamed out, "Where was fucking *God* when he needed her? Wish I'd never met you.

Piss off to fucking India! You're not doing any good here so fuck off!" He suddenly remembered having all the same feelings when he finally lost his little sister, when Stumpy bluntly blurted it out. He whispered, "Sorry, Sis. So sorry, I didn't mean it. Please stay." He curled up in the middle of the gateway and sobbed. Life was hard for God's moon-dreamer, her little pinky-tickler, her rampant pussy-packer, her space-man, her adopted conscience, her God. But then he thought of her book. Poor Stuart was just one of millions every week. The people in East Pakistan right at that moment, and the children of the Ukraine, dobbing in their own parents for food. But they didn't kill themselves, they fought on. "Is that all you are, Sis? Just faith." He broke from his sobbing and began to smile. "That *is* all you are, blind faith." He sighed, "Wish you were here for me now, cos when faith is all that's left, I'm going with Stuart. I know you're listening, but wish I could cuddle you. You could talk dirty to me, like when you were in your naughty mood, and you could drink my sweetest tears, and giggle. And just giggle, and giggle. Funny ain't it. You went off to discover something you knew nothing about, love, and I had to come right back here to discover what I didn't know about, faith." His forrid creased as he frowned. "But why didn't you give Stuart some faith? Is it because you're a fraud? People are shit scared of God, but I'm not, I know what she is. She's just faith. That's all you are." A smile crept in. "And, of course, a sexy little kitten." He looked around, in case somebody was listening. "Be good if we weren't brother and sister. Could get married, and have a sister for Catan. She'd love that, a little baby sister." The tears slowly returned, so he got up and stealthily made his way back to his dorm. Nobody approached him.

Knock, knock. "Who's there?"

"I'm Jenny, the housekeeper. I've got something for you."

Peter opened the door, and the pretty young lady presented him with a transistor radio.

"Wow. Where's that from?"

"A little girl and her three friends delivered it. She said you asked for it."

"Sis. Brilliant!" Then he realised that Katie was in the clinic. "Who was it?"

"She said that she's your girlfriend's twin sister. Had a funny London accent, but beautiful grey-green eyes, which seemed so hypnotic.

Catherine! He plugged it in and sat on the bed searching for stations. "God, I almost met Catherine. God's *real* conscience." But the radio quickly took over his resources and he forgot all about Catherine, and Stuart and Katie. His old favourite Radio Caroline had ceased broadcasting, but he managed to find Luxembourg. "Brilliant. Just brilliant."

He lay on his bed, listening to the hits of April 1971, drowning his conscious mind in the music and the lyrics. He floated off to another dimension. Ringo Starr wafted in with 'It Don't Come Easy'. "Yes, I like that," Peter whispered to his radio, and then the next tune rolled in. It was 'Brown Sugar' and he pulled his lips out as far as they could go as he accompanied Mick Jagger and the Stones. Then, through the crackly music came a quiet voice.

"Peter." It was feint, but he could make out his name. Then, "Peter." It was *definitely* his name, behind the music.

He asked the radio, "Who's there?" He listened hard.

"It's me." It was a strained whisper.

Peter began to get frisky. "Who's me? This a game?"

"If you want. Who do you think it is?"

He spoke into the radio, "I know who I hope it is. Is it Stuart?"

The radio answered, "No, stupid," but then the track ended and there was silence.

Peter almost wet himself straining to hear the voice again. But the DJ finally shut up and another track began; 'Indiana Wants Me'. "Well, you still there?"

The radio answered, "Not going nowhere."

With baited breath, Peter asked, "Are you Stumpy?" He waited for a reply.

"Who's Stuart. Can I meet him?"

"No. Now are you Stumpy? You've got his voice."

"Of course I'm Stumpy. I'm your twin brother."

Peter was totally enchanted, and floating. "Can we talk every day?"

"Don't know. Maybe."

"Well, as often as possible." Peter began to giggle. "Can all twin brothers do this, you know, contact each other? It's like a dream. Will you visit every day? Please."

"Lot's of bloody questions. But I've got one for you, because I'm getting worried about your state of mind."

"Go on, then. Anything. Ask me *anything*."

"Ok." A moment silence, and then he asked very deliberately, "Why are you talking to that bloody radio?"

Then, a hand banged down on Peter's shoulder and he screeched, and almost hit the ceiling. He swung around. It was him!

"Stumpy!"

They almost flew, and then tried to squash the life out of each other.

"I can't believe it. It's you. High five!" They fived, but somebody started banging on the door.

"What' going on?" It was the housekeeper.

Peter flew into bed, as she opened the door.

"What's the noise?" She looked around the room.

He whimpered, "Sorry, miss. I had a nightmare. I thought one of those ghastly monsters from the colony was in here." He hid his grin. "They're *horrible*."

"Oh, poor Peter. Come here." She sat down on the bed, and pulled him to her chest. Wow, his head was snuggled right between her firm breasts, and they were warm, with a slight smell of fresh perspiration. He wanted to suck them. "Is that better? Poor dear."

"Almost. A bit longer, and I'll be better." He was in heaven, but suddenly he noticed through the dark a big white set of teeth grinning at him from between the wall and the wardrobe, and a thumbs up. He asked her, "Will you come back if I have another one, miss?" His voice was pathetic, and begging. "Please."

"I'll be back later. Now settle down." The young lady, no more than about twenty, pulled his covers up and gave him a kiss, right on the lips. "Sleep tight, honey." She quietly left.

"Wowee, Peter," Stumpy whispered, loudly. "I think your gonna shag tonight."

Peter gaped his mouth open. "What do I do? I bet she's had loads."

Stumpy sat on the bed and tried to wink, but, as usual, failed. "Well, do as your mummy told you when we were around the campfire. Lay back, and think of England. It stops you shooting too early."

"Does it? Hey you, she told me that in private."

"Nothing's private with me, pal. You're me brother."

They lay down on the bed just pondering their lives, and wondering what the hell they were going to do, with a ten foot tall monster in their bedroom. Stumpy hadn't thought of that. And where was Stumpy going to go when the housekeeper came back for her nightcap.

"You're not watching me. I won't be able to get it up if you're watching."

"I'll shut my eyes. Honest guv." Stumpy grinned. "I can help you out if you get lost."

"Piss off!" Teenagers don't share, not in that department. "Anyway, you haven't got a knob."

"I was just thinking of pointing out where the honey pot is, because you've never been there."

Just as Peter was about to explode, he remembered who he was with; the last member of a civilisation which did nothing but play. "Guess you'll just have to shut your eyes, and keep quiet."

They both relaxed on the bed, Stumpy with his feet hanging over the end, waiting for a knock on the door. The sun rose, and still no knock. Peter was feeling dejected.

"I'm not going to care, cos I've got my old mate back. Nothing else matters right now."

"Sorry, mate, but I think she's too old for you anyhow. What we going to do today?"

Back to pondering about a boy in an approved school harbouring a dangerous monster from a far away planet. Stumpy would have to stay in the room, all day, while Peter went to his classes. That seemed a good plan. But Peter luckily remembered that the housekeeper always enters his room, just to check the state, and Stumpy would not be able to hide beside the wardrobe during the daylight hours.

"It's only quarter to six. You'll have to get out and hide in the woods before anybody else gets up." And so that was the final plan. Peter led the giant by the hand through the school grounds, and over the fence. "Keep a low profile in those trees. I'll be back when it's getting dark." Stumpy slipped into the thick woodlands. It was a mixture of pine and chestnut, developing over the years a clean but peaty forest floor. Stumpy dug himself into the ground and waited, totally invisible from the surface.

Half a day later, Peter went in search of his mate. After checking for dog-walkers he loudly whispered, "Stumpy. I'm back." He heard some rustling, and peered through the trees. As he did, a ghostly figure sat up out of the ground, grinning from ear-to-ear, and the soil fell away from him. "You're ok. Thank God." They crept off deeper into the woods to ensure privacy, and sat in conference. Peter began. "Now, I've got a plan, not much of one, but it's a plan. I've got to get hold of Uncle. He's our only chance. Once it's dark we can move through these woods, and down into the valley, where there's a lane. That lane comes out on Dedham Road, and just up on the bend there's a phone-box there, and it's quiet, not many houses. We'll have to hope that Uncle is in the Wig, having a beer, cos that's the only place I can think of phoning to talk to him. You still with me?"

"Always. It's a good adventure so far." Stumpy jigged his shoulders with the excitement. "But what's your plan, once you've spoken to Uncle?"

Peter had a big sigh, and then grinned. "No idea. Got any?"

Stumpy put his forefinger on his chin and thought hard. "Same as you. No Idea." He then snapped his fingers. "We could go and live with the wolves in the Belgian Congo, and eat pygmies. Like in your story." He sat with a smug smile on his face. "Got a better one?"

Peter frowned, and punched Stumpy on the arm. "That's for being a clever dick. It's a great idea. Go to somewhere where there's no people. Like the jungle."

"With Mister Wolf? We can help him catch the pygmies, and live happily ever after. Sounds like heaven."

Peter just grinned and chilled out, in the knowledge that his green giant twin was the most innocent and naïve being that he had ever had the pleasure to know. Green all over, including behind the ears. "We'll *maybe* find a wolf to be mates with."

Once it was dark enough to hide their presence, they set out down into the valley, and found the lane. They hurried along the road to the junction, only once having to jump into the hedge while a car passed, and there it was, the telephone box. Peter found the number from directory enquiries. "Stumpy, keep out of site, in case a car comes. And I've only got one shilling, so don't disturb me. This is a one-shot chance."

Their luck was in, and Mrs Hickey got Uncle to the phone.

"Quick, Uncle, you've got to speak to Katie. You won't believe what's turned up. Stumpy!" He managed to get the urgency of the situation across to Steven and some basic arrangements before his money ran out. It was all down to Uncle Steven to come up with the goods.

Having moved back into the woods by the school, they set out their immediate plans. Peter suggested, "You stay here, until we get news from Uncle. All we've arranged is for him to speak to Sis."

Stumpy looked hard into Peter's face. "Is that all? Haven't you got any good ideas?" His voice was sad, maybe disappointed.

But Peter had none, and as he began to realise the predicament that they were both in, a tear appeared in his eye. They had a loving, brotherly cuddle. But Peter had to get back to school as he couldn't take the chance that they would send people out looking for him.

"Keep buried, and I'll see you first thing in the morning, before my classes." He left, and got back into his room, unnoticed. "Please God, Katie. Hear my prayer." He knelt beside his bed, with his bible in his hands. "Please help our bestest friend. He has nowhere in the whole World to go. Nowhere."

He was very, very tired, having had almost no sleep the previous night, and he just drifted into a deep sleep. In his dreams he floated the universe with Katie, and they settled down in a beautiful, green pasture, surrounded by towering trees which kept the world out, and the sun stroked their young bodies with life. And as they sat in their paradise, Katie's mummy approached. Her body floated around the two children, enclosing them in love, and she put her radiant ginger head and emerald face to Peter's, and kissed him. He became mesmerised as he and Katie blended in as one.

Peter woke to the sound of his alarm clock tinkling, and he jumped out of bed with a renewed vigour. "We *can* do it." He crept out and found Stumpy. "We *can* find somewhere where there's no people. I *know* we can. Katie's mummy told me last night."

"Really? That's such good news, Bruv."

"But we've still got to wait for Uncle. Don't know how long for, but you must keep hidden at all times. If they find you, they'll kill you, or put you in a zoo, or cut you up to experiment. And let's hope that Hutney is too dead to get involved. He knows about the izaline."

They had their cuddle, Stumpy towering over the little teenager, did a high five and then split.

Meanwhile, Steven visited the clinic, and Katie. She lay on her blanket like a vegetable.

"Please help us, Katie, if you can. Peter phoned me at the pub, and was terrified about something big. Stumpy is here!"

Her emotionless face slightly changed. Uncle was sure that she smiled, and so he stroked her cheek. She had truly gone back inside her shell.

"Please help us. Peter says the monster will be killed if he's found. I've only met him when they gave me the claw, but I somehow feel that I owe him everything. Please help us."

Katie's grey-green eyes found Steven's, and burned into his mind. He was sure that he heard her say *'I'll speak to Catherine'* but he wasn't sure. Then he heard her say *'Tell the boys I love them. That's all they need to know, right now.'* Poor Uncle was not convinced, until he heard *'Hire a transit. Tomorrow.'*

"I will. I'll get a transit." He gently pulled the lethargic body up and held her to him, her head on his shoulder. "Why? I could've looked after you." And then he heard, from within, *'You are looking after me, by believing in me. You keep my soul alive with belief. You, and billions of others.'*

Although poor Steven was confused, and dying, he finally believed. "I'll do anything you ask. Just help our Peter and make sure he goes to heaven, where he deserves."

Katie managed to smile, but said no more.

Back at the school, Peter received a message. He had a visitor. Nervously, he went to the head's office, and gently knocked. The door opened, and the head stepped outside.

"Peter. There is somebody in my office who says that she has some urgent news about your sister. So I let her in. Would you like me to stay, in case it's bad news?"

Peter shook his head, so the head kindly went off to the classrooms to allow them privacy.

A little blond girl sat in front of the desk, with her back to him. Peter asked, with a shake in his voice, "Who are you?"

She turned around, and wow, she was just like Katie, but perfectly formed. The flowing blond hair, the big grey-green eyes and the grin. "I'm Caferine," she stated. Her voice was soft, but she had a ragged south Essex accent. "I've come to talk." She bit her bottom lip. "Did you get yer radio?"

Peter just stared.

"I'm like me twin ain't I." She giggled. "You can talk. I won't slap ya, honest."

The shock waned, and he sat down beside her. They pulled their chairs around to face each other, and just grinned for a while. Then he asked, "What about Katie? Is she ok."

"Yeah, pucker. She's doin' a loada work on our project plan. So she's happy. She asked me to help yer out over Edward's boy."

But Peter still couldn't believe how alike they were, but for the physical disabilities of Katie. He couldn't stop staring at her.

"Yeah, I can see what yer finking. We are. Exactly the same, but completely different." She chuckled. "We're one. But you know all that, so let's talk about Stumpy. He's in the shit, right up to his eyeballs." She went quiet, looking into Peter's head, with hypnotic effect. He said nothing, but the conversation continued. "Yes, they'll do him in if they find him. We 'ave to get the poor darling out the way." She bit her bottom lip, and then "If you feel more comfy, you can talk."

Peter seemed to wake up. He replied, "Yes I'd like to talk. You can stop raping my mind. Katie wouldn't like that." The two of them shared a grinning session. "You look like Katie. You're lovely."

"Thanks mate. Gayla, sorry Katie, has told me all about yer. Thank you. The whole world owes you a big one."

Peter went a little bit red, and looked down at his feet. "We never did anything."

"Whatever! You did it for me sister." She put her hand on his, and squeezed it. "Stumpy should've stayed with his dad. But he didn't so now we've now gotta sort it." The girl maintained her stare into Peter's eyes and head. "You know what'll happen if they find Stumpy? So they can't. We've gotta make sure of it."

"Can I talk with my mouth?" Catherine grinned at him and nodded. He asked, "Why can't you send him home? You're God. And you're back together, to full strength. Why don't you just send him home?"

"I know. We sit up on our frone and rule with an iron hand. Well, that's what Edward did, and where's he? You lot were made in our own image and we 'ave to let you get on with it, just like we do. It's our law. So what I'm gonna do for yer is influence. Our little girl in Bengal has made some arrangements, and you two can go and live in a solitary area in western Africa. And if anyone sees yer, you'll become legends, like a yeti, or big-foot." She shuffled closer to Peter. As she bit her bottom lip, she moved onto Peter's lap and looking straight into his eyes she asked, "Will you do what's right, when the time comes?"

The young lad, with an even younger girl on his knee, hesitated.

"Stumpy needs to go home, Peter. He can't stay 'ere. All we can do is hide him. Know what I mean?" Peter shook his head. "Well, we can get him to western Africa, but you'll have to look after him. He's your ward, your responsibility. He must never be captured by man. Never."

Peter pulled Catherine to him. "You're just like Katie. Suppose you are Katie, really." They hugged each other. "How many Gods are there?"

"In our domain, only one. Me and Katie." She pulled herself back, enough to see his face, and she laid her hand on his cheek. "I can see why me sister loves yer." She held her hand there for quite a time, until he eventually smiled. She whispered, "I'm sorry fer getting you into this mess. I hope you can fergive me, and still love me sister. It spurs her on." She hesitated. "She'd lost it proper, and then you gave it back."

Peter just carried on smiling into her beautiful face. He almost forgot that it wasn't Katie sitting on his knee, until she broke the moment.

"So you're goin' to western Africa. What you gotta do?"

"I know. I've got to look after Stumpy. I think I'm all he's got. But perhaps we can meet up with mister wolf, and all live happily ever after, dining on Mbuti pygmies."

She chuckled, just like Katie. "That's just a fairy-tale. Sorry." She cocked her head. "Well, the wolf bit is. Just be at the Boxted playing fields, near the fens, at seven tonight."

Catherine kissed Peter goodbye, and the head returned. He asked, "Is everything all right with your sister, Peter? If you want to talk, you can trust me."

Poor Peter was not able to trust anybody apart from his families, the Knasebys and the Qeervys, and he was beginning to realise that Stumpy and Mo's gift of life to Katie was maturing as a repayable debt. And he would have to commit to pay in kind. "I'll do it, Stumpy. I'll give you my life."

He was given the rest of the day off by the head, to relax, and as he lay on his bed, he tried desperately to get to sleep, in the belief that Katie's mum might be waiting, to give him a bit more of her spirit. But he couldn't sleep. He fidgeted, sweated and tossed around as the stress hung heavy over him. He was to give the ultimate gift to Stumpy, in return.

They sat in the wood, excited, but muted.

"Do you know the plan yet?"

Peter shook his head. "I only know part of the plan. My part."

"Tell me?"

He looked up into the giant's eyes. "You gave me and Katie your life of a God, and Mo gave his life. And now you're like me. It's what you always wanted, to be like me. And now, I'm going to be like you. I'm giving you *my* life, 'til the end, the very end. I'll stay with you until the end, and forsake everything else." He laughed as he spoke, but cried. "We'll be one apart, 'til death." He reached up high, and they did a high five. They were a true team.

Peter waited at the end of the poplar trees, looking across the playing field, not really knowing what he was waiting for. Through the twilight he could see children playing on the swings and slide, but nothing else, until a little girl popped out from between the trees.

"What are you doing?" She asked, her long ginger hair blowing in the breeze.

Peter suddenly relaxed, and irresponsibly replied, "Waiting for God. Who are you?"

"I'm Tracy." The eight year old grinned. The eight year old, with brilliant ginger hair, living in Boxted. She stuttered, "You're silly. You won't find God here, this is the playing field."

Peter grinned, and asked her, "What do you want to be when you grow up?"

"A mummy. With lots and lots of children who will all love me, like a mysterious Queen." With that she turned and ran towards home, to the opposite side of the field. Peter giggled at the irony.

At last, with the sun gone, a vehicle entered the field and drove around the perimeter to Peter. It was Uncle, in a red Ford Transit. Peter rushed down to the fens and fetched his mate, and they were away. With Stumpy in the back, hidden from view, they set off, towards their new life in the jungles.

"I've got to drive you to Oxford Street, in London. There's a place there which has not been built long, and it's empty, and that's where you'll hide and then be picked up from. I think the place is very tall, and has been empty for about three years or so. And Katie's girl, or her friends, have organised that, instead of the architect bloke making his monthly visit by helicopter, *you'll* be picked up instead. The world'll just think it's the routine visit." They drove for some time down the A12. "The place is called Centre Point, and the security bloke will let me in, give me some keys, and then go. You've got to go up the lift to the roof, and lock all the doors behind you. You'll be hiding on the roof until the helicopter turns up to collect you. Then you'll be flown to your hiding place in Africa." Uncle was sad that his nephew was leaving. "When we get there, can I look at Stumpy before you leave me?"

Peter stretched over, and held Uncle's arm. "Of course. You might see him on telly, if we get seen in the jungle, and they go looking for the yeti. They'll think he's the yeti. But we'll have to wait to see what the future really has." He sniffed. "I'll be sad to leave you, Uncle. But try not to worry about us. We're gonna stay together for life, whatever happens, cos we're one. 'Til the end of the earth. Well, until death, and that's the real end."

They crawled down Oxford Street, which, even at that time of night, was thronging with tourists, London taxis and buses, and the lights shone from everywhere. Then they saw Centre Point.

"Wow. How can something be so high? Look Stumps." They all admired the concrete skyscraper, which looked down at them like a giant insect's eye, each window simulating a uniform optical cell. The eye of the spider. "We're going up there, Stumps."

They pulled over, and a security man waved them around behind the fountain, and behind another transit.

"This van'll give you some cover. That's the door to go through, and lock every door behind you. And I've been warned, if I see your cargo, I'll get lost. Know what I mean, Guv?" The security man left them to it. They skulked behind the two vans to the open door and went in.

Uncle Steven gasped at his first full sight of Stumpy. Ten feet tall, and dark green with a leathery outer, but an inside like soft putty. He was never designed for the cut-throat environment here on Earth.

They all held each other, and the two humans shed some tears as the lift doors opened. "You must go, now." The doors closed, leaving a broken man to walk away, alone.

They locked everything behind them, as instructed. And there they were, on the roof of one of London's tallest buildings, towering above everything, well, almost everything. They were mesmerised as they looked down on the lights, which shone as far as they eye could see, in every direction, and then as if rising from the cinders of a smouldering fire, they looked across, and upwards, to the BT Tower. Stumpy was astounded at the beauty of the rocket shaped building with its red nose, white cabin windows and the two red rings which sat at the head of the enormous dark shaft. "Did men make all this? They're clever."

Peter had never really noticed any of man's major creations until then and Stumpy's admiration for the smouldering metropolis was catching. "Look, that must be Saint Paul's," he shouted, "and it's nearly as high as us!" They found the blankets which had been placed up there for them and wrapped up. They stood for hours, just watching and maybe dreaming, and the mood changed with the sky as it took on its various light forms. A sight which they were never to see again.

"We'll be in Africa soon. None of this over there."

"Why not?"

Peter grinned. "This is all man. Man is your enemy, and mine, and the *solitude* of the jungle is our future. Take it all in, while you can."

They eventually slept under the stars until the sun rose, as they did. The city looked completely different in the daylight, and the people were out and about early. Oxford Street and Tottenham Court Road were buzzing with life by about six thirty, the millions of humans coming and going in the endless routine of life. As impressive as all it was, it looked more threatening by day.

Stumpy caught something in the distance. He could see an object in the sky which seemed invisible to Peter. "It's probably just a plane," remarked Peter. But the giant never took his eyes off it, and it eventually got close enough for Peter to see. "It's a helicopter!" They suddenly expected. "It's probably ours!" The two of them began jigging about, staring hard at the spot, which was getting larger, and heading their way. As it became clearer their faces screwed up with rapture and they shouted. But it seemed to slow, and turn, and wait.

"He can't see us!" Stumpy began to panic and ran to the corner closest to the helicopter, waving and shouting. The craft turned back towards the tower. "He's seen us, Pete! We're going to Africa! Yeehaaaa!"

But it stopped short of them, and hovered. And as it turned, Peter could see what it was, a Metropolitan Police helicopter. Oh shit!

"Stumpy!" Peter stared at the helicopter and the helicopter stared back. "Please, Stumpy. Come here."

He went to Peter, who put his arms around the waste of his twin and cried. The helicopter slowly edged forward, to get a closer look at the two roof-top intruders, and then turned away.

Stumpy slowly asked, "What's the matter, Bruv? Have I upset you?" Peter carried on crying into his brothers chest. "Please tell me, else I'll start to cry as well." He held Peter tightly for what seemed a very long time, until his brother had reduced to sniffing and sobbing.

"Stumpy. My brother." He was still crying, but smiling, almost in ecstasy. "My adopted twin brother. I've promised to look after you, and look where I've got you. On top of the World, quite literally." He stayed on Stumpy's powerful chest. The tears subsided. "A change of plan, Bruv. A big change."

They moved back to the Tottenham Court Road end of the building, and looking down could see police cars accumulating around the fountain.

"When will the helicopter be back?" Stumpy frowned in anticipation.

"There's something we need to discuss." He began laughing. "It's a big pile of shit we're in, and we need to discuss it." He got up and made sure the doors to the roof were securely locked. "Now, that helicopter, it wasn't ours. It was a police helicopter, and got a full frontal view of a monster dancing around on one of their buildings. His mates have already turned up down there."

Stumpy's face dropped. "Are they after me?" He was beginning to grasp their predicament. "Why?"

"You're different and they can't handle that. You must know that from the colony. Sorry. But we're in big trouble. They're gonna come up here, after you." He thought for a while, then, "You know, I've only really loved three people in all of my life. Stuart, and they made him kill himself, Katie and she's my God, and you, and you're my brother and my best mate. It's just us. It's all we have."

The police helicopter was back. They had a loud haler which shouted, "You down there! Stay where you are! We are coming up to speak to you. Stay where you are."

Peter snuggled up to Stumpy. "Hold me, for one last time."

"Are they going to eat me?" His thick green skin was furrowed across his brow. "I don't want to be eaten. Don't let them eat me. Please Peter, don't let them eat me."

Peter knew that they wouldn't eat him, but would probably do much worse. "Catherine said that I mustn't let them get you. She knows best, she's God. And I promised, so, got any ideas? We need to get off this roof before they break through the doors."

Stumpy put his index finger on his chin. "Same as you, none." But then he flicked his fingers. "But there is somebody else in our lives. We could go and see Daddy!"

Peter pulled himself away enough to place a good punch on Stumpy's arm. "That's for being such a smart arse. A *brilliant* idea. Do you know the way?"

"Not sure, but I know we can find it. I bet it's that way." He pointed to the edge of the building. "Shall we try?"

They held each other tightly and both began to laugh. "Then show me the way, big boy. Let's go."

Stumpy took Peter by the hand and held it so tightly. "Must *never* let go. Never. Let's do it. I bet Daddy's waiting for us."

The doors began to bang and bend as the police thumped them with their battering ram. Time was running out.

So they looked at each other, then ran, hand in hand, and leapt. They flew over the edge of the building, and set out on their journey to the new life, their laughing faces distorted by the speed of the air flow. "We're coming, Daddy!" They looked at each other's faces as the gravity pulled them ever faster and the wind blew their mouths up like balloons, and they laughed and laughed. "Weeee, we're coming, Daddy." And the concrete got closer, and the people scattered, and got closer, and they suddenly reached the ground.

Colin Hodgson

19 -- NO MORE CRYING

March 1972, Essex, England.

As Uncle Steven and Katie entered the graveyard the rooks called. They circled overhead looking down on the two visitors with intrepid interest but when Katie twisted her deformed neck up to look at them, and waved, they quietened and returned to tending their young. It was a cold spring morning.

The tiny eight-year-old held on to her uncle's hand to steady her walk, one leg slightly dragging, and she swayed with every step, but her face gleamed as she slowly headed towards the grave. And on the other side of the graveyard, snuggled below a stately old conker tree, was her khaki army tent.

"I need to sit down, Kate," whispered Uncle.

The frail old man lowered himself onto a bench, and Katie, grinning, struggled on by herself. The journey across the grass was gruelling.

"I'm nearly with you," she uttered.

As the grave became within reach, Katie stopped and looked over to the little tent and observed, "A new dawn approaches." She took the final painful steps and dropped down onto the grave, laying face down on the un-tended mound. She whispered, "I hope you are behaving yourselves." The chit-chat went on for several minutes. "I'm going home soon, just to change, but I'll soon be back. I'll think of you both wherever I am." She held her ear to the earth. "Don't be silly. Now I've got your emotions, I'm never gonna be without them. Love you, my impetuous pinky-tickler." She started to giggle, but was distracted.

"What are you doing? Get off the grave!" shouted the vicar. "Come on, off with you."

She strained to turn her head enough to see the vicar's legs towering up over her. "I'm talking to my friends." She pushed herself over and rolled off the mound. "I'll miss my friends, and their love." The little blond girl lay on her back and grinned up at the vicar.

"Well you can't treat a grave like a playground."

"I can, it's *God's* playground, and I'm talking to my friends." Her speech was slurred and the cold ground was sending her into shivers, so the vicar held his hand down, and she took it.

"Come on, child, I'll take you to your father."

"He ain't my father. He's Uncle Steven."

The vicar could not understand her deformed speech, and so just smiled. As he looked towards the bench he exclaimed, "Oh, he's gone."

"No, he's still there. He would never leave me."

The vicar helped her to walk over to the bench, and she stressed, "Look, this is Uncle Steven." But the vicar could see nobody sitting there. He just humoured her.

"Where do you come from, child?"

"I'm from heaven, from right around these parts, and from many others." She winked at the vicar. "I'll be ok, you can leave me now."

He frowned, but said goodbye and walked over towards the vicarage. The rooks circled and called as they followed his progress out of the graveyard, and they then went back to their young.

"Uncle, it's time for me to get back to my project, so you can slip off now." She wrapped her arms around his neck. "The boys are ok now, and Stumpy's safe with Peter, and they said they love you. So if you'd like to go now, it's ok, and you can be at peace."

He smiled through his pain, and held his hand out. With a strained croak he said, "It seems a long time ago, only last year, but Stumpy gave me this. He asked me to make sure you get it." He pulled one of Katie's hands to his, and placed the izaline claw, Edward's key, into her grasp."

"Thanks, Uncle. What did he say?"

"He didn't say anything, he just asked me." He grinned. "It'll get you in when you need to." He coughed to clear his congested chest. "But I can't find your book. So sorry."

She kissed his cheek as his eyes closed and the breathing ceased. He had gone to join Old Dick. Chuckling to herself she struggled back over to the grave and said her goodbyes to the boys, kissing the soil, before crawling into her khaki tent and the little blond God was no more.

Suddenly the rooks left their nests and began their caws, circling around, high above the graves. Something had arrived. And the throng became louder and more desperate as the tent flap opened. Out crawled a barefoot little Indian girl. She was wearing a white kurta, like a night shirt, and short, pale blue pyjamas on her legs. And she looked around the yard and began giggling.

"Gayla!" An excited call came from the churchyard gate. "Gayla, over here!"

The little Indian girl looked around, and then she rushed towards the gate, and towards Catherine. "I'm back!" They both danced around each other, and then cuddled. "I'm back. It was a brilliant adventure. I'll tell you all about it on the way to Bengal." And Gayla and her conscience laughed and chuckled, as one apart, and conducted by the choir of rooks in the Kingdom of Heaven, and elation ruled.

And on that cold March day in nineteen seventy two the little Indian girl walked away from her Uncle and from her one true love, arm-in-arm with her conscience, and fully loaded with her new-found emotions. "I'm not gonna cry any more," she sung. "Catherine, take me to Bengal, and never mind the horses!" And God laughed His way all the way to India, together with Himself. And, maybe, the World lived happily ever after.

----------------------------The End--------------------------

Colony